DEATH IS SLEEPING WITH MY WIFE

BY

RANDALL J. FUNK

<u>ALSO BY RANDALL J. FUNK</u>

Death is a Clingy Ex

Death Lives Across The Hall

Death Wears A Big Hat

Published in the United States by Ghost Light Press, L.L.C.

www.randalljfunk.com

ISBN:

Cover design by Ann McMan

First edition

Special Thanks to:

Anne Tressler, for her consultation on the legal matters involved in the book.

Samantha Papke, for her assistance in preparing the manuscript.

Everyone at Fabulous Fern's for all the years of great memories.

Steel Toe Brewing, for hosting my Sunday beer-and-writing sessions.

Ann McMan, for her terrific cover design.

Kris and Ben, for their patience and love.

Everyone who has bought *Death is a Clingy Ex*, *Death Lives Across The Hall* and *Death Wears A Big Hat* and has helped me to start this adventure.

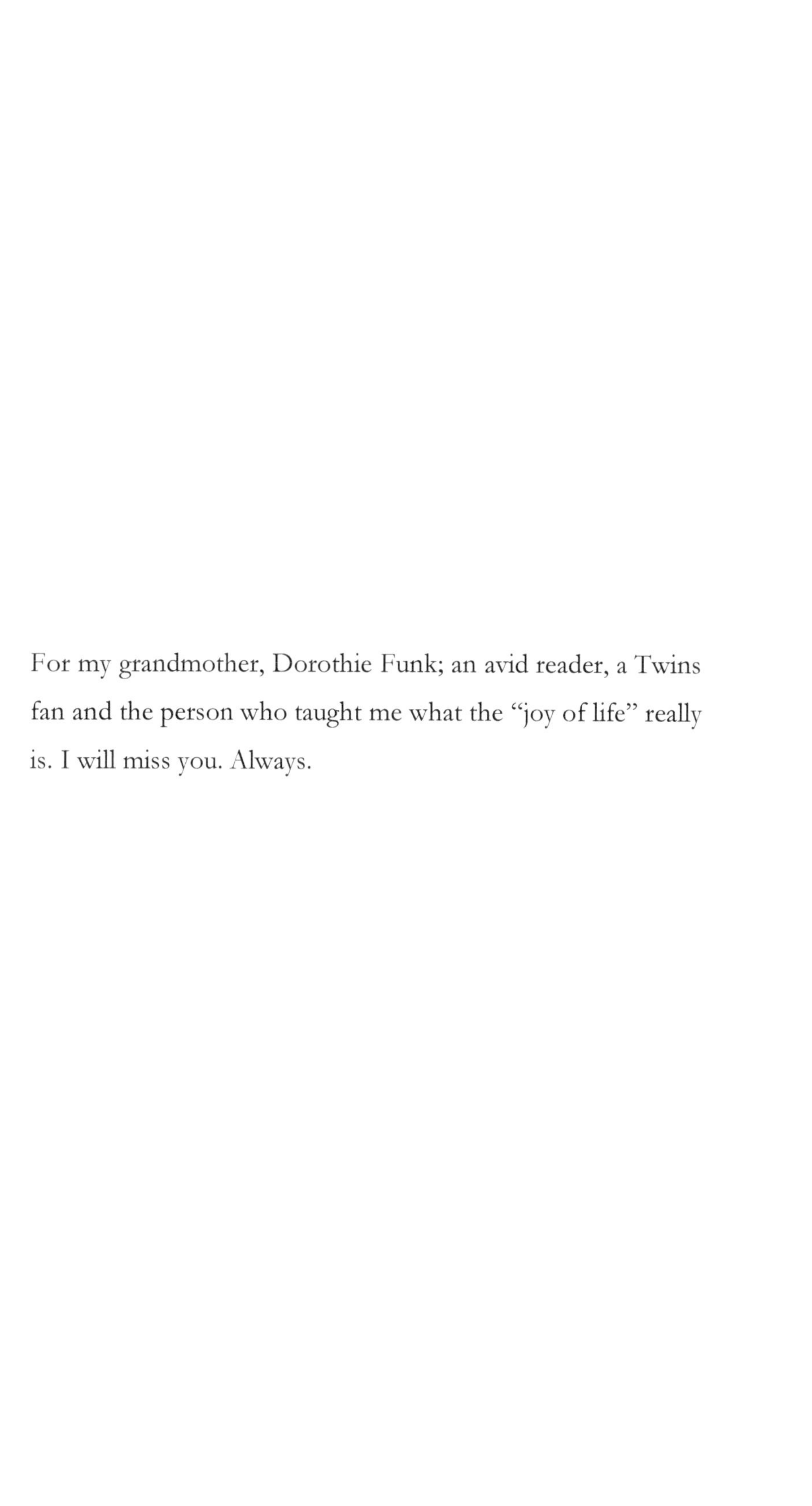

For my grandmother, Dorothie Funk; an avid reader, a Twins fan and the person who taught me what the "joy of life" really is. I will miss you. Always.

CHAPTER ONE

Every now and again, we run across a situation that makes us wonder, "How well does anyone know anyone?"

After all, what criteria do we use to make these decisions? Yes, some are willing to trust everyone until presented with overwhelming evidence to the contrary. We generally call these people "children" or alternatively, "children under the age of five." And yes, some will not trust anyone about anything under any circumstances. We call these people "cops" or alternatively, "my uncle Mel." The rest of us reside somewhere in the middle.

But what makes us decide if someone is trustworthy? What evidence do we use? Do we have a personal checklist or do we just trust our instincts and hope for the best? Circumstances can play into it. For example, the guy selling wristwatches in the alley has a harder time establishing credibility than, say, the pastor collecting donations for a food drive.

But what happens when everything we supposedly know goes pear-shaped? The pastor has been embezzling money from the church. The guy selling the wristwatches works at a homeless shelter. It's then, in the spirit of self-involved people everywhere, we wonder how we didn't spot these things earlier. If we're honest, we realize how lazy our criteria really are. We trusted the pastor simply because he's a pastor. We didn't trust the guy selling the wristwatches because, well, look at him. We never thought to look beneath the surface and see what truth might be lying beneath.

This, by the way, is a thing all politicians rely on.

My name is Joe Davis. I get paid to write stuff like that. That little riff springs to mind the second I realize I'm sleeping with another guy's wife.

It's always a shock when your cell phone rings in the middle of the night. First thoughts are generally, "What the hell is that?" and "Who died?" My phone is leaning against the antique Fonzie lamp on the nightstand and it sounds like a bomb going off. I snap awake and bump into the person I'm sharing my bed with. There's a moment where naked skin brushes naked skin before I get my wits about me. I pick up the phone.

"Yeah?" I say. I'm not at my friendliest when I'm woken up.

"Where's my wife, motherfucker?"

Okay, clearly, this isn't a sales call. "Excuse me?"

"You're Joe Davis, right? Asshole who writes for *The Daily Bugle?*"

"Well, I'm, I'm Joe Davis…"

"You're sleeping with my wife, fucker!"

Norah props her head on my shoulder; her slim body warm next to mine. "Who is it?"

"Some guy who says I'm sleeping with his wife."

"Oh shit! It's my husband!"

Yeah, I should have put that together faster. Again, I'm not at my best in the middle of the night. Norah slides to the other side of the bed and pulls the covers over her head. Meantime, Screamy McScream is still on the line.

"You motherfucker! I will…you fucker! Put Norah on the phone!"

I hold the phone away and turn to Norah. "He wants to talk to you," I say. Her head shakes under the covers. I carefully return the phone to my ear. "I think that's a no-go."

The guy unleashes another string of expletives, then adds: "I'm going to destroy you. You hear me? By the time I'm done with you, they won't hire you to be a dog catcher."

"Do we even still have dog catch—"

"Fuck you!" And on that note, he rings off.

I stare at the phone. My hand falls to the bed. Norah pokes her head out from under the covers.

"Sorry about that," she says, "I suppose we should talk, huh?"

"That might be a good idea."

For the first time since Norah and I started dating again a few weeks ago, I'm questioning that decision. I have a policy against getting back together with ex-girlfriends. It rarely works, either in my own experience or in other people's. You can talk about how things are different, but at some point, the relationship will be torpedoed by the very same factors that destroyed it in the first place. No matter what self-help books tell us, people don't change that much.

I made an exception with Norah. Our original breakup wasn't ugly. She got busy with work and we sort of drifted apart. There hadn't even been a *Breakup Moment* so to speak. Just an *I'll call you next week* and next week never arrived. Not the kind of breakup that's going to still rankle after two years. So, when we bumped into each other at a local coffee shop and one thing lead to the next, getting back together didn't feel all that weird.

Although, this more than makes up for any weirdness the relationship lacked up to now.

Norah stares at the phone on my lap. Her blue eyes wide and liquid. When she frowns, her lip sticks out in a pouty sort of way. It's cute, I'm not going to lie to you. She runs a hand through her blonde hair. It cascades down the side of her face, curtaining her eyes.

I can't find a better way to open the conversation. "You're married?"

She nods, barely. "Yeah. Pretty much."

"So the guy on the phone was…?"

"Brady. My husband."

I glance toward the bedroom window. Moonlight filters in, illuminating the erector set of stairs and decks lining the back of the converted brownstone where I live. I half-expect this Brady guy to be charging up the stairs, heading for my third-floor apartment. The good news is that said erector set has been known to groan in a slight breeze, so it's not conducive to launching a sneak attack. I turn toward Norah.

"Not to go all Adam Sandler movie on you," I say, "But don't you think this was something you should have mentioned sooner?"

"I'm sorry. I know I should have. But things haven't been going well with Brady. And it was so nice to see you again. And I didn't know how you'd react."

I hold up the phone. "I can't imagine that scene being any more awkward than this one."

Norah bites her lip. "I'm sorry."

I've got an instinct to put my arms around her. It's killed by a voice in my head screaming, "You idiot, the husband you didn't know she had five minutes ago threatened to kill you four minutes ago!" (Sometimes you *should* listen to the voices in your head.)

"How long have you been married?" I ask.

"About a year."

"And how long have things been bad?"

"Almost a year." Norah leans against the headboard and draws her knees up to her chest. "It was one of those whirlwind things. Two months from first date to wedding date. I didn't think it through."

Norah brushes her hair aside. The soft light dances in her eyes. Sadness creases her face, making her look like a broken china doll. No doubt. Norah is a beautiful woman. Why does there always have to be a catch?

"You think your husband will really kill me?" I ask.

"I doubt it."

I've got to be honest: there are more reassuring answers to that question. "You doubt it?"

"How well does anybody know anybody?"

See what I mean? Norah slides out from under the covers and rummages around for her clothes.

"I suppose I should go," she says.

"Where would you go? Home doesn't sound like a good idea."

"I guess not."

Norah stands there, a pair of blue cotton underwear in one hand and a pink half-shirt in the other. I'm searching my better instincts while also wondering if I have any better instincts left. I throw back the covers on her side of the bed.

"You had a place here before the…the phone call," I say, "You might as well stay. Start fresh in the morning."

Norah drops the clothing and slips back into bed. She lays facing me. I stare at the ceiling, watching her from the corner of my eye. Norah is, without doubt, a beautiful woman. An All-American girl with a mischievous streak. The gentle look in her eyes causes a flutter in my stomach.

"Thanks for letting me stay," she whispers.

"It's no big deal. I'm not going to throw you out in the middle of the night."

"You're a good person."

"I'd love to agree with you, but…"

I close my eyes, maybe hoping this is all a dream. Five bucks says I'm going to wonder the same thing in the morning. Best to forget about it for now. Sleep on it. There's some movement in the bed. When Norah speaks, her face is close to mine.

"I'm sorry this happened," she says.

"What? You and me or—"

"No. I don't regret anything about you and me. I'm sorry I messed things up."

My head rolls toward Norah. Her face is warm and shadowy in the moonlight. I try to think of something to say that will make things right, something that won't leave her feeling abandoned. Something that won't leave *me* feeling abandoned.

"We'll see how things look after we get some sleep," I say, "Sound good?"

Norah lays her head on the pillow and I close my eyes. Her face is still close to mine. A second later, her lips brush my cheek. I look at her, but I don't move.

"What are you doing?" I ask.

She kisses me along my jawline and moves to my neck. I'm tempted to push her away. But that feeling fades quickly.

"I just want us to be okay," she whispers.

"We are."

"Show me."

"Norah, I don't think this is—"

"Shut up."

Norah glides on top of me. My hands stroke her face and cup her cheeks. No doubt. Norah is a very beautiful woman.

And I am a very stupid man.

***

"Here's what I don't get," Mike says, rummaging through my freezer, "When did we decide pizza and buffalo wings go together? I gotta assume the pizza companies started this. I understand upselling and all, but how is diarrhea a marketing tool?"

Mike's been my best friend since about five minutes after we got to college. Through fifteen years, one of the constants in our friendship has been his rummaging through my food supply at every opportunity. In this case, he began with a search for grape soda (I only keep the stuff on hand out of consideration for Mike) and has gravitated to snacks.

"You're welcomed to the pizza and wings," I say, staring at the computer screen on my desk, "I'd prefer you take the diarrhea elsewhere."

That draws a groan from Carol at my breakfast bar. (As you may have gathered, I have an open-door policy when it comes to my friends.) She spins on one of the stools lining both sides of the bar. Her cool blue eyes bore into me.

"If we could get back to the point," Carol says.

"What point?" Mike says, his Cro-Magnon head briefly reappearing from my freezer.

"How Joe's become an adulterer."

I turn away from a column that stubbornly refuses to write itself. "I assume you'll be ordering my scarlet letter on Amazon?"

Carol responds with a little *tsk-tsk*. "What *would* your mother say?"

She's teasing, but that cuts a little close to the bone. I love my parents and get along well with them. But I've always sensed their disapproval of my lifestyle. Thirty-four years old, not married, working a job that pays my bills but little else, living in a one-bedroom apartment in the heart of a dangerous city. (Okay, it's St. Paul, but my parents are from northern Minnesota. To them, the Twin Cities is one big den of iniquity.) An affair with a married woman is not going in the *Plus* column.

As if I needed this distraction. I write a thrice-weekly column (*Cup o'Joe*) for *The Daily Bugle,* a former independent newspaper that now functions strictly as a website. The column covers all manner of subjects; social, ethical, political. All done with the sort of depth and reasoning one normally finds in a Daffy Duck cartoon. But hey, it's a living (sort of).

Mike and Carol have more respectable professions. Mike works in real estate and Carol's an ad writer. Their income levels are where the resemblance ends. Mike's like a bulldog who'd rather eat and fart than protect the house. Carol brings to mind a Sunday School teacher who will occasionally knock back shots with you. With the two of them here and a beautiful May afternoon unfolding on Summit Avenue outside, it's clear I'm not going to be productive today. I close the document I'm (not really) working on and walk away from the computer. Carol turns on the stool to follow me.

"I guess that's it for you and Norah?" she asks, briefly checking the mirror to make sure her ponytail is intact.

I step into the thin kitchen and pour a cup of coffee. "It was a hell of a thing to find out."

"What did you do after her husband called?"

"Well, we, uh…y'know, I couldn't throw her out in the middle of the night. And it's not like she could go home. So, I let her stay."

Carol fixes me with her piercing gaze. "Uh-huh," is all she says.

I run a hand through my hair. "And then we had sex. And this morning, we went to breakfast at The Tav and did a crossword puzzle. Oh, and we went for a bike ride by the river."

The room is quiet. Mike flips the freezer shut. "I gotta be honest: I wish my breakups were that smooth."

Carol rolls her eyes toward Mike. "So do I." It's a bit pointed because Mike and Carol dated once upon a time. Their breakup came as quite a shock. To Mike.

Carol steps around the breakfast bar and blocks my exit from the kitchen. "Joe, you haven't broken up with Norah?"

"I haven't not broken up with her."

"Meaning?"

"I haven't broken up with her."

Carol puts her hands on the hips of her black slacks. "Joe, it's one thing to sleep with a married woman when you didn't know she was married. But now you're doing it with full knowledge of the situation."

"Yeah, but the marriage obviously isn't going well. If she's sleeping with me, how happy could she be? Wait, that didn't come out right."

I take a seat at the breakfast bar. Mike grabs a grape soda out of the fridge. He and Carol surround me. It's like facing a Board of Inquiry. Mike cracks the soda, spilling some of it on his Green Lantern t-shirt and greasy blue jeans.

"I'm not going to get on your case," he says, "It's not like I've got a lot going in the dating department. That chick I met online didn't work out at all."

"Didn't hit it off?" Carol asks.

"No. She had a unibrow."

Carol and I look at each other. One of us has to take this. "A unibrow?" I say, "That was the deal-breaker?"

"Wouldn't it be for you?" Mike says.

I look to Carol. "It would be."

Carol folds her arms across her wine-colored blouse. "You're really going to let appearances be that important?"

"Appearances are one thing," Mike says, scratching his mangy goatee, "Someone's born looking like they got beaten with a big stick, they can't help that. But there's no excuse for letting a unibrow happen. That's just careless."

"You're unbelievable," Carol says.

"Hey, those are my standards," Mike says, "I'm sure someone will make Sheena The Cave Woman very happy. But it ain't gonna be me."

Carol starts to say something but gives up, probably realizing it's a lost cause. She joins us at the breakfast bar. "Doesn't sound like any of us are doing well," she says, "I kicked another one to the curb."

"This was who? David?" I ask, "What happened?"

"He wanted to borrow money."

"For what?" Mike asks.

"Bail," Carol says.

Mike and I exchange a look. It's like when grandma cuts one at the dinner table. Best to say nothing. I'm tempted to lecture Carol on her terrible taste in men, but Exhibit A is sipping grape soda at my breakfast bar. She decides to wheel back around to *my* misery.

"Have you thought about the publicity you're going to get if this gets out?" she asks.

Truthfully, I hadn't. My job doesn't make me a household name in the Cities. But it *does* afford me a small bit of celebrity. Quite a few people know my name because of the column and my occasional radio and podcast appearances. It's not much, but it strokes the ego.

"You think it's going to hurt me?" I ask.

"It isn't going to help," Carol says, "Your whole persona, such as it is, is based on people thinking you're a nice, average…well, Joe. Someone like them."

"And *they* don't sleep with married women?" I ask.

"They like to think they don't."

That's true. When you're on a pedestal, no matter how small the pedestal, you lose any *There but for the grace of God* leeway people might give you. This could be a problem. Huge celebrities can recover from a thing like this. A minor leaguer like me might find himself out of a job before the public finds themselves in a forgiving mood.

"And what about Norah's job?" Carol asks, "Won't she get in trouble?"

"I don't think it's any of their business," I say.

"But if you get bad publicity," she says, "Norah gets bad publicity. And then the school gets bad publicity."

Ugh. Hadn't thought of that, either. Norah teaches English at Cornette Academy, a private school in Minneapolis. If this becomes a public kerfuffle, the school administrators aren't going to be pleased. With the school year coming to an end, it might be a simple matter of terminating Norah's employment. This situation has become the gift that keeps on giving.

Carol is still lasered in on me. "What are you going to do?"

"I don't know," I say, "Maybe it will all blow over. The husband's got to realize I don't have anything to do with his marriage being bad. I'm just the by-product. Maybe he won't raise a stink."

That gets a chuckle out of Mike. "You really think it'll go down that way?"

"The guy can't be entirely unreasonable, right?"

Before anyone can answer, there's a noise outside, coming from the front of my building. Someone's shouting. This isn't unusual in and of itself. People in my building occasionally shout down from the windows or hail each other on the street. But there's a belligerence to this noise. Mike, always quick to move toward the sound of belligerence, leads the way to the arch windows at the front of the apartment. Lenny, my alpha cat, has been lounging near the open middle window. He runs off as soon as people invade his space. Mike opens the window nearest my desk. The voice coming from the street sounds vaguely familiar.

"Hey asshole! I want to know where my wife is!"

Mike looks back at me. "It's for you."

I step past Mike. This must be Brady, Norah's husband, ranting and raving on the tiny front lawn of my building. Despite the invective, he's not a particularly intimidating fellow. Skinny arms stick out from his white t-shirt and his head looks a tad too large for his body. The swept-back brown hair adds a few inches to his height and I think that's intentional. The beady eyes and the angry set of the jaw give him a malevolent look. His voice is surprisingly deep and harsh. Carol peers over my shoulder.

"Oh, he's good-looking," she says. I turn toward her and she adds: "What? It's just an observation."

While I *do* wish Carol would be more discerning about the men she finds attractive, that's not the priority. The screaming crazy man on the front lawn is. I'd rather not deal with this, but it doesn't seem like it will go away on its own. I lean out the window.

"Um, hi," I say, trying to sound friendly, "I, uh, I think you're looking for me."

"Where's my wife?" is how Brady responds.

"Um, I'm not sure. Listen—"

"Is she there?"

"She is not. Look—"

"No, you look, fucko," Brady says, waving a balled-up fist at me, "You think you're hot shit because you're on the fucking internet? Let's see what all your little geek fans think when they find out what a fucking scumbag you are. You think anyone's going to want to read your fucking column then?"

"I guess I'm hoping—"

"Fuck you!"

Brady bounces on the balls of his feet, as if he's ready to run up the side of the building. Before we can continue the conversation, someone comes out the front door. It's our buddy, Lars, my downstairs neighbor and the building's superintendent. This isn't exactly like sending in the cavalry. Lars' scarecrow physique and quasi-pompadour don't inspire fear. It's like sending Trotsky out to fight your battles for you.

Lars also tries the friendly approach. "Hey brother, I gotta ask you to dial it down. You're disturbing the—"

That's as far as Lars gets before Brady punches him in the face. Everybody at the window jumps. Carol puts a hand over her mouth.

"Oh my God," she says, "He killed Lars!"

"You bastard!" Mike says.

I look at them. "Really? We're going twenty-year old jokes now?"

Lars stumbles back a few feet, drops to one knee on the grass and then gets to his feet. He weaves toward the front door, done with the fisticuffs. Brady's big hands saw the air as he motions for me to join him on the front lawn (and Lars on the disabled list.)

"Come on down, asshole!" he shouts.

Everyone's looking to me to solve this. I guess I *did* bring this on, what with me sleeping with the guy's wife and all. I lean out the window, still trying to be amiable.

"Hey, Brady," I say, "I understand why you're upset."

"Fuck you!"

"Yes. All of that. But I can't have you screaming and yelling and punching the superintendent. That shit just don't fly. If you don't mind, I'm going to have to ask you to leave before I call the police."

"Fuck you!"

"That's the word on the street." I wave my phone out the window. "I'm calling them now. I don't think you're going to get inside the building before they get here."

Mike says, at full volume, "What about the backdoor?"

I glare at Mike, who realizes he's stepped in it. Thankfully, it looks like Carol and I were the only ones who heard him. Brady glances down Summit, as if the cops could show up at any time. He uses his middle finger to point toward my window.

"You wait, motherfucker," he says, "You're going to get yours."

Brady stalks off, kicking a trash can as he rounds around the corner of Summit and Dale. I close the window. Just as I do, the door opens and Lars stumbles in, holding his jaw. He's weaving, quasi-pompadour drifting from side to side and his eyes glassy. Carol, the closest thing we've got to a nurturer, goes over to him.

"Lars, are you okay?" she asks.

"He hits real hard," Lars says.

"Do you need a doctor?" I ask.

"He hits real hard."

Carol guides Lars to the sofa while Mike heads into the kitchen to get an icepack. He grabs a beer for good measure (though I'm not sure if it's for him or Lars.)

"Hate to tell you," Mike says, "But I don't think that guy's coming to his senses."

I glance toward the backdoor. "Clearly," I say, "The conversation is a work in progress."

CHAPTER TWO

One of the more disquieting realizations in life is that we're not as safe as we think. You ever realize the military can seize control of the government at any time and there isn't a damn thing we can do about it? This whole thing we call democracy is done on the honor system?

Or how we'd never run into one of those situations you see in the Trending section on Facebook. Man's Testicles Removed By Jealous Wife. *Surely, no one would do something like that to us. And yet, we could be just one misinterpreted text message away from such a fate.*

Or we could be crossing the street the day Milton at the home office has decided he's had all he can take and he's going to make an example out of the next son of a bitch that walks in front of his car.

Crime, death and destruction are everywhere. If you haven't been touched by them, it's because you haven't been noticed yet.

Sleep well.

"As far as I'm concerned, dealing drugs is a customer business," Lars tells me, "There is no reason for someone to be rude."

This wasn't how I wanted the conversation to go. Lars circles around his apartment, which is located right below mine. It's slightly larger, housing a second bedroom which Lars uses for additional bric-a-brac, knick-knacks and tchakis. Beyond that, the place is a dump.

The same can be said for Lars. He's wearing a ratty bathrobe over shorts and a t-shirt. One of his pipe cleaner arms swings about. There's a decent-sized black-and-blue mark on his cheek. But the assault has not diminished his energy. He moves in a short elliptical pattern, looking like a bantam rooster standing guard over a trash pile.

"I'm sorry to hear about the problems with your dealer," I say, "But about the guy who wants to kill me—"

Lars bulldozes over my concerns. "Seriously, does Billy think he's the only pot dealer around? Because I could take my business elsewhere."

I'd prefer to talk about ways to prevent Brady from getting into the building and killing me. But I've known Lars long enough to know this conversation will not proceed unless he gets all this out. I plunk down at his breakfast bar.

"Why are you having trouble with your dealer?" I ask.

Lars glides over to me, bathrobe billowing out behind him. "It's a deterioration of customer service. See, I was one of Billy's first customers. Back then, I'd go over to his place, we'd transact business and then smoke a bowl. Lately, though? He doesn't have time to smoke up. It's all business and no personal touch."

"Have you talked to him about it?"

"Absolutely! I don't go in for this passive-aggressive nonsense. I told him, 'Hey, why don't we smoke up? Unless you're too busy or you think you've got something better to do.' He just gave me some kind of look and threw me out." He lays a hand solemnly on the countertop. "That's why I'm going into the drug business."

That's not what you want to hear from a friend and neighbor. "Going into the drug business? What are you talking about?"

"I'm going to be a dealer, brother. Why should I put up with middle men?"

"The whole drug industry is based on middle men," I say, "Unless you plan on growing something here."

Lars' eyes light up and I know I've screwed up. Lars' entire life is a string of ridiculous get-rich-quick schemes, interrupted by an occasional nap. I shouldn't be feeding him ideas. But the ball is rolling downhill.

"Grow my own weed," he says, his pacing at Mach 5, "That is a brilliant idea! Who knew you had it in you? To hell with Billy and his fallutin' ways. I'm growing my own shit!"

Herculean as the task may be, I need to get Lars back on track. I can't reason with Brady, so my thoughts have turned to security. With no direct conduit to building management, I'm forced to talk to the superintendent. I thought Lars would provide a sympathetic ear, given his recent fisticuffs with Brady. But when Lars is plotting, even tenant safety gets moved down the priority list. (Assuming they're ever *on* the priority list.)

"This is a seminal moment," Lars says, his hands rapping out a rhythm on the breakfast bar, "You think Pablo Escobar got started this way?"

"Look, much as I'd love to discuss Pablo Escobar and drug trade semen, can we talk about why I came down here?"

Lars stops. "I thought this was a social call."

"Not really, I—"

"See? You're no better than Billy. Must everything in life be a transaction? Is there no such thing as simply socializing without some form of quid pro quo?"

"Are you finished?"

"No, but society might be." He flops down at the breakfast bar. "What's on your mind?"

"It's about that guy who punched you. Brady."

"He's bad news," Lars says, moving his hand to his cheek, "You made a hell of an enemy there, brother. All because you're sleeping with this man's wife? Or is there something you haven't mentioned?"

"No," I say, "The adultery pretty much covers it."

"Huh," Lars says, "People should be more open-minded. A significant other isn't your possession. They should be allowed freedom within the relationship. Including sexual freedom. You remember Didi? From a few years back? You could have had her if you asked."

I nearly slide off my stool. "Why didn't you tell me?"

"You didn't ask."

Briefly, I'm filled with thoughts of Didi, a pixie of a woman with short hair and big breasts (a combination that's always driven me wild). Then I remember I already have a girlfriend and I didn't come down here to talk about Didi.

"I'm concerned about this guy," I say, "He's nuts and he knows where I live."

Lars pours himself a scotch-and-soda. "I get it. You want me to kill this guy."

"No! I want to know if the building is secure."

"Fine. But let's not take killing off the table. We'll think of it as Plan B."

A headache is developing, as one often does when I find myself in any conversation with Lars that runs longer than two minutes. I pinch the bridge of my nose.

"Can you call management and see if there's anything they can do?" I ask

His face scrunches up. "I don't know. They aren't into spending unnecessary money. How do you think I got the superintendent gig?"

That explains that. Money often funds the Peter Principle. "Can you at least ask? It might make me feel better."

"I can ask. But I can't promise anything."

I run a hand through my hair. (It's a nervous gesture I've done since I was a kid. At the current rate, I'm going to need Rogaine in a few weeks.) For the first time since I got here, Lars notices my distress.

"You know what you need?" he says, "Something to take your troubles off your mind. Have you considered smoking a bowl? I can get you a great deal."

"Sorry, I only deal with middle men."

I walk out the door. Behind me, Lars mutters, "The road is long. The path is steep."

***

There's a couple sides to the coin that is Norah. There's a side that's cool and controlled. Her face freezes and her eyes will go cold as she thinks. There's also a side that's passionate and animated. Her face lights up, her laughter fills the room.

Right now, I'm dealing with a mix of the two. Norah's passionate, certainly. But the passion takes the form of abject panic.

"Brady's going to get me fired," she says, standing at the arch windows in my apartment, hugging herself, "I don't know what I'm going to do."

I'd like to help. Consoling someone in the throes of strong emotion has never been my strong suit. I usually subcontract that work to booze since pouring drinks *is* my strong suit. I've given Norah a vodka press, but she's not inclined to drink it. I stand next to my futon, helpless.

"You're sure he's going to get you fired?" I ask.

"That's exactly what he said. He's got a meeting with one of the school administrators and he's going to tell them the whole thing. And they're just tight-assed enough to fire me." She puts a hand to her forehead. "I love teaching. I love my kids. We're working on *Macbeth* right now and you can just see it come alive for them. It's so exciting." She sits on the ledge next to the window. "What am I going to do?"

I don't know what to say, other than: "I'm sorry."

Norah holds out her hand and guides me to a spot next to her on the ledge. She lays her head on my shoulder. "Don't be stupid. You didn't do anything wrong. It's my fault for not telling you."

We sit in silence, Norah resting comfortably next to me. Her hair is pulled back into a ponytail and a single strand falls across her face. I brush it away and kiss her forehead.

"What are you thinking about?" I ask.

She picks at a rip in the knee of her jeans. "Just…wondering how it all came to this. I mean, a year ago. That's it. I was just married. And now all of this."

Squiggy, my beta cat and the one who responds most to people's moods, lays at Norah's feet. With his black-and-white coloring and obsequious manner, he's like a butler coming to lend aid and comfort. Norah pets Squiggy's head and gives him a sad smile. She huddles into her flannel shirt, pulling it closed across her white long-sleeve tee.

"I thought Brady was a decent guy when I first met him," Norah says, "He was funny and driven and, I don't know, charismatic. It was a whirlwind thing, but it felt right." She turns slightly, bringing her feet up the little space on the ledge and turning her back to me. "And then I realized how self-involved he was. When we were dating, he focused on me. When we were married, he focused on his business. And his free time. I might as well have been a piece of furniture. He expected me to be around when he wanted me around. And I had to let him decide when those moments would be." Norah lays the back of her head against my shoulder and stares at the ceiling. "All the thinking I was doing before…before I ran into you again. It all revolved around how I didn't want to be divorced. I wanted the marriage, but I didn't want Brady. Does that make any sense?"

"It does."

Norah's eyes are wet. "Guess that's what I get for getting married so soon."

I kiss the top of her head. I sympathize with Norah's regret, if not her haste. It's part of the reason my process for deciding on a spouse is only slightly less involved than the process for becoming a CIA agent. And, I'm sure, part of the reason I'm still single.

"I've got to ask," I say, "We've, uh, we've spent a few nights together. Where did Brady think you were?"

"He travels a lot for work. Conventions, trade shows, meetings. He was supposed to be out of town the night he called here. He got back early." She swings her legs to the floor and faces me. "You know how he found out about us? He hacked my email. Saw a note from you. Hell of a guy, my husband." Norah lays her hand on my knee. "I'm sorry I didn't tell you. We hooked up again and I didn't have any plans or expectations. It felt free. And fun. Things just…happened."

I guess John Lennon was on to something. I lay my hand on Norah's. We look over my apartment and I can't help feeling how natural it is to have her here. But that's a little scary, so I switch gears, slightly.

"How's your brother-in-law's place?" I ask.

Norah accepted an offer to temporarily live at her brother-in-law's house in Eagan. From what I understand, Doug, the brother-in-law, has a big enough place that the lower level can function as its own apartment.

"It's pretty comfortable," Norah says, "I can barely hear Doug coming and going. And it's got its own entrance, so I get plenty of privacy. Just what I need right now, to be honest."

"Does Brady know you're there?"

"Doug's going to tell him tonight. I don't think Doug cares. He and Brady don't like each other. They're in business together, but that's about it."

Huh. There's that old saying about not doing business with family and friends. I'll have to remind my father of that the next time he nags me about coming home and working in the family hardware store. Norah turns toward me, tucking one foot under her.

"Where are we in all of this?" she asks.

It's a good question. We've been on automatic pilot the last couple days, trying to get things sorted out. We haven't really dealt with the subject of us. By all rights, I should take Carol's advice and walk away. But I can make up my own mind.

"I've missed you," I tell her, "I like having you here. I don't want that to change."

A corner of Norah's mouth lifts. "Doesn't sound like breakup talk."

"It does not. So if it's okay with you, can we drop the breakup talk?"

She puts her forehead against mine. "That's okay with me."

We sit like that, enjoying the silence. As it's wont to do, though, real life intrudes. Norah glances at the clock over my TV set. She lets out a sigh.

"I should probably get going," she says, "I've got to get up early for school."

She grabs her purse off the futon and I walk Norah to the front door. I'd love to go home with her, but this isn't the time for that. Although the kiss Norah gives me tells me she'd be fine with it. Instead, I stand on the landing and watch her disappear down the stairs. The lightness I'm feeling is leavened by the awareness that Norah is still, technically, married to a maniac who wants to fold, spindle and mutilate my person.

What have I gotten myself into?

***

It's been a few hours since Norah left and I'm struggling to sleep. Without her, the apartment feels empty. I'm sprawled out on the bed, listening to classical music, trying to relax. The building is quiet. Fonzie's presence on the nightstand is comforting. He gives me a thumbs-up, keeping the world safe from the nerds. And the cats are at my feet.

Two cats, litter-mates, run my household: Lenny, a handsome butterscotch tabby who's got a jock's ego and none of the grace, and Squiggy, the former runt of the litter and my imaginary butler. They're stretched out at the foot of the bed, their favorite place to sleep when spring has sprung. Between the cats, The Fonz and the music, I'm able to doze.

I'm not sure how long I've been out when I hear something on the deck. It's a scuffling sound. A second later, there's a *thud* right outside my backdoor. This is followed by a rattling that goes all the way down the erector set of stairs and decks behind the building. Someone running away.

I'm certainly awake now.

I run to the bedroom window. I can't see anyone in the parking lot and the window doesn't afford me a view of the deck. I give some thought to calling the police, but I don't know what the situation is out there. Might just be one of my neighbors coming home drunk and screwing around (perhaps literally) on my deck.

I look around for a weapon, just in case. All I've got is an old tennis racket that's served as a surrogate guitar more than sporting equipment. Lenny and Squiggy, cowardly bastards to the end, relocate to the underside of the bed. I'm on my own.

I step into the hallway and listen for further noises. I don't hear anything, but it doesn't ease my anxiety. I crouch near the door and strain to listen. Still nothing. If it's a neighbor, maybe they passed out. Or maybe they fell down, got up and moved on. Then again, there wasn't the usual laughter and loud conversation that accompanies someone coming home drunk. I don't know. Maybe I'm just being paranoid. Or maybe somebody's trying to draw me out of the apartment and kill me. Got to keep all possibilities on the table. I decide to take a look. It's me and the tennis racket against the world.

I crack open the backdoor and peek out, half-ready for it to be kicked in. I'm in luck. Nobody's waiting on my deck, poised to kill me.

There is, however, the matter of the dead body.

CHAPTER THREE

We love to think that, as intelligent people, we wouldn't give into a thing like panic. After all, if you have the capacity for reason, you should be able to see trouble for what it is and immediately find a solution. Surely, only the lesser lights give into something as puerile as the heebie-jeebies.

Sadly, the opposite usually holds true. When faced with a situation that appeals to basic emotions rather than intellect, our fallback mode is panic. It's that piece of grit that interrupts the workings of a perfectly good microchip. It's sad to watch an otherwise intelligent person get turned into a pants-wetting ditherer.

Like me after I find the body.

At first, I'm not sure I'm looking at a dead body. But the growing pool of blood underneath it clues me in. The guy is lying face down. He's outfitted in black from head to toe: sweater, pants, shoes, stocking cap, gloves. He doesn't look familiar, which shouldn't come as a shock as very few of my acquaintances sneak on to my deck and drop dead.

"Hey," I say, maybe hoping the guy's still conscious, "Hey, are you okay?"

I'm not sure what answer I'm expecting ("I'm kicking ass. Don't let all this blood fool ya.") But I don't get one. The Common-Sense Gene kicks in. I run back inside, grab the cordless phone off the breakfast bar and place a hasty call to 9-1-1, babbling my way through the conversation. The operator is patient and speaks a fluent Panicky Guy. She assures me the police are on their way. She offers to stay on the line until they get here, but I figure the guy on the deck isn't going anywhere and there's only so much conversation you can have with a 9-1-1 operator. I tell her I'll be fine.

The truth is, I'm a mass of indecision. I start down the hallway, thinking I may to give the guy first aid. Then I stop, thinking he may already be dead and I'd be tampering with a crime scene. Then I start moving again, thinking if the guy isn't dead and I don't do anything to help him, *that* might be a crime. Then I stop again, because I don't know any first aid more complicated than putting a Band-Aid on a boo-boo. Finally, I move again, figuring that leaving someone alone while they bleed out on my deck is just inhospitable.

When I get to the deck, the pool of blood is even larger. The guy's head is lying in it, so if I had to guess (if you're *really* going to make me guess) I'd say his throat has been cut. I fumble for his wrist, carefully avoiding the blood because it's A. evidence and B. gross. I'm not an expert, but even I know when there's no pulse to be found. This guy's not just merely dead, he's really most sincerely dead. I tiptoe around the perimeter of the blood. I kneel down and take a peek at the guy's face.

And I'm looking at Norah's husband, Brady.

I jump back, crashing into the railing at the edge of the deck. The damn thing is all that's holding me up. My knees are weak and I think I'm going to vomit. Somehow, I've got both goosebumps and sweat on my arms.

There's a knock at the front door. It must be the cops. I stumble down the hall, trying and failing to come up with a decent explanation for why the guy whose wife I'm sleeping with is now lying dead on my deck. I lean into the peephole and discover it's Lars at the door. Strangely enough, I *want* to see him.

"What are you doing up here?" he asks, standing there in his boxers and a t-shirt, "There's something dripping on to my deck."

"It's blood."

"Are you slaughtering an animal?" It's a serious question.

"It's the middle of the night. Why the hell would I be slaughtering an animal?"

"For fresh meat, obviously. Why else would one slaughter an animal?"

I pull Lars into the apartment, lest I throw him down the stairs. "The police are on their way," I say, "Someone got killed on my deck."

Lars' head snaps back. "The police?" He snaps his fingers. "My pot plants!" He bounds down the stairs and back into his apartment.

I head back out to the deck and squat as close to the body as I can. Assuming Brady fell straight down, he was killed on the edge of the deck, right where it meets the general walkway. I think back to when I woke up. The stairs were rattling. The murderer making a getaway? There was no sight of anyone in the parking lot. The murder got out of here fast. I spot something in Brady's gloved hand. Unless I'm mistaken (and there's not a lot I could mistake this thing for) it's a small handgun. One that Brady was probably here to use on me.

The urge to vomit rises again. I head for the bathroom, just in case. Before there can be any chucking of the up, though, there's a knock at my front door and then an army of cops invade my place. (Then again, the apartment's pretty small. *Three* cops would seem like an invading force.) I'm guided into the living room while some cops head out to the deck and establish a crime scene. Through the open front door, my neighbor across the hall can be seen peering out, probably wondering what the hell is going on. Other neighbors gather on the stairs. Lars steps into my doorway and gives me a pronounced wink, oh-so-subtly indicating his pot plants have been hidden. He goes to work on dispersing the crowd. Meantime, a plainclothes cop walks through the open backdoor. I recognize the guy.

"Counselor," he says, strolling up, "As I live and breathe."

It's Sergeant Frank Pike of the St. Paul Police Department, Homicide Division. I make no attempt to hide my chagrin.

"Y'know, it's no sin to take a night off every once in a while," I say.

"And miss all the fun? It's been literally weeks."

Months, actually, but who's counting? Last fall, Pike was the lead investigator when Mike was accused of murdering his neighbor. Pike was convinced of Mike's guilt and wouldn't listen when I tried to tell him otherwise. (But then, we didn't get off on the right foot. The *counselor* nickname is a remnant of Mike passing me off as his lawyer when we first met Pike.)

A smirk twists Pike's bulldog face. "Let's chat."

"I'm not going anywhere," I say.

Pike slips his hands into the pants pockets of his rumpled gray suit. He's several inches shorter than me, but the way his cold blue eyes stare over his wire-rim glasses cuts me down to size.

"What happened here tonight?" he asks, his voice taking on an edgy, slightly amused quality that makes me think he excels at both good cop and bad cop.

I go through the whole story. Pike listens intently, his face giving away nothing. When I'm done, he fingers his cheap blue tie.

"Did you know this guy?" he asks.

There's a split-second of indecision before I fall back on a lie. "No. No idea."

"According to his wallet, his name's Brady Perkins. That mean anything to you?"

"Doesn't ring a bell," I say.

Pike gives me the cop glare; cold and hard. He's either trying to read me or he's waiting for me to break. Maybe both. I give him nothing in return. He runs a hand through what's left of his hair.

"Okay," he says, "Hang on a second." He calls to one of the uniformed cops, who hands him a plastic evidence bag. Pike holds the bag toward me. It contains Brady's handgun. "Brady was holding this. Can't tell if you were his final stop or if he was looking for someone else." Pike's eyes narrow. "You're *sure* you don't know this guy?"

Pike knows there's something I'm not telling him. I shake my head, the old playing-dumb *Gee, teacher, I had my homework when I left the house* gambit that's served me well over the years. Pike turns toward the front door.

"I'm going to have to talk to your neighbors," he says, "See if anyone knew this guy." He snaps a business card into his hand and offers it to me. "Give me a call if you think of anything."

"I probably still have your last card."

Pike heads out the door. "Have a good night, counselor. I'll be in touch."

That's what worries me.

***

I met Mike in college. He was a military brat and the only child of an overly-protective mother. He was woefully unprepared for life and mildly unprepared for college. He promptly discovered the joys of a life free of constant supervision. He threw himself into college with a fervor that would make the guys from *Animal House* consider some lifestyle changes. He hasn't changed much since.

So it's a little sobering (pardon whatever pun happens to be there) when Mike's taken aback by something *I* did.

"You lied to the cops?" he says, drawing looks from the other customers, "Are you insane?"

"You lie to the cops all the time," I say.

"Little white lies. Not stuff that would get me thrown in jail."

"You *did* get thrown in jail!"

"For First Degree Murder, not lying!"

In Mike's world, that must make a difference. We break off the debate and he sits back in the café chair, ignoring his mug of dark roast. We're at Glacier's, my favorite neighborhood coffee shop. It's a converted café with checkerboard tile floors, brass rails and picture windows. It draws the young and artistic denizens from the upscale side of Cathedral Hill, a brick-and-mortar neighborhood overlooking downtown St. Paul. Glacier's is kind of sleepy right now. Just a few wannabe writers exuding more angst than productivity.

"What should I do?" I say, keeping my voice down, "Call up Pike and tell him the truth?"

Mike grabs my arm. "Dear God, no! Are you kidding me? Let him figure it out on his own. The truth is *always* on a need-to-know basis."

Panic expands like a bubble in my chest. The words *obstruction of justice* pop into my head. I see jail bars and cells with rough, lonely individuals and, worst of all, a shared toilet. All for the crime of starting up with an old girlfriend.

I push my latte aside and stare at the table top. I didn't get a lot of sleep, what with my residence being a crime scene and me loaded with enough adrenaline to kill a Batman villain. I turn things over in my mind. Brady was at my apartment to kill me. The gun made that obvious enough. But who killed *him?* And why? More directly, how long is it going to take Pike to put me and Norah together and figure out *why* Brady Perkins was on my deck?

A shit-eating grin splits Mike's goatee. "For what it's worth," he says, "I had my own little adventure last night."

I should have known we were never going to get far from Mike's self-concern, no matter how much jail time I'm facing. But I'm completely open to hearing about his latest (likely sexual) misadventure. As long as it takes my mind off *my* latest sexual misadventure.

"What happened?" I ask.

Mike slides his coffee aside. "Here's the story. I stop into the office last night—"

"Wait a minute. You were in the office after hours? You're barely there during regular hours."

"I wasn't working," Mike says, looking offended at the thought. "I left my Kindle there. Anyway, the place is deserted—pretty much like I expected—except there's some chick in Alan's office."

"Alan's your boss, right?"

"Right. Anyway, the chick in question is *smoking* hot. I poke my head in Alan's office. Just to be polite."

"Of course."

"Of course. She tells me she's there to use her dad's computer. Get a little privacy. And then I realize, this is Haley,

Alan's daughter. I haven't seen her since she was, like, seventeen. She has *really* grown in five years. And she was a hot seventeen, don't get me wrong."

"Wouldn't dream of it," I say.

"Anyway, we get to talking and we hit it off. Pretty soon, she tells me, 'My dad keeps some whiskey in the bottom drawer of his desk. You want some?' I'm like, 'Sure.' I didn't want to be rude."

"Your manners are impeccable."

"I try," Mike says, loosening his work tie, "So, we have a couple of belts and things are getting rather friendly. We're not sloppy, but there's a definite buzz going. Then we have one of those moments where we're looking at each other and we're not saying anything and *boom*, we're playing tonsil hockey across the desk."

Tonsil hockey. Lovely. "You were making out with Alan's daughter in Alan's office?"

"It gets better. We fumble around for a minute or two and she says, 'You want to come back to my place?' I'm like, 'Absolutely. Let's go.' We get in our cars and I follow her home. I'm thinking she's got an apartment or something. But I forget: she's just finishing college. Her place is Alan's place. I recognize it because I was there once."

"Holy shit."

"Yeah. I've got a woody that could spear fish, but even *I'm* thinking this is a bad idea. Haley's got a room downstairs with its own separate entrance. Great and all, but this is still Alan's *house*. Place isn't *that* big. It's not like Alan can't see me coming and going."

"So to speak."

"So to speak. I follow Haley downstairs and I'm getting the creeps. Alan hasn't been all that thrilled with my work lately. Last thing I need is something like this. I'm trying to think up a nice way to break it to Haley. But then she unzipped my pants and grabbed my rod and I kind of lost my train of thought."

I sip my latte. "That'll happen."

"Five minutes later, we're on Alan's pool table and she's riding me like I'm Secretariat." Mike exhales a breath. "I didn't even know Alan *had* a pool table."

On the bright side, if Alan finds out about this, I won't be the only one accused of murder. Meantime, Mike takes a self-satisfied look out the picture window to Selby Avenue. The weather is warm and dry. Somewhere, the lilacs are blooming. Not the time of year in Minnesota for murder and mayhem. But here we are, engaged in copious amounts of both.

Mike finishes his coffee. "I guess Haley and I are dating now."

"You sure that's a good idea?"

"I don't care. The woman is sexual crack, Joe. You can try and make me go to rehab, I'll say, 'No, no, no.'"

Egads. "You think Alan will understand?"

"No. That he will not. He's got that whole Daddy's Little Girl thing going toward her. And like I said, he doesn't care much for me to begin with."

"A situation that's not likely to change when he finds out you've defiled both his daughter and his pool table."

Mike gazes at a couple of young women who have just stopped in, from jogging if the sports bras mean anything. He gives them an appreciative glance. That's Mike for you. A sex drive with an auxiliary human being attached. Before I can say anything, my cell phone buzzes on the table. It's Norah. I have to take this. I rush out to the sidewalk to answer. Norah's first words come out in a rush.

"What the hell is going on?" she says.

"I don't know. Brady turned up dead on my deck last night."

"He was trying to kill you?"

I guess Norah knows about the gun and the very reasonable supposition how Brady intended to use it. "The cops told you," I say.

There's rushing air on the other end of the line, telling me Norah's pacing whatever room she's in. "They came to

Doug's place in the middle of the night. Woke us both up. They said Brady was found dead on your deck and that he had a gun on him."

"That's the case," I say. Norah doesn't say anything to that. If not the for the sound of the rushing air, I'd suspect the call's been dropped. The silence gets uncomfortable, so I ask: "Are you all right?"

"My husband just died. How am I supposed to be?"

"Sorry. Dumb question."

"No, I'm actually asking. I didn't like him, but I didn't want him dead. I don't know how to react. It's like my thoughts and feelings are in a blender."

I glance around, making sure no one's come along to overhear us. "Where are you now?"

"I'm at Doug's. I didn't go to work today."

"I'd like to see you."

There's a pause. "You think that's a good idea? It's just…Brady gets killed at your place and then we're seen together? How do you think that's going to look?"

Norah's got a point, though I'm a little disturbed she's making it. Seeing someone you like should never be the act of a guilty person.

"Do, uh, do you want to see me?" I ask.

After a second, Norah answers in a soft voice. "Yes."

"Do you want me to come to Doug's?"

"No, I don't think that would be good idea. Not yet." Norah lets out a breath. "Look, the hell with it. You want to meet at a hotel?"

Normally, I'm not a hotel guy. It feels sleazy and I generally can't afford one. But if there was ever a time to make exceptions…

"I can do that," I say, "Name it."

"How about the Ambassador Suites? Downtown? In about two hours?"

"I can do that."

"See you then."

I pocket my phone and stare at the traffic. A part of me thinks seeing Norah right after I've lied to the cops about knowing her is a colossal mistake. But a stronger part of me needs to see her, as if connecting with her will make sense of all this. When everything around you has gone crazy, what do you crave more than a little sanity?

Assuming anything I do at this point could be called sane.

***

The Ambassador Suites is an old-school hotel on the east end of downtown St. Paul. It's a little spendier than I'd like, but it's better than meeting at a No Tell Motel. (*That* would feel sleazy.) Norah's already checked in by the time I get there. I make may my way past the sunken garden area in the center.

The rooms are grouped in tiers ascending above the garden. I take the glass elevator to the eighth floor. When I walk into the room, Norah's on a balcony just big enough to hold two people. She's sitting in a chair, smoking a cigarette.

"I didn't know you smoked," I say, stepping through the sliding glass door.

"Neither did I," she says, "Seemed to be the thing to do. You want one?"

"No thanks."

"Suit yourself," she says, taking a deep drag.

I take in the view of downtown St. Paul. It's a mix of modern steel-and-glass and old school brick-and-mortar. Norah stares at the cement floor of the balcony. Her hair is pulled back into a ponytail that's already starting to fray. I lean against the balcony rail.

"Did the police ask about me?" I ask.

"They asked if I knew you. If I'd had any contact with you. That sort of thing." Norah tosses the cigarette over the balcony and drops her head into her hands. "I lied. I said I didn't know anything about you. I didn't know why Brady would be over at your place. I…panicked."

"So did I."

Norah's head pops up. "What do you mean?"

I tell her about my chat with Sergeant Pike. She stands and tries to move around, quickly realizing there's no room to accomplish that.

"We've both lied to the police," she says, "That's fucking great."

Norah goes into the room. I follow, not saying anything. Having dealt with more than a few explosions from girlfriends, I know it's best to let the volcano cool on its own. Norah paces the floor, one hand on her hip and one on her forehead.

"It's not going to take the cops long to figure out why Brady was at your place," she says, "They're going to know we were lying. And then it's a short jump to them thinking one of us killed him. If they're not thinking that already." She drops the hand from her forehead. "What exactly happened last night?"

"I was in bed," I say, "I heard a noise out on my deck. I went to check it out and…there was Brady."

"You didn't see anyone else?"

"No. I thought I heard someone running down the stairs when I first woke up. But they were long gone by the time I got out there."

Norah stops and stares past me at the St. Paul skyline. Her face has that cold look. She doesn't move or blink. I feel very alone. When Norah speaks, it sounds like she's talking to herself more than to me.

"It could have been self-defense," she says.

Panic stabs through me. Sure, I could make a case for self-defense. I shouldn't need to, since I didn't kill Brady, self-defense or no. But even a successful defense means getting arrested, sitting in a jail cell, having my name dragged through the public mud and then hoping like hell a jury of my peers (the same peers I've made a living out of mocking) doesn't think I'm guilty. And sleeping with the guy's wife and lying to the police about it isn't going to work in my favor.

Holy crap, I'm in real trouble.

"I didn't do it," I mumble.

Norah's head snaps, as if she's just woken up after falling asleep in class. She slides her arms around my waist.

"I didn't think for a second you did," she says, "I'm sorry. I'm just freaking out."

"Seems like the appropriate response," I say.

I sit in the easy chair and Norah guides herself on to my lap. She pulls her hair out of the ponytail and drops her head on to my shoulder. We sit there, staring at nothing in particular.

"It doesn't even seem real," Norah says, "I'm actually mad at Brady. Like this is another one of those shitty things he does. I can't get my head around the idea he's gone. That he went to your place to…" She stops, unable to finish the thought. "And I'm scared. We should have told the police the truth." She gently bumps her head against my shoulder. "Stupid, stupid, stupid."

I kiss her forehead. "I know. But this is a learning experience. Our next murder will be so much smoother."

Norah's head comes up. She's fighting off a smile. But she loses the fight and it devolves into a full-out laugh. A second later, I'm laughing. Yes, I know. It's not appropriate and it doesn't reflect well on us; laughing in the face of murder and all. But if there was ever a moment where the tension needed to be broken, this is it. Norah leans against me.

"We're horrible," she says.

"Can't argue with you there."

The laughter continues for several more seconds before subsiding. Norah strokes my cheek, her face close to mine. She's smiling and, for the first time since I got here, there's a lightness in her eyes.

"Missed you," Norah says.

"Likewise."

We kiss, letting some of the tension melt away. The room feels like a sanctuary. As long as we're here, as long as we're together, everything's going to be fine. We move into the bedroom and slide on to the bed. After a few minutes, we come up for air and Norah lays her head on my chest. A cool breeze blows in from the balcony.

"Baby," she says, "I don't want to kill the mood. But a thought just hit me."

Nuts. In my experience, every time someone tells you they don't want to kill the mood, that's exactly what they're about to do. I try to play it cool, but from where Norah's positioned, she can probably hear my heartrate pick up.

"What thought is that?" I ask.

Norah props herself up on an elbow. "I didn't kill Brady…"

"That thought *just* occurred to you?"

She gently swats me. "I mean, I didn't kill him and you didn't kill him."

Norah lets the next thought go unspoken. But now it's occurred to *both* of us. The thing that, in our panic about lying to the police, we haven't stopped to consider. Norah didn't kill Brady. I didn't kill Brady.

Then who did?

CHAPTER FOUR

My uncle Gordie once explained his opposition to the internet. He said a buddy of his asked for his address. When Gordie gave it to him, the buddy punched it into a search engine and Gordie got a look at his house (well, trailer) on Google Earth. Gordie was so off-put by the experience, he refused to use the internet anymore.

"Gordie," I asked, "Does your not being on the internet mean your house can't be seen? That's kind of like a dog hiding his head and assuming the rest of him is invisible."

Gordie had no answer for that. Probably because he was busy cracking open another case of Schlitz.

The loss of privacy is something we've all learned to live with. The generation coming up behind mine will probably have no memories of a time when the internet did not routinely compromise our privacy, much in the way my generation has no real memories of the Cold War (except for Rocky V, which proved that no conflict, great or small, could not be solved by a good ass-whuppin'). The key to getting through these times is to live your life, regardless of the consequences. If the FBI wants to know how many porn sites I've cruised, that's their problem. If my major appliances expose how often I sing Frank Sinatra while doing the dishes, then I feel sorry for the pencil-neck who has to record the experience. It's not going to change my life or my masturbation habits (unless I get a note from the Feds, asking me to knock it off).

Then again, it's easier to think like that when you feel you have nothing to hide.

Norah takes off for school first thing in the morning. I question if she should go back so soon. She tells me getting back to work is the best way to deal with things. I let her go and sleep in for a little while before getting my stuff together and heading out. I'm halfway across the hotel lobby when someone gets up from a sofa and approaches me. It's Sergeant Pike of the St. Paul Police Department.

"Counselor," he says, "Did you enjoy your evening?"

Pike's smirking, but back of that is a look of cold scrutiny. His eyes are red, likely from lack of sleep. His clothes are rumpled (although that's their normal state). I'd better watch what I say. Everything will go through Pike's personal polygraph.

"It was a nice night," I say, "Can I help you with something?"

"I was hoping you had a minute to chat."

"Here or downtown?"

"Here's fine." Pike points toward the hotel bar, just off the lobby. "Shall we?"

Pike leads the way into the bar. As could be expected, the place is empty this time of morning. It's done up in the style of an English pub: wooden table tops, stained glass around the hanging lamps, straight-back chairs. We stop at the bar to get a couple of beverages. Pike grabs a coffee. I figure they probably serve the kind of Folger's sludge that would gag a coffee snob like me, so I order an orange juice. We take our beverages to a table near the window.

Pike doesn't waste time. "When were you going to tell me you've been sleeping with Brady Perkins' wife?"

"Um, I was going to get around to it. Sooner or later."

"You lied to me the other night. When you said you didn't know the guy. You realize that's obstruction of justice, don't you?"

I'm forcing myself to remain calm. Think pleasant thoughts. Duckies, bunnies, pro wrestling. If Pike was here to arrest me for obstruction of justice, we wouldn't be hanging out in the hotel bar.

"I panicked," I say, "Until a few days ago, I didn't even know Norah *had* a husband. I only met the guy once when he was alive and that was him threatening me from the front lawn of my apartment building. So, when I said I didn't know him, I was sort of telling the truth."

"Y'know, the District Attorney has a real fondness for people who *sort of* tell the truth."

I try not to let Pike see how hard I'm gripping the table. "Am I under arrest?"

Pike's cold glare remains steady. "Let's chat a little and then I'll decide. Meantime, if I get the slightest idea you're not telling me everything you know, I'll handcuff you right here."

My mouth has gone dry and the pulpy orange juice does nothing to help. "That, uh, that sounds good."

"Good. Tell me the whole story then."

I give him everything. Me dating Norah without realizing she was married, the threats against my person, Lars getting punched in the face, waking up in the middle of the night to hear what I later realized was Brady's murder. When I'm done, Pike takes his glasses off and wipes them on his suit coat.

"You own any knives, counselor?" he asks.

"Just for cooking. They're all present and accounted for."

"We're reasonably certain Brady Perkins was killed with a hunting knife of some kind. Serrated blade."

"You don't know for sure?"

"We haven't found it. If the murderer ran away from your place, they took the murder weapon with them."

"I don't own a hunting knife. You're welcomed to check my place."

Pike replaces his glasses. "Must have been a scary situation for you. Living alone, building not exactly secure, someone threatening you. And Brady Perkins came to your place loaded for bear."

"You think I killed him in self-defense?"

"It's understandable if you did."

"I appreciate that," I say, "But I didn't kill him."

Pike swirls the coffee in his cup, still staring at me over the top of his wire-rim glasses. He pushes the cup aside.

"Here's my problem," he says, "You're the obvious one to build a case against. You're sleeping with the guy's wife. He was threatening you. He showed up at your place, ready to kill you. But he winds up dead instead. And when you're asked about him and the wife, you lie and say you don't know either of them."

My face has gone completely numb. Pike looks concerned I'm about to pass out. He puts a hand out, as if he can steady me with the Jedi Mind Trick.

"I'll be straight with you," he says, "Just for a second and completely off the record. I don't think you killed Brady Perkins. You say you panicked when you lied. I believe you."

The relief flooding through me makes me want to cry. If I started blubbering, though, Pike would probably haul me in, for the blubbering if nothing else. I just say, "You do?"

"I think you're smart enough—but only just smart enough—to realize that self-defense makes a better argument than, 'Gee, officer, I don't know how the corpse got here.' And, much as this gives me a pain in my ass to admit: after everything you did to get your friend out of jail last fall, I find it hard to believe you'd be this clumsy about murdering someone yourself."

"Thank you. Assuming that was a compliment. It's a little hard to tell with you."

"Call it a compliment. It's the only one you're getting out of me."

"Understood."

Pike pushes his glasses up to his forehead and rubs his eyes. "But your girlfriend is another story."

So much for the relief I was feeling. This is the exact thing Norah was worried about. "Norah didn't do it," I say.

"What makes you say that?"

"Because I trust her," I say.

Pike waits for more of an answer. I don't have one and the silence lets me wallow in the shallowness of my own response. I try to think of another reason, a crusher that will render the idea of Norah as a suspect completely and totally absurd. But I've got nothing. Pike slides his glasses back on to his face.

"I guess that solves that," he says.

Pike looks more than a little smug. It's enough to tempt me to throw my orange juice at him. (But with this much pulp, it could be considered a lethal weapon.)

"Did you stop her this morning, too?" I ask.

"No. I thought I'd talk to you first."

"But you talked to her the night of the murder, right?" I say, "She was home. I'm assuming Brady's brother can back that up."

"He did."

"There you go."

Pike folds his hands in his lap. "Alibis are a little overrated. Plenty of innocent people who don't have one. Plenty of guilty people who get someone to cover for them."

"You think someone's covering for Norah?"

"Maybe. She's got a hell of a lot of a motive, I know that much. You know that Brady Perkins hired a divorce lawyer?"

"Norah mentioned it. Said the lawyer was a real shark."

He sniggers, as if to say *You don't know the half of it.* "Sheila Grant. You want to take someone to the cleaners, that's who you hire. She handled my divorce. It was carnage."

"You hired her?"

"No, my ex-wife. Barely left me with a pot to piss in." The thought amuses me, but since Pike still has the option of taking me to jail, I keep it on the downlow. "Divorce lawyer aside," he says, "There's plenty of other stuff. Bad marriage, boyfriend on the side, threats about losing her job. Maybe physical threats. I haven't found out for sure, but it wouldn't surprise me."

"Brady was an asshole. I'm sure a lot of people had motive."

Pike gazes out the window, watching the passersby. His voice takes on a speculative tone, but I'm sure it's for my benefit.

"If you're trying to get away with killing your husband, what do you need?"

"Guns, knives. Maybe that big rock from *Raiders of the Lost Ark.*"

"Also helps to have some schlub take the fall for you."

I glare at Pike, but he doesn't seem to notice. He drains his cup of coffee, then kicks the chair out and stands up.

"You have a good day, counselor," he says, "I'm sure I'll see you soon."

Pike walks out of the bar, tossing a napkin in the trash as he goes. I take a swig of the orange juice and nearly gag on it. On the bright side, I'm still on the right side of incarceration. But how free should I feel? Brady Perkins' actual killer is still running around and Pike's looking at the wrong suspect.

Who's going to find the *right* suspect?

***

"The thing is," Carol says, working on a drink at my liquor shelf, "Sometimes you have to do something just because it's wrong."

I don't like where she's going with this. I'd love to tell you I don't have a sexist bone in my body, but that would be a lie. I do my best, but certain instincts get the better of me. I'll give Mike the floor to ramble on about some distasteful sexual adventure. But if Carol starts talking about something similar, I feel like my mother's sitting me down to talk about the birds and the bees. (Although, my father made such a hash of that talk, Mom might've been the better option.)

I decide to suck it up. "Maybe you need to start from the beginning."

Carol drops an olive into her martini and sashays across my living room floor. "I had a meeting the other night with a client. It's a hardware chain. They're rolling out their summer ad campaign. The CEO is one of these rich kids. Inherited the business from his father. Never had to work a day in his life, but thinks he knows everything there is to know about business."

"Sounds like a real loser."

"He's nice to look at. Trick is to not pay attention to what he's saying."

"Kind of like the time Lars and I got high and watched *2001: A Space Odyssey.*"

"I've got no frame of reference for that," Carol says, "Anyway, the usual happens: we have a few drinks—mostly me—we have a few laughs—mostly him—and then he invites me up to his room. I say no. He tells me his wife will never find out. Like I give a rat's ass, but whatever. We do this every time he's in town."

"Sounds ghastly."

She gives it a flip of her hand. "It's fine. He doesn't get aggressive. Just self-pitying. Anyway, I turn him down and he finishes his drink and goes up to his room. I've still got half a drink left and I'm not going to let it go to waste. So, I just hang out at the bar. And then I meet this guy."

Ah. The plot thickens. "Tell me about this gentleman."

Carol takes a swig of her drink. "He's wearing a suit, but his hair's a little shaggy. And he's got a Van Dyke that's going a little gray. Whole ensemble makes him look pretty smug. But he's got these beautiful blue eyes. They make him look kind of…kind. I guess."

I'm not digging this whole thing in general, but it's hard not to get caught up in Carol's enthusiasm. "All right, I'm getting the picture."

"He says to me, 'I'm a natural born killer and I'd like to buy you a drink.' And it's *so* goddamned hokey, but he's got this glint in his eye like he *knows* it's hokey. I tell him, 'Sure, I'd love to have a natural born killer buy me a drink.'"

I wonder if these are the kinds of stories parents tell their kids about how they met. I hope not. "After you were done with the cheap-ass dialogue, where did it go from there?"

"That's the thing. We kept up the cheap-ass dialogue. I should have laughed in his face. But there was something about him. Like I could see the real him under all the layers of bullshit. He was just…vulnerable. All he wanted was to talk to me. It was…cute."

Huh. Pathos as an aphrodisiac. It would explain why that angsty douche with the guitar back in college never seemed all *that* lonely.

"Then what?" I ask.

"We're hitting it off, getting pretty toasty. And he says, 'My place is only a few blocks from here. You want a nightcap?' I'm thinking, 'This is stupid. Why would I do this?' Then I realize, 'Shit. I really *want* to do this.' But I'm still playing coy. And he says, "You want to go for a ride instead?""

"A ride?" I ask.

"I was wondering the same thing. He tells me he's got a motorcycle. A little mid-life crisis thing. I'm thinking, 'Why not?' So we did."

I pour another beer into my Grand Brewing pint glass. "And that's all you did? You went for a ride?"

"Yep. First the bike and then each other."

"I see."

Carol lounges on the arm of the comfy chair. "He's got a little place over by Ford Parkway. This morning, he took me to breakfast. And there was a bouquet of flowers delivered to me at work."

"Very sweet."

She stops her martini short of her lips. "Are you being sarcastic?"

"I don't think so. But these days, even *I* have trouble figuring that out."

Carol gazes off into space, her dopey grin firmly in place. It's good to see her happy. I can't help feeling a twinge of jealousy, given how fed up my love life is at the moment.

"What's this guy's name?" I ask.

"Alan."

That sets off a little alarm bell. "Alan? Mike has a boss named Alan."

"There are a lot of people named Alan," Carol says, "Although this Alan *is* Mike's boss."

I nearly drop my pint glass. Carol ignores whatever distress I'm feeling. She tosses her hair back and looks away from me, toward the arch windows. I set my beer down on the breakfast bar.

"You're dating Mike's boss?" I say.

"It's a little early to call it *dating*. But there's definitely something happening."

"You really think that's a good idea?"

Carol's tone gets a little icy. "It's not his business. It's mine."

"Aren't you the same person who was ready to remove Mike's nutsack when you found out he was dating Jeannette?"

Last summer, Mike covertly dated one of Carol's friends. It eventually blew up in his face, to the point where his trip to jail in the fall probably seemed like a relief. Not surprisingly, Carol doesn't see eye-to-eye with me on this.

"This situation is totally different," she says, "When Mike and I broke up, we had a very specific agreement about our friends. He knew it and he violated it. We didn't say anything about bosses."

"Isn't that just a loophole?" I say.

"I'll take a loophole over an open violation."

"I don't think Mike's going to see it that way."

"Too bad for Mike."

Yep, this discussion is going nowhere at Indy Car speed. Carol seems to really likes this guy and she's not going to let Mike stand in the way. I knock back a goodly amount of beer and something occurs to me.

"I thought Alan was married," I say.

Carol wags her finger. "He *was* married. They're separated. Divorce pending."

"Pending? Doesn't that mean, technically, you are also seeing a marr—?"

"Don't go there."

"After getting on your high horse about me and Norah—"

"Shut it."

"You go out and start knocking boots with a guy—"

"Shut."

"Who in the eyes of the law—"

"Zip."

"Is still a married individual?"

Carol stalks over to the breakfast bar and stands opposite me. She sticks her martini glass under my nose. "This is one of your martini glasses, Joe. It can be used for consuming beverages *or* it can have a number of other household applications. For example, you could use it as a small stool after I permanently wedge it up your ass."

My eyes flick to the glass. Then I hold up my hands up and back away. "I wish you and Alan the best of luck." If Mike finds out, they're going to need it.

I move around my living room, making sure things are clean and straightened. (Despite the messiness of my life, I try to keep my apartment as clean as an operating room. Orderly work space, orderly mind.) Carol watches me, the martini glass tucked under her chin.

"How are you and Norah doing?" she asks.

"We're hanging in there. We had a nice night together. A nice phone call today. I think hanging in there is all we can hope for."

"Have you heard any more from the police?"

I busy myself straightening the framed poster of *The Godfather* on the wall. "Just Sergeant Pike of the St. Paul P.D. He seems to enjoy slapping me around."

I give Carol the rundown on my chat with the good sergeant. She twists her mouth to one side as she listens. When I'm done, she chuckles, humorlessly.

"You get away with everything, don't you?" she says, "You sleep with another guy's wife. You get the girl and the guy is dead. You lie to the cops about the whole thing and the lead investigator lets you off with a warning." She slugs the rest of her martini. "Must be nice."

"Strangely, *nice* isn't the word I'd use to describe the situation."

Carol toys with the martini glass. "What are you going to do?"

I roll the bottom of the pint glass on the breakfast bar, like it's a top of some kind. I'm avoiding eye contact—and really, this entire conversation—with Carol. I'm going to be honest with her and I already know how she's going to respond.

"Norah didn't kill Brady and I didn't kill Brady," I say, "And since the cops don't seem interested in anybody *except* me and Norah…I thought maybe I should look into it."

Carol's head falls back, like someone just karate chopped her. She makes the same sound I used to make when my mom would put Brussel sprouts in front of me at the dinner table.

"Look into it?" she says, "As in, *I will bring The Hound of The Baskervilles to justice*? That sort of look into it?"

"I don't believe there's a hound involved. But that's the general idea."

Carol sets her elbows down on the breakfast bar. "You're going to do this again? You realize, it's like performing brain surgery with a pen cap and a high school biology book? This should be left to professionals."

"I didn't hear you complaining last winter."

Carol ran into some trouble of her own in January. It had us running around the Twin Cities for a night, ducking the cops and almost getting killed about fifteen times. Y'know. Like you do.

Carol's fingernails claw the countertop. "That was different. The police weren't looking in the right direction. I was innocent and…okay, I see what you mean."

"Very magnanimous of you."

"But are you certain the police are looking in the wrong direction?"

"Meaning?"

Carol looks in the little mirror in the hallway, straightens a few stray hairs. "I know you didn't do it," she says, "But…are you *completely* sure about Norah?"

Great. Everywhere I go, people are trying to turn me against Norah. And now we can add Carol to the list. "Yes, I am," I say, cold as I can make it, "I know her."

We stand there, staring at each other. The tension in the room is palpable and we're not used to it. At least not with each other. Carol looks down, not wanting to confront me, but not wanting to give in, either. I lean on the breakfast bar.

"Norah's staying at her brother-in-law's place," I say, "He told the police she was at home the night of the murder."

"They've cleared her?"

"No. But it's good enough for now."

Carol scrutinizes me. "You needed an alibi from her?"

"No. But you did."

She raises her hands, conceding the point. Carol glances at the liquor shelf, briefly considering another. She does the smart thing, though, and simply puts her glass in the sink. When she comes back, she grabs her purse and throws it over her shoulder. She stops at the door, her hand on the doorknob.

"Something you might want to consider," she says, "Whoever killed Brady—no matter who it was—probably wanted it to look like you did it."

I glance down the hallway, in the direction of the deck. She's right. If someone wanted to kill Brady and deflect the blame from themselves, they've found a hell of a way of doing it.

"I guess that's a theory," I say.

"And if the theory is correct and Pike isn't going to arrest you, then the real murderer might still come after you." She opens the door, her face softening. "Just be careful."

I give her a reassuring nod. Now, if only I could reassure myself...

***

"The problem is that the drug crowd doesn't draw what we might call *the right element*," Lars says, leaning on the railing of my deck, "Management might frown on that. And by *might*, I mean they absolutely will."

I'm not sure which part of this conversation I like the least: Lars' latest dipshit business venture or that we're having this conversation on my deck. The deck, particularly after dark, now gives me the willies. The giant bloodstain does nothing to help the situation. Lars is oblivious to all this.

"I'm thinking I need to rent another place," he says.

That *does* get my interest. "Wait. You're moving?"

"No, I'm going to get a place on the side."

"On the side? If you weren't the super, you wouldn't be able to afford the place you have now."

Lars gives that an airy wave. "It's a principle of business."

"Which one?" I ask, "*Let the buyer beware? A fool and his money?*"

"No! *You gotta spend money to make money.*"

"Doesn't that imply you *have* money in the first place?"

"I've already found a backer," Lars says, "Chuck's coming in."

I try to hide my grimace. Chuck is Lars' friend and frequent business partner. Lars refers to Chuck as his *idea man* and he means it as a compliment. Given that Chuck's ideas have included a dating service for arranged marriages, a circus that *promoted* animal cruelty and a meat substitute of unknown origin (Mysteryfu), the rest of us view him in a slightly different light.

"Where did Chuck get the money to back you?" I ask.

"He's working on it. He knows a good enterprise when he sees one."

"Of course," I say, "Dealing drugs. Nobody's ever thought of that before."

"Exactly. It's…wait. You were being snarky, weren't you?"

"That's what I got from it."

I know I should be more supportive of my friends, be it relationships or business ventures. But sometimes being supportive of your friends in detrimental to society. That's certainly the case with Lars. Closer to home, I'd rather he helped get my deck back to normal.

"Have you talked to management about this?" I ask, waving toward the huge bloodstain.

"You bet. I'm the super. That's my job." He squats down next to the stain. "It's going to take an industrial cleaner to do it. They asked me to give it a shot."

Oh dear God. "Did you say you would?"

"I have to. I'm the super. That's my job."

I'm tempted to jump off the deck and get it over with. I can see how this whole thing will play out. Lars will try to clean the deck, probably using Windex or the generic equivalent. Flummoxed, he'll try something harder, like Pledge (or the generic equivalent). He'll float the idea of setting the deck on fire, at which point management will hire someone qualified to handle the cleaning. But we have to go through the charade first.

"Just get to it sooner rather than later," I say

"I'll try. But I've got a lot on my plate right now."

"But you're the super. It's your job."

My cell phone rings, thankfully ending this conversation. Lars salutes me and heads for the stairs. I take the phone out of my pocket. According to the caller ID, it's Lance, my editor at *The Daily Bugle*. Great.

"Hey, buddy," is Lance's standard annoying greeting, "Sorry to be calling so late. I know you creative types burn the midnight oil, though. Am I right?"

"Actually, I was just going to bed."

"Great, great," he says, not hearing a word I said, "Listen, buddy, I heard something kind of bothersome. Something about you and a married woman and a dead guy. Am I right?"

This gets better and better. "You have the general idea. What about it?"

Lance starts to get mealy around the mouth. "Um, here's the deal: I talked to a few people at the office. We've got some concerns."

"Concerns?"

"I…I don't want to go into it over the phone. You, uh, you think you could come into the office tomorrow?"

The office? never get called into the office. In fact, unless I'm late with a column or they want me to make a publicity appearance, the office never calls me at all.

"Can't we do this now?" I ask.

"No, it's, uh, it would just be better if you came in. Tomorrow."

What the hell is going on? "Okay, I can be there. Do I need to bring a lawyer?"

Lance laughs louder than my half-assed joke requires. "Nothing like that. Just a little confab. You know how it is."

"No, I don't. Maybe you could explain it to me."

Lance's force (such as it was) is diminishing. He doesn't do conflict well. "We, uh, we can talk about that tomorrow morning. Does ten o'clock work?"

"I've got a breakfast date at ten. I can do eleven-thirty."

"Eleven-thirty. Sounds good, sounds good. We'll, uh, we'll see you then."

"I'll bring donuts."

I ring off with Lance, dreading the coming pow-wow. Chatting with someone as relentlessly cheerful as Lance is bad enough under normal circumstances. Explaining my personal life to him is going to be sheer torture. Maybe I can lace the donuts with arsenic.

This miserable little reverie is broken by the sound of footsteps on my deck. It's got to be Lars, returning to clean the bloodstain. In the middle of the night, no less. The idiot has no sense of time. I storm to the backdoor and whip it open, ready to tell Lars where to get off.

And I find a guy on my deck, holding a knife.

The guy jumps a little. In the thin light, I can only see a blob of black and the gleam of the knife. We stand there, neither of us moving.

"Oh hi," I say. Because I'm not sure how else to open this conversation.

He steps my direction. I try to flip on the deck light. I miss my first swipe, but it's enough to spook the guy. By the time I get the light on, he's sprinting for the stairs. I charge after him.

Judging by the little I've seen, the guy has some girth to him. And I'm a fast runner. I should be able to catch him. But the twists and turns in the erector set of stairs give him a slight advantage. Speed is no good when you're in a constant state of slowing down. We sound like a herd of water buffalo going down the stairs. Nobody else has their deck light on, so things get darker as I descend. I round on to the last set of stairs and put on a burst of speed to the bottom.

And find I've lost the guy.

I look around, trying to catch my breath. There's some spill from the streetlights in the alley and over on Dale and Summit. But the parking lot is mostly dark. I doubt the guy had the time or the speed to reach the alley. He couldn't have stolen a car this fast. He *could* have ducked back toward the building, but he probably doesn't have the keys. And there was no time to pick the lock to the backdoor. I'm not sure where to go.

While I'm thinking about it, the guy clobbers me.

I drop to my knees on the grass. The guy hit me with something. Hard enough to feel it, but not hard enough to knock me goofy. He looms overhead. My hand goes to my throat, guarding it from the knife. I start to turn my head to get a look at him. He kicks me in the ass, stopping me. I stare at the grass.

"You killed Brady Perkins?" I ask.

"No, dipshit. You did. That's gonna be proved sooner or later. Whether you want it to or not."

His voice is muffled, like he's trying to disguise it. The guy circles me. A pair of black moccasins stalk past. I keep my hands where he can see them. No time for false moves.

"You're the one who killed Brady?" I ask.

"No!" he says.

I start to look up at the guy. "Then why are you here?"

One of the moccasins collides with my ribcage. It doesn't take the wind out of me, but it hurts like hell. When the muffled voice speaks again, it's very close to my ear.

"If you're smart, you'll walk right into the police station and tell them you did it. That's where you're going to wind up sooner or later. That or dead. Choice is yours."

Holy shit. Threatened with death right outside my apartment building. And I had such high hopes when I moved into the place.

Somewhere nearby, a voice rings out. "Hey! The fuck you think you're doing?"

The gravelly growl is familiar. I sneak a peek. So does my attacker. The object of our fascination is a tall, elderly man silhouetted standing in the back doorway. His still-muscular arms drop out of a simple white t-shirt and hang down to the legs of his crisp blue jeans. He seems somehow relaxed and coiled at the same time.

My attacker barks at him. "Get back in the house, old man."

An instant later, the old man seems to conjure a hand cannon out of thin air. "You want to run that by me again, shithead?"

My attacker figures out this is not someone to be trifled with. He raises his hands and slowly backs away from me. The old man follows the attacker's movements with his gun.

"Listen, pop, we don't have to—" And that's as much as the attacker gets out before the old man's gun goes off.

The attacker lets out a high-pitched scream and runs across the parking lot, disappearing into the night. I get to my feet, legs barely holding me up. The old man returns the gun to wherever it came from.

"You okay, boy?" he asks.

"I'm fine," I say, "Thanks, Mr. Albertson."

CHAPTER FIVE

It's time we faced it: at some point, our parents simply outlive their usefulness.

Naturally, we still love them. But the main components of the parent-child relationship are survival and guidance. Once we're out on our own, we (theoretically) don't need our parents to provide basic living materials. As for advice, I'm sure, say, Descartes still had a few decent words to the wise when his kid got older. But for most of us, our parents' advice is largely confined to, "You probably shouldn't do that" and other pearls of wisdom. So we're stuck with these people who provide no basic necessities or decent advice and yet we're required to have them in our lives. Because nobody's come up with an alternative.

And yet, when the fecal matter hits the cooling unit, our first instinct is to think, "I want my mommy."

In the absence of my mom or dad, I'll take Mr. Albertson.

Old Man Albertson is a legend around my building. According to the rumors, he hasn't left the building in fifteen years. His reclusiveness is not due to helplessness or anxiety.

The world outside has nothing to offer him, so screw it, he'll stay in his apartment and watch the Military Channel, thank you very much.

Mr. Albertson takes my arm and guides me into his apartment. The place is spare, neat as a pin, outfitted with your basic furniture (TV, couple of chairs, dining room table.) The only decorations are a couple of framed service medals and a picture of John Wayne on one wall.

"Grab a seat," he says, pointing at a straight-back chair.

My head hurts, but I'll live. The abject terror of the last few minutes has left my legs weak, so I drop into the chair. Mr. Albertson returns from the kitchen with some ice cubes wrapped in a towel and a bottle of Budweiser. Beer snob that I am, I'm not sure which I should be putting on my head and which I should be drinking. I crack the beer. (Guy just saved my life. I'm not going to insult his taste in beer.) Mr. Albertson turns the Barcalounger away from the TV and sits directly across from me. He cracks a beer of his own and studies me with his steely blue eyes.

"Who was your friend?" he asks.

"No idea. I found him out on my deck and he took off running. I went after him."

"Bad idea. He was holding a knife."

"I didn't think it all through," I say.

Old Man Albertson takes a contemplative sip of his beer. "This have something to do with the guy who got killed outside your apartment?"

Since the news of Brady Perkins' murder has probably gotten all over the building, it's naturally going to get back to the guy who never leaves said building.

"It had something to do with that," I say, "At first, I thought it might be the real murderer. But he had a chance to kill me and he didn't. He seemed more interested in me confessing to it."

I tell Mr. Albertson my side of the story. I'm not sure how he's going to react to the more sordid aspects, such as my having an affair with a married woman. Any guy who irons his t-shirt and blue jeans is a guy who values propriety. But he's silent while I give him all the info. When I'm done, he sits back in the lounge chair.

"Sounds like you're in a world of shit," he says.

"I'm getting the same impression."

Mr. Albertson uses his beer bottle to gesture toward the back. "You going to call the cops about this thing?"

"I don't know. Did you get a good look at the guy?"

"Can't say I did. He was wearing black. Maybe six feet tall. Fat ass. What do they call that? Pear-shaped? Might have had a beard"

"So, like any ten guys you could find watching a ballgame over at The Tav?"

"I don't go to The Tav. But I would guess so. How about you?"

"No," I say, "He slugged me before I could get a decent look." I adjust the makeshift icepack on my head. "I'll tell the lead investigator about it. He seems to think I'm innocent. But without a decent description, I don't think I'll make it a huge issue. All they'll do is take a statement and promise to get back to me. Like when my bike was stolen. And then they'll never get back to me. Like when my bike was stolen."

I chug the rest of my beer. I hand Mr. Albertson both the bottle and the icepack. He brings them into the kitchen while I get to my feet. I'm still a little shaky, but otherwise in decent working order.

"Thanks for bailing me out," I say.

"It was nothing. Guys like that shit their pants at the first sign of real trouble."

"Hopefully, he'll think about that before coming around again."

"Just in case he *does* come around again," he says, leaning against his kitchen wall, "You got anyone keeping your apartment safe?"

"I've got Lars."

"It's been nice knowing you."

He's hit the nail right on its pointed little head. Having Lars protect you is like running to the deck of the Titanic and discovering the captain has converted the last lifeboat into a man cave. I assure Old Man Albertson I'll be okay and head for the door.

"By the way," he says, "Tell your friend Lars he's asking for it if he keeps growing marijuana out on his deck."

"You know about that? How?"

"I have a life outside of you, Joe."

I can live with that. As long as I continue to *have* a life.

***

"I've got to tell you, Joe. I've heard better suggestions."

When undertaking a murder investigation, one hopes to get the approval of the girlfriend. Then again, unless you're Nero Wolfe or Philip Marlowe, I guess the chances are remote. Still, Norah's objections cast a bit of a pall over breakfast.

"The police aren't focused on anybody but us," I say, ignoring my ham and cheese omelet, "And after last night, I really don't want to sit around and wait to be arrested or killed."

I haven't told Norah that the police aren't focused on *us* so much as *her*. She seems to be getting over her initial panic and I don't want to screw that up. Besides, I get the feeling Pike's given me a reprieve more than a dismissal. If the pressure mounts to bring in a suspect, he might start liking the case he can build around me.

Norah holds a piece of wheat toast halfway to her mouth. "This guy who attacked you. You have no idea who he is?"

"None."

"But looking into this thing is pretty risky, isn't it?"

"Someone came to my place and threatened me. Things are risky whether I do something or not. I'd feel better doing something."

Norah gazes toward the street, temporarily ignoring her spinach-and-feta frittata. We're on the patio at The Highland Skillet. And by *patio*, I mean four wrought-iron tables placed on the sidewalk. They're around the corner from Snelling Avenue, but not immune to occasional bus fumes. Still, it's a beautiful day in the neighborhood, what with the sun and the warmth. I reach for the salt. Just as I grab it, Norah reaches for her coffee. She doesn't see me until she's accidently knocked the salt shaker out of my hand.

"Sorry," she says, hurrying to pick up the shaker.

"Not a problem," I say, tossing some salt over my shoulder (thankfully, the table behind us is unoccupied), "This is strictly an issue of table coordination. Everything would flow better if you used the hand God intended you to use."

Norah sticks her tongue out at me and clenches her left fist. "I am using it. Beware the Hammer of the Gods, Joe Davis."

I wave my hands like a damsel in distress and we start giggling. I love dating women who are left-handed and there's nothing sexual about that (so get it off your mind, you sick bastard). It gives me a natural opening for teasing and, thankfully, Norah takes it in the playful spirit it's intended. (I once had a drink thrown on me by someone who *didn't* see the humor in it.) Norah ends the giggling with a little sigh.

"All right, go ahead and investigate," she says, "But if you get yourself killed, I'm going to be really mad at you."

"Noted."

Norah goes back to the frittata. "Where do you start?"

"With you."

Her fork freezes on her plate. "I thought you're trying to prove I *didn't* do it."

"I am. But I need to find out more about Brady and you're the first person I came to."

A smile plays at one corner of her mouth. "Is that why you invited me to breakfast?"

"Yes. That and the possibility of sexual favors at a later date."

"Later date?"

"You have to be back at work in forty-five minutes. Otherwise…"

"Later date it is."

I can't think with an erection, so I give it a minute before getting back to business. Thankfully, Norah doesn't start playing footsie under the table or there'd be no getting back on track.

"So, Brady," I say, "He was co-owner of a sporting goods store. His brother being the other owner?"

"Doug. Yeah. The store was where Brady spent most of his time and energy. He lived for the business."

"Which store is it?"

"Pro Sports. Down in Bloomington."

"How long have they owned it?"

"About five years."

I dab at my mouth with a napkin. "And he and Doug don't get along?"

"I don't think they've ever been close," Norah says, "They only went into business together because they had more money collectively than either of them separately. From what I gather, they were equal partners but Brady acted like he was in charge."

"And Doug resented this?"

"He did. But like I said, I think the resentment goes back a long way."

I pick at the omelet. "You think Doug would talk to me?"

Norah sips her coffee as she thinks. "If I asked him, sure, but I get the feeling he doesn't approve of…us. He hasn't said anything, but don't expect a hero's welcome."

That's all right. The last time I got a hero's welcome was when the guys in the dorm found out I slept with Jenny Ryan. And even that seemed more like an excuse to have a kegger than an actual celebration.

"Can I drop by today to talk to him?" I ask.

Norah seems very tired. "I don't know. Brady's visitation is tonight. The funeral's tomorrow. I'll check with Doug. But I'm not sure what he'll say."

"Just do your best. Time is of the essence and all that."

"Understood."

Since I've gotten what I can out of that topic, I let it go. Better to pass the time without constantly reminding ourselves that either the cops or the Angel of Death could be joining us at any moment. Norah glances at her phone, checking the time.

"You have to get back?" I ask.

"Not just yet," she says, "I'm in no hurry."

"How is it at work?"

"The faculty is fine. I get a few *she's back awfully soon* looks, but everyone's good. The kids, on the other hand, are wonderful."

"Really? That's a shock. What with everyone telling us this generation is the end of civilization as we know it."

Norah flips her hand. "They're not. Believe me. They're great kids. So many of them stop and ask me how I'm doing. I don't know if they know about…you. But I don't think it really matters." She turns her face to the sun. "They're why I love my job."

I can't help smiling. I don't know if I had a teacher like Norah when I was in high school. I probably did but didn't appreciate them. I just hope her students realize how lucky they are. Someone smart who loves them with a heart as big as all outdoors. You can do a hell of a lot worse.

After paying the check, we step out on to Snelling, ready to head our separate directions. Norah looks at me, concern creasing her brow.

"Are you going to be all right?" she asks.

"I'll be fine," I say, "I've got an old tennis racket, two cowardly cats and an idiot neighbor to keep me safe. What could possibly go wrong?"

Norah laughs, but doesn't seem comforted. I cup her face in my hands as I kiss her. Her hands rub mine as we part.

"You be careful," she says, smiling up at me.

"Yes, ma'am."

After another quick peck, Norah strolls down the street, heading for her car. She glances back and gives me a little finger wave. If I had any doubts about whether all of this is worth it, the little lift in my heart answers the question.

*****

I've been working for *The Daily Bugle* for over five years and I've been to the office twice in all that time. And one of those was my job interview. My interactions with my bosses are generally via phone and email. Exactly the way I like it.

The *Daily Bugle* office is in Uptown, a hipster hangout rapidly being supplanted by the gentrified Nordeast. Given its proximity to the chain of lakes and to downtown Minneapolis, I doubt Uptown will ever go completely out of style. Judging by the number of unwashed poseurs floating about, it's holding its own.

The Bugle is on the second floor of Calhoun Square, right in the heart of Uptown. The reception desk is visible as soon as I walk through the glass doors. Beyond that is a general office area with a few executive offices on the far side. A series of windows look out on Uptown. There are old front covers in frames on the wall, hearkening back to the days when *The Bugle* was in print. The receptionist is a college-age dude named Kyle (according to the nameplate on his desk). He's thin and wears a striped shirt and a thin, black tie. His brown hair is swept back and gelled into place. He spins his chair toward me as I enter.

"Hi," he says, in a voice more chipper than I'd like, "How can I help you?"

"I'm Joe Davis. I'm here to meet Lance."

Kyle's eyes light up. Then they darken and he looks like someone told him President Kennedy's been shot. "It's nice to meet you, Mr. Davis," Kyle says, rummaging around the desk, "I was—*am!*—am a big fan. I'll let Lance know you're here."

Kyle picks up a phone, then reconsiders and heads for one of the offices at the back. The butterflies in my gut are forming a conga line. If Lance comes out of that office holding a file (one that likely contains a severance package), I'm urinating on the floor.

Fortunately, Lance is not carrying anything when he comes out of the office. Unfortunately, he doesn't look any more comfortable than Kyle. He tugs at the sleeves of his sport coat and looks around. He plasters on a grin and throws a hand out.

"Joe, good to see you," Lance says, looking past me, "You look well."

Quite the compliment, given this is the second time Lance and I have seen each other in person. He's pretty much the way I remember. Just about my age and height, slightly unruly brown hair, needle nose, a lot of teeth. He walks with a slight stoop, as if he'd prefer to go through life anonymously. His eyes are furtive and his gestures spastic. He'll make some neurotic woman or man very happy one of these days. (Assuming he hasn't already. I know *nothing* about this dude.)

Lance clears his throat. "You got a minute?"

"I have several," I say, "That's why I'm here. You invited me. Remember?"

Lance gives that a forced laugh. "That's right. I just…got distracted by a thing. The, uh, the conference room is open. You want to go in there?"

"It's your show."

The conference room is on the other side of the reception area. It's a little room framed on one side by a picture window, meaning everyone in the office can see our conversation. I can't help noticing how many of them are making an effort *not* to look at me. I'm remembering when I got fired from a Gas and Go. I walked in for my shift and my soon-to-be-former co-workers made a point of not looking at me. I had the sensation I was a dead man walking.

The same feeling I have right now.

Lance sits at the end of the conference table. I sit adjacent to him and he immediately moves to a seat right across from me. I guess he wants something between us in case I get violent. My *accused murderer* reputation is already preceding me. Lance tugs at his cuffs.

"We, uh, obviously," he says, "We've got a little problem."

"Since I'm the guy suspected of murder, I think the problem's all mine."

Lance winces. I'm usually dismissive and snarky with him, but never in person. Does he react this way when I give him the verbal back of my hand over the phone?

"I should tell you that the editorial staff and the board have been meeting…" he says.

"Both of you?"

"And we're very uncomfortable with the situation you're in."

"I know the feeling."

Lance lays his arms on the table, still not looking at me. "What I'm saying is, whether you're guilty or not, this looks bad. Even if the murder charge turns out to be nothing—"

"I'm kind of banking on that."

"The fact you were…*with* a married woman…it reflects poorly on all of us. It makes our staff look immoral."

"So what? The entire readership is immoral. If we didn't get hits from perverts, we'd get no hits at all."

Lance shoves both hands into his hair. "That's, that's not entirely accurate."

"Really? When *The Bugle* was still in print, the last ten pages of every edition were ads for sex lines. I know. I saw them. And called many of them."

That probably wasn't the right thing to say, given I'm trying to talk my way *out* of a sex-related jam. But I can't resist calling out hypocrisy and being a smartass. Lance's hands massage his hair. He's either nervous or has a scalp condition.

"I'm afraid you're suspended until further notice," Lance says, suddenly, "I don't like doing it. I'll be the first to tell you it sucks. But the board and the editorial staff—"

"Both of you."

"Have decided it's for the best. But it's not all bad. We're suspending you *with* pay."

I'm sure I'm sporting the *Who farted?* face. "*With* pay? Lance, you guys only pay me when I submit a column. If I'm not submitting columns, how it is a suspension *with* pay?"

"Well, our legal team says we're covered."

Terrific. *The Bugle*'s legal team consists of Lance's ambulance-chaser uncle. It's more legal representation than I have access to. Sure, my brother Kevin is a lawyer, but that would mean calling him and begging him to help me. I'd rather get fired. After being *set* on fire.

I stand up from the table. "In that case, I guess…good luck to you."

Lance bounces to his feet, relieved. "That's, that's really very, uh, nice of you. Sporting, you might say."

"I might. But I won't."

I walk out of the conference room and head for the front door without looking back. Kyle at reception averts his eyes. Lance's footsteps fade behind me.

"I, uh, I hope this whole thing blows over soon," he says, "I'd love to have you back."

Yeah, I'm hoping for one of those. But maybe not the other.

***

So, now the job that barely pays my bills no longer pays my bills. That means an afternoon of abject panic before meeting Brady's brother, Doug. Still, I'm able to talk myself off the ledge. I don't make a lot of money and tend to live paycheck-to-paycheck, but my parents schooled me on the virtues of paying your bills on time and squirrelling away a little for a rainy day. May's rent has been paid and all of my bills are current. *The Bugle* owes me for a few recent columns. If I live like a monk for the next few weeks, I should be able to pay June's rent. That means, worst case scenario, I'll have sixty days before things reach a breaking point with bills and rent. By the end of the summer, I'll need to either be back with *The Bugle* or find another job (which, judging by resume, will probably mean working at McDonald's…so strike what I previously said about a *worst* case scenario).

Doug's place is located on a cul-de-sac in Eagan, a conservative suburb south of St. Paul. It's one of those places that indulges in the fantasy this country never left the Fifties. Husband is the breadwinner, mows the lawn and ogles the neighbor's wife. Wife stays home, takes care of the house and spends afternoons with her tennis instructor. Kids get good grades and smoke reefer under the bleachers at the football stadium. Truly, the stuff that made America great.

The house is nice enough. Multiple stories, big backyard, perfectly manicured lawn. A path leads around the side of the house. Norah is waiting for me when I pull my Saturn Ion into the driveway. She's already in her wake wear: a black dress, hair pinned back in an attempt to look matronly. Total failure. She still looks hot.

Norah takes my hand and leads me down the path around the house. Her basement apartment has a separate entrance in the back. The yard is filled with tasteful lawn furniture. A gazebo would not be out of place. The whole thing is screened from humanity by a tall wooden fence. It's as Stepford as the rest of the neighborhood.

The basement apartment is comfortable, but nothing to write home about. The ceilings are low, giving the place a cramped feeling. The living room and kitchen are separated by a breakfast bar, much like my place. The carpeting is beige and the sofa a deep red. Tastefully bland.

Doug stands up from the sofa when I enter. Even at his insane, raging worst, Brady at least appeared professional. (Lying on my deck with his throat cut wasn't a good look, but you know what I mean.) Doug has none of that. He's taller than Brady, but also heavier. His patches of stubble may or may not someday coalesce into a beard. He might have once been capable of having the same kind of swept-back hair as Brady, but he's lost quite a bit of it. It sticks up from his head like a collection of wacky waving inflatable arm men. He slouches and he seems to swim around in his black suit. Nothing's out of place, but he's one of those guys who manages to look slovenly even when everything is in place.

"Joe, this is Doug," Norah says, flicking her hand, "Doug? Joe."

Doug cradles his right hand, which is wrapped in white athletic tape. It's an excuse not to shake mine. He immediately returns to the sofa. Norah looks at me and shrugs, as if to say, *You're on your own.*

"What happened to your hand?" I ask, sitting in a nearby chair.

Doug slides the hand into his lap. "Car door."

Norah hovers between us, staring at the floor. None of us seem sure how to open this interview. I clear my throat.

"Thanks, uh, thanks for meeting me," I say.

"Norah said you're trying to find Brady's murderer?" Doug says.

Why does it sound so damn silly when someone *else* says it? "I'm, I'm looking into it."

Doug has the decency to let it go at that. "What would you like to know?"

That ends the *Getting to know you* portion of our show. Let's play our game, shall we? "I have some questions about Brady," I say. Doug's eyes, dark and downcast, slide toward Norah, who puts a hand on my shoulder. I'm guessing she had to cajole him into meeting me. "You were here the night Brady was killed?" I ask.

"I was," Doug says, "The police woke us up in the middle of the night."

"Must have come as a shock."

"I was more concerned about how Norah was taking it. She was fine, so I was fine."

I reach up and put my hand over Norah's. "I understand you and Brady didn't get along."

Doug frowns, (although that appears to be his standard look). "Brady was a dink. He ran the business like he was the only owner. He treated people like shit. You ask around and that's what everyone's going to tell you. Nobody liked the guy."

I'll be honest: there's always been a little tension in my relationships with my brothers. But the only time I remember speaking about one of them with the same contempt Doug has for Brady was when my younger brother Owen was learning to walk and his first steps caused him to tread on the Lego car I'd just built.

"But you went into business together," I say.

"And that's all it was," Doug says, "A business arrangement. We needed each other's money and credit. End of story." Reacting to the look on my face, he adds: "I know. He's my brother and I'm supposed to love him and blah, blah, blah. All I know is: I didn't ask for him to be my brother and family was never a good enough reason to put up with somebody's bullshit."

Interesting philosophy. Brings to mind Noel and Liam Gallagher. Or Ray and Dave Davies. Or any two British brothers with the misfortune of forming a band. Norah, it seems, has heard enough. She edges toward the stairs.

"I'm going to give you guys a minute," she says.

She gives me a fleeting look before practically running up the stairs, leaving me alone with Doug. He glowers at me (or more accurately, the floor, since he doesn't seem big on making eye contact). This seems like a good time to address the elephant in the room.

"Obviously, you know about me and Norah," I say.

Doug looks toward the wall. "That's her business, not mine."

"I appreciate you understanding."

"I didn't say that."

Zoinks. The little bit I know about interrogation is that you want to have the upper-hand at all times. But Doug's every word and gesture from the second I got here has been designed to remind me I'm not welcome. It keeps me off-balance. I shift in the chair, trying to find a comfortable position.

"Did everyone at the store think Brady was a…a dink?" I ask.

"Probably. He didn't work closely with most of them. Just me and Stephanie."

"Stephanie?"

"She's the store manager," Doug says, "Good worker. Not that Brady figured that out."

"You think she'd talk to me?"

"You'd have to ask her," he says, "She's at the store afternoons and evenings. She just changed shifts."

"Because of Brady?"

"No. Just a work thing." Doug's eyes fall on a backpack lying on the floor. With the butterfly stickers on it, it's obviously Norah's. His eyes widen and some of the sullenness falls away. "Brady didn't value much of anybody," he says, "I guess Norah was an exception. For a while. Brady had a manipulative streak a mile long. He knew how to be charming when it suited him. That's the problem with being an asshole, though. Sooner or later, that side of you is going to come out. It did with Norah."

"Did you see a lot of them?" I ask.

"At first. During the summer, Norah would come to the store every day. She'd bring Brady lunch or they'd go out to eat. Then it became a couple of times a week. And she'd hang out with me more than Brady. Whenever I saw them together, Brady would snap at her, get pissy."

From my little bit of experience with him, Brady could go beyond pissy. I can't help remembering Norah hiding under the covers when he caught us, as if she'd be willing to crawl into the earth to hide from him.

"Is that why you offered Norah a place?" I ask.

Doug rubs his stubble. "I don't approve of having an affair. I need to say that. But Norah was in a rough spot. I wanted to help her out."

"How did Brady react?" I ask.

"He wasn't pleased. Not that I gave a shit." Doug cradles his hand. He glances at a clock on the wall, then gets up and clomps toward the stairs. "Norah and I have to get going. I'll get her for you. Don't take too long saying good night." He stops at the bottom of the stairs. "I'd appreciate it if you didn't…um…y'know, while Norah's staying here."

"Your house, your rules."

Without looking at me, Doug gives that a curt acknowledgment and heads up the stairs. I hear a few words exchanged between he and Norah, something about when they need to leave. Norah comes back down to the apartment. She hurries across the floor and drops into my lap.

"How'd it go?" she asks.

"Fine. We're making plans to go to Tijuana. Raise some real hell."

Norah gently punches my arm. She lays her head on my shoulder and kisses me on the neck. "I think we need some quality time," she says, "It's been a few days."

"You may be on to something."

"I'm free later. I have to be up early, but I can bring an overnight bag."

There's absolutely no way I'm saying *no* to that. I give her a quick kiss to seal the deal. It's only when I'm heading out the door that I realize what's about to happen. I'll be spending the night with a guy's widow right after the guy's visitation.

Next time I visit my parents, I'm going to have to redact this entire episode.

CHAPTER SIX

*I'll be the first to admit that I have a problem with supporting my friends. Probably because I know so many f**king idiots.*

The challenge is to support someone when you know *the idea they've come up with is a bad one. It takes a poker face worthy of Phil Ivey. Sadly, I've got a poker face worthy of Don Knotts. For example, my friend Lucy was working on a book that was a rewrite of Agatha Christie's* Murder at the Vicarage. *The big twist was that the Miss Marple character would be replaced by a pair of twins. Fair enough, I guess, if you could obscure things enough to get it past the Christie estate. But Lucy didn't bother to change* anything *else about the book. The characters, the plot, the setting, they were all exactly the same. The only difference was there were now* two *elderly ladies solving the crime rather than one. And they were never out of each other's company, either. It was the literary equivalent of poking the readers' eye so they'd see double. Lucy never figured out what a colossally poor idea this was. Nor did she get what I was driving at when I talked about my idea to re-do The Hardy Boys as triplets.*

And that idea seems brilliant compared to Lars and his pot enterprise.

"The key is to treat the cannabis plant like any other plant," Lars says, pottering around his deck with a spray bottle, an apron and a floppy gardening hat, "They need plenty of water and sunshine. The key at this stage is to keep them in a warm climate. Seventy-five to eighty degrees is ideal. It's a little cool today, so I should really have them inside. But the sun is nice and bright, I just had to give them some fresh air."

He baby-talks to one of the plants, using the same voice I occasionally use with Lenny and Squiggy. I'm not seeing any buds, but we're early in the process.

"Now, you know I'm the first one to support agriculture and the small businessman," I say, glancing at the pots of...*pot* lining the deck, "And what you've got here is truly impressive. But are you sure this is going to yield enough to turn a profit?"

Lars stops spraying one of the plants. "Joe, you have to understand business. You don't get in on a 3M level right away. You start small and work your way up. With a little love and care and diligence, I can turn these wonderful little guys into some primo shit. Once I've done that, I'll develop a small base of loyal customers and grow the business from there."

"And where is this small base going to come from?" I ask, "You already deal to me and Mike. You got other customers I'm not aware of?"

"Just the two of you and Chuck. But I've got a source that can hook me up."

"Who is this?"

"Billy. My old dealer."

I'm already deeper in this conversation than I want to be, but I can't stop now. "Billy? I thought the whole reason you're going to deal is because you're pissed at him."

"Nothing's changed there," Lars says, merrily spraying the plants, "But Chuck pointed something out: I'm probably not alone in my dissatisfaction with Billy. Surely, he's been pissing off other customers. That's how you draw a base. Build on the dissatisfaction of your competitor's customers. Give them something they're not getting from Billy. There's a potential goldmine there."

I could point out the folly of someone as socially inept as Lars basing a business on the personal touch. But any attempt to talk Lars out of this would be foolhardy. As a fool, Lars is nothing if not hardy. Meantime, I've let this business distract me from the reason for my visit.

"Have you talked to management about security," I ask, "I don't want to get jumped again."

He rearranges the potted ganja. "I haven't spoken to management as such. Since opening my new business, I've been reluctant to interact with them. But I've made some discreet inquiries around the building. Trying to see if there were any witnesses to the attack."

Not that I'm hopeful, but: "And what have you found?"

"I'm afraid I've come up with a bumper crop of bupkus." He sets down the spray bottle and takes off the floppy hat. "The Boscoes in 4C saw something. Jay said the attacker was a short guy with a ski mask and a beard like a rhododendron. But Jaye, Jay's wife, said she doesn't remember a beard."

I'm about to dive into this Abbott-and-Costello routine when I remember that the Boscoes are both named some variation of *Jaye*. My condolences to whoever had to perform *that* ceremony.

"Anybody else see anything?" I ask.

Lars pours himself some lemonade. "Mr. Scott in 7C said the attacker was an old guy with steel gray hair, a white t-shirt and a gravelly voice."

"He just described Old Man Albertson."

"Old Man Albertson attacked you?"

An enormous headache is developing in my sinuses. "He was the one who *saved* me."

"Suit yourself," he says, "Frances Urquahat in 5D said she saw some creep skulking around the building. Described him as about six-one, early thirties, brown hair, thin. Good-looking, but a little scruffy. Had a St. Paul Saints t-shirt on."

We can turn that headache up to eleven. "Lars, she just described me."

"Why were you skulking around the building?"

Should have seen that coming. "In other words, you haven't found anything useful?"

"Not as such. No."

I head for the walkway that will lead me to the stairs and up to my deck. "Just do me a favor: keep an eye out for anything strange. I don't want to bring the cops into this until I have something concrete."

Lars sets his lemonade glass down. "You can count on me, brother. I'll stay on this. We're going to take this S.O.B. down!"

Right now, I'd be happy if the guy just left me alone. Much like my neighbors.

***

"The problem is, sexually, she's an animal." You can count that as a phrase I never thought I'd hear from Mike.

We're heading down Highway 494, toward Bloomington. It's early evening and rush hour has just passed. This means 494 is mostly a parking lot rather than completely a parking lot. We're on an intercept course with Pro Sports and a chat with Stephanie, the manager. I'm hoping to get more information on Brady. Mike's tagging along, less to help me than to drone on about his new girlfriend. I'm forced to play along.

"How is the animal thing a problem?" I ask, fighting to change lanes.

"Because she lives at home. You ever tried making love to a really loud girl when her parents are just down the hall?"

"You remember when I went home with Jenny Warner for the weekend?"

"When her father chased you out of the house?"

"Yep. Long bus ride home."

"Was it worth it?"

"Most definitely."

Mike taps his knuckles on the window. "This could be worse than getting chased by a fat guy with a baseball bat. Haley's dad is my boss. If this gets fucked up, I could be out of a job."

"You don't think it was a mistake to take up with her?"

"Have you seen this girl?"

"I have not."

Mike rocks in his seat. "She's beautiful. Seriously out of my league. And she's twenty-two. How often does a guy in his mid-thirties get to be with a beautiful younger woman?"

"If you're George Clooney, it happens all the time."

"I'm not George Clooney."

"I didn't think I needed to clarify that."

Mike gives me a sour look, then continues. "It's not just the stuff at home. She's got a thing for doing it in odd places."

I don't want to hear this, but I probably can't stop him. "When you say *odd places*…"

"You ever done it in a car?" Mike asks.

"What's so odd about that?"

"Her father's car?"

"One time."

"On the hood?"

Nothing to say to that, but: "I have not. No."

"In the garage? *His* garage?"

"No. That's new territory."

Mike pats his hands on the dash. "For me, too. Not that I'm complaining. It wasn't as comfortable as the desk at Alan's office, but…." He shivers at the memory. "And don't get me started on Alan's exercise bike. *That* was tricky. No worse than his weight bench. Better in some ways."

Mike's foot is tapping and he's chewing his fingernails. Talking about sex tends to get him fidgety with excitement. (Not the worst kind of excitement, I suppose.) Meantime, I try to concentrate on the landscape of retail spaces.

"I'm sensing a theme in these, uh, encounters," I say.

"They all involve something of Alan's?"

"You've noticed it, too?"

"I have indeed. Didn't take me long to figure out Haley has daddy issues. First time she cried out, 'Fuck me! Fuck him!' I thought, 'Something's going on here.' She talked about it a little. How Alan was wrapped up in business most of the time. Neglected the kids. Missed plays and ballgames and recitals and the like. And—she didn't come right out and say this—but she suspects Alan hasn't been all he could be, uh, fidelity-wise."

I just manage to get to the exit ramp. "You think she's right?"

"Oh God, yes. It's known far and wide that Alan will chase anything with two legs and a vagina. And even the legs are negotiable. Every Christmas party is like a *Mad Men* episode. I swear the company lawyer must spend the holidays swigging Pepto Bismal."

Guess that explains why Alan's getting a divorce. Seems like the kind of thing I should let Carol know about. Maybe the next time she gets on her high-horse about Norah's infidelity.

Pro Sports comes up a few blocks later. It's a hell of a lot larger than I expected. The store's in a strip mall, but to be more accurate, it practically *is* the strip mall. There's a little coffee shop and a tobacconist on one side, but Pro Sports occupies roughly two-thirds and a second story of the mall.

Mike gapes as we pull in. "Whoa. You need decent money for a place like this."

"So it would seem."

"And Norah threw over a guy with this kind of earning potential for *you?*"

"So it would seem."

Mike whistles through his teeth. "This guy must have really fucked up."

I'll have to thank Mike for his ringing endorsement. Some other time. We walk into the store and stare at the enormity. It's more like a warehouse. There's all manner of sporting goods, from team sports to camping and mountain climbing equipment. There's even a climbing wall. It would not be out of place to see the *Spirit of St. Louis* hanging from the rafters.

"Where do we go?" Mike asks.

"I see something marked *Information* about halfway back. Why don't we start there?"

The girl at the information desk sets aside the book she's reading and bounces to her feet. Even doing that, she doesn't rise far above the desk itself. Her brown eyes light up as we approach. She's trim and athletic, the kind of person you'd expect to work in a sporting goods store. Her demeanor is…um, *Perky* sounds like a such a condescending description, but she really fits the bill. Her ponytail bobs behind her and a set of perfectly straight teeth greet us.

Mike steps past me. "Hi…" He looks at the nametag on her white polo shirt. "Amy. How's your day going?"

If you've known Mike for more than five minutes, you know the nametag thing was an excuse to sneak a look at Amy's chest. She seems oblivious to it. In fact, the way she situates her hands on the information desk and leans forward only accentuates the target of Mike's stare. (Not that I'm, uh, noticing this myself.)

"It's going great," Amy says, "What can I help you with?"

Mike jerks a thumb toward me. "My friend here would like to talk to your manager."

Amy's smile fades. "Sure. Is anything wrong?"

I wave away her concerns. "Nothing at all. It's just a few, uh, business questions I have."

The white teeth return to their full brilliance, off-set by the deeply-tanned skin (too deep this early in the season to be natural). "No problem," she says, picking up the phone next to her, "Stephanie's in her office. I'll page her."

Mike strikes up a conversation with Amy while I pretend to check out the nearby sporting goods. (I'm so caught up in preparing for the chat, it takes a minute to realize I'm staring at athletic supporters.) Stephanie arrives at the information desk. She's roughly my age, about five and a half feet tall. She's prim and tanned. She wears a polo shirt and a pair of coach's pants. Her dark hair is tied back into a ponytail that hangs just below the nape of her neck. She wears no makeup and is one of those fortunate souls who looks better without it. Her arms are muscular and she greets me with a firm handshake.

"What can I help you with?" she asks.

"I wanted to talk about Brady Perkins."

"And you are?"

"Joe Davis. I, uh, I know Brady's wife. Widow now, I guess."

Stephanie has a slight smile, but it's off-set by the intensity in her eyes. I'm being scrutinized. "Are you the one who's been seeing her?" she asks.

"It's kind of—"

Mike steps behind me. "Yep, they've been sleeping together." I shoot him a glare and he holds his hands out. "What? You're having sex with her. Am I supposed to nuance that?"

I turn away, wondering why I let Mike come along. "I am involved with Norah," I say, "It's a complicated deal and if that means you don't want to talk to me, I'll understand." I won't, but I'm trying to be reasonable here.

"Why do you want to talk about Brady?" Stephanie asks.

"I'm trying to find out who killed him," I say.

"My number one suspect would be you."

"There's a lot of that going around. Would you mind? I only need a few minutes."

Stephanie bounces lightly against the counter as she thinks. She flicks her head toward the stairs and says, without a great deal of enthusiasm, "Come up to my office."

We head toward the back of the store. I glance back and see Mike chatting up Amy. Just what he needs. Another girl in his life. Stephanie leads me up a flight of stairs and down a hallway to her office. She moves with an athlete's easy grace and control. Her office is small and windowless with no hint of decoration. There's just enough room to hold a desk and a chair. The fluorescent lighting overhead is not turned on. Stephanie has opted for a couple desk lamps. She slides behind the desk while I wedge myself into the chair across from her.

"What do you want to know?" she asks, turning her computer screen away from me.

My knees are only a few millimeters away from the desk. I grip the arms of the chair like I'm on a rollercoaster.

"What kind of boss was Brady?" I ask.

Stephanie says, carefully: "He understood business and he was attentive."

"And beyond that?"

"He was an asshole."

Good. I like it when a conversation gets frank. "Was that the general consensus among the staff?" I ask.

"Brady didn't deal with the staff too often. He'd make the rounds every now and again, ask people how things were going. But I did the hiring. I handled the books and the accounts. I talked to the employees. Brady talked to me. Simple as that." Stephanie raises one corner of her mouth. "Have you talked to Doug?"

"Briefly. He wasn't a fan of Brady's, but I'm guessing that's not a newsflash."

"It's not"

"What was it like to work with Doug and Brady? With their not getting along?"

Stephanie shrugs. "It was fine. It's not like they had knock-down, drag-out fights in the middle of the sales floor. They didn't talk much and never had a kind word to say about each other."

"Did they both talk to you?" I ask.

She sits back and toys with a pen, something she must do when thinking. "Doug would make conversation. Brady only talked to me when he needed something. Or when I had done something wrong. Which was often, as far as he was concerned."

"Did he lose his temper?"

"No. He was more condescending than anything. He'd talk about the store having standards. It was all I could do to remind him that those weren't really standards. They were one pissy man wanting things done a certain way."

"But you didn't tell him that."

Stephanie's thick eyebrows go up in amusement. "I like having money for groceries. So, no. I didn't tell him that."

Fair enough. "Would he act the same way toward Doug?"

"Pretty much. As far as Brady was concerned, Doug knew sporting goods, but was incompetent as a businessman. And Doug thought Brady was good with numbers but didn't know people to save his ass. They were both right, by the way. But if I had to choose someone to talk to, I preferred Doug."

Seems like everyone, except me, prefers Doug. (I choose *None of the Above*.) I try to cross my legs, but realize I'd have to be Plastic Man to pull that off. Meantime, Stephanie sets the pen in a precise spot on the desk and adjusts her shirt over her midsection. She slips a surreptitious glance toward the computer screen. I get the feeling she's looking at the clock on the computer. One of these times I'll have to chat with someone who wants to chat with *me*.

"Did you see Norah all that often?" I ask.

"Yes, I did," Stephanie says, rearranging some papers on the desk, "She came in every now and again, brought Brady lunch. By the end, she hung out with Doug more than Brady."

"Did Brady ever talk about Norah?"

She gives that a slight shake of her head. "I figured they weren't happy. You could read it in the body language. I *did* notice Norah looking a little happier the last few weeks. Turns out it was because she was…uh…"

"Bumping uglies with yours truly?"

"That would be my guess."

There's the goofy thing about this situation. I'm flattered I make Norah happy, but I also realize that makes me look guilty. It's a case of screwing up in reverse.

"The, uh, the night Brady was killed," I ask, staring at the wall, "What, uh, what were you up to?"

I try to make it sound casual, but I fail miserably. If I had any doubts on that score, the look on Stephanie's face removes them. She stares at me with those intense eyes, as if someone left a flaming bag on her doorstep.

"You want an alibi?" she asks.

"Just wondering what you were up to," I say, "Nothing more than that."

Her eyes study the ceiling as she debates answering. She says: "You saw Amy down at the reception desk? We went out for a drink. An after-work thing."

I stand up (as best I can) and thank Stephanie for her time. She gives me a dry handshake and leads me out of the office. When we get back to the store proper, I find myself looking around the store again.

"Quite the place," I say, pointing toward the climbing wall, "Rock climbing and everything."

"We've got a climbing club," Stephanie says, "We go out on the weekends, weather permitting. We practice here."

"You do rock climbing?"

"I used to. I had to quit recently." She points at her knee. "Tendonitis. Probably just needs some rest. We'll see."

I don't think she should be all that optimistic. I've been a runner for a goodly number of years and have seen quite a few of my running partners drop out due to tendonitis. Rest doesn't do them any good. But I'll let Stephanie entertain her fantasy.

Mike's still at the information desk, chatting up Amy. She seems more interested in Mike than her actual job, but the place is pretty slow. She spins toward us as we approach.

"Hi, Steph," Amy says, "You ready to go to dinner?"

"Absolutely," Stephanie says, "I just need to let Justin know and then I'll be right back."

Stephanie and Amy offer their goodbyes and Stephanie disappears down one of aisles. I grab Mike and start for the door. He mouths something to Amy. I'm assuming it's *Call me*. I don't say anything until we get to the parking lot.

"Don't you have enough on your plate?" I say.

"I have nothing on my plate. My thing with Haley is casual revenge fucking. It'll run its course and that'll be that. No rules that say I can't have some fun in the meantime."

"You checked that with Haley?"

Mike gives me the annoyed look I'm oh-so-familiar with. "Thanks for your input, Mother Superior. I suppose you're not interested in what I found out from Amy?"

Give the man credit: he can certainly re-route a lecture. "What is that?" I ask.

Mike glances back toward the store. "If I remember what you told me, this Brady guy got his throat slit by a hunting knife? Did you notice they sell hunting supplies? When I was chatting with Amy, I asked her about the business and Brady and if anything funny happened lately. She told me one of their hunting knives had gone missing."

I stop walking. "Maybe a customer walked off with it."

"Unless this customer found his way into the backroom, opened a box of the damn things and walked off without anyone noticing, I don't think that's how it went down."

"And they don't know who took it?"

"They do not. Bet you dollars to donuts that missing knife is the murder weapon."

Holy shit. If Mike's right and the missing knife is the murder weapon, it means that Brady's murderer *definitely* had a connection to the store. I don't regret bringing Mike along.

"Is that all Amy told you?" I ask.

"I got her phone number and a few hints as to what turns her on, but—"

"So, that's a *no*."

We climb into the Saturn and head out. We don't say anything until I'm back on 494. I tap the steering wheel.

"Interesting that Stephanie never mentioned the missing knife," I say.

"Maybe she didn't think it was important."

"I come in there, tell her I'm trying to find out who murdered Brady and she doesn't think to say, 'By the way, the potential murder weapon has gone missing from our inventory'?"

Mike flits his hand. "Maybe she thinks you did it."

"She's going to have to get in line."

CHAPTER SEVEN

Over the course of your average friendship, you endure many trials and tribulations: job losses, disagreements over significant others, losses of friends and family. But the most trying of all these, without doubt, is helping someone move. For all the bantering Mike and I have done over the years, the closest I ever came to ending our friendship was the time I helped him move. Allow me to explain.

When he graduated from college, Mike's parents bought him a fifty-five inch TV. Now, we're not talking one of those lovely fifty-five inch flat-screens we have today; the kind that can be neatly placed in any briefcase or carry-on bag. No, this was an old school gigantic TV that could have applied for statehood. Mike loved the damn thing, despite the fact he nearly had to sleep in his car because the TV took up most of the available space in his first apartment.

After a year at that hovel, Mike decided to upgrade to a slightly-larger hovel. This required help in moving, the biggest item of which was the TV. It had to go from one third-floor apartment…to another third-floor apartment. When I showed up for the move, I discovered all of our other "friends" (Robbie, Stoner, T.J.) had found excuses for getting out of the move (work commitments, family commitments, colonoscopy). It was up to me and Mike to haul around the Titan Tron. By the time we got the damn thing to his new place, I couldn't lift my arms to accept the beer he offered, let alone punch him in the face (which I wanted more than the beer).

I'm just glad Norah's not into big screen TVs.

"Why don't you bring those boxes out to the front porch?" she says, "They're full of Brady's stuff, so don't worry about being careful with them."

The weird thing about being at Brady's and Norah's house is that I feel like I've returned to the scene of the crime. Even though I've never been here before. Helping her rummage through Brady's stuff isn't helping the situation.

"Is all this going somewhere?" I ask, moving a few boxes to the front porch.

"To his mother. She can decide what to do."

I set some boxes on the front porch. The house is attractive, but not huge. It's on a tree-lined street in south Minneapolis, not far from Highway 35W. There are two floors, a good-sized living room and dining room, a kitchen with plenty of counter space and a small study. The second floor is a converted attic containing a master bedroom. There's a hot tub in the backyard.

"I would've thought Brady preferred the suburbs," I say, walking back into the living room.

Norah is busy wrapping the china in the dining room. "He did. *I* preferred Minneapolis. This place was a good compromise."

I take a few more boxes out to the front porch. Norah's working to keep up, not packing things as carefully as she could. This isn't the most comfortable task I've ever performed, but it's worse for Norah. She keeps looking around like she's breaking into her own home.

There's a lull in the action, so I wander around the place. Various prints of Renaissance art lean against the walls of the living room. These seem more Norah than Brady. The study is without decoration, probably Brady's domain. The guest room upstairs is filled with books and movies. Norah's space. I meander back down to the dining room and watch Norah wrap the china. She brushes some hair off her face.

"There's beer in the fridge, if you want," she says.

"I want."

I grab a bottle of Grand Maibock out of the stainless-steel refrigerator. I pull up a high back chair from the glass dining room table and take a seat.

"It's a nice place," I say, "You don't want to move back in here?"

"This is Brady's house. All I see here is him." She roughly shoves some china into the box, "I'll find a place. Doug's nice, but I need some place that feels like home."

Norah wraps more china. "Besides, I only lived here a year. And most of it was miserable."

"That bad?"

Norah sets the china aside and talks to no one in particular. "You realize how many nights I'd lay in bed with my back to him, crying myself to sleep. Hoping he wouldn't wake up and ask me what was wrong?"

"Would you have told him?" I ask.

"What good would it have done? Did you ever deal with a bully when you were in school? Did you ever tell them how much they were hurting you? Of course you didn't. Because you knew it would just make things worse." She taps the box with her foot. "And when I did something that made me happy, how did he react? He was going to take everything away from me. It was like a tornado came into my life and blew every damn thing apart."

I sit on the floor next to Norah. "I'm sorry."

Norah pats my leg. "Nothing to be sorry about." She grabs the china again. "If you don't mind, some of Brady's paperwork is in his desk in the study. It's just got to go into boxes and then out to the porch. Would you mind doing that?"

"Not a problem."

The study is dominated by a large desk along one wall. There are no filing cabinets, but with desk drawers the size of storage units, they probably weren't needed. I pull open the bottom drawer and discover files stretching halfway to Terre Haute. Several cardboard boxes sit open on the floor, waiting for the paperwork. I'm guessing it will all wind up in a dumpster or a bonfire, whichever Norah finds more amusing.

Per instructions, I'm not careful about chucking the paperwork into the boxes. When you don't have to be delicate, jobs like this don't take that long. In short order, I've cleared out the drawers. In the interest of being thorough, I pull open the small middle drawer under the desktop, just to make sure it's empty. The only thing it contains is a small key, attached to an orange plastic keychain. There's a three-digit number on one side of the keychain and the name *Universal Fitness* on another. Norah leans in the doorway.

"Are you ready for a break?" she asks.

My hand closes around the key. "Sounds great. What did you have in mind?"

"Dinner at The Stone Mill?"

"Perfect."

I wait in the foyer while Norah grabs her purse and a light jacket. She glances at the rapidly-emptying living room as she walks toward me. There's a strange look on her face, something akin to wistfulness.

"Are you okay?" I ask.

"It's nothing. Just anxious to get out of here. I'll be fine as soon as I get a martini."

That *will* solve most things. I take the key out of my pocket. "You recognize this?"

Norah looks it over. After a few seconds, she hands it back. "Not at all. Where did you find it?"

"In the study. I assume it belongs to Brady?"

"If it was in the study, it did." A shiver runs through her. "Can we just get out of here? I don't want to think about Brady for a while."

"Understood. Should we come back here later and finish up?"

"How about we forget it entirely and go back to your place?"

I pocket the key. "I think I can make that work."

***

You wouldn't think the (hopefully temporary) loss of a job that rarely took up more than a few hours of my day would play havoc with my schedule. Maybe it shouldn't. Maybe I'm just letting it mess with my mind. But I'm having trouble filling my days. I keep walking over to my desk to get started on a column but have to reroute myself when I realize there's no call for it. The days are beginning to seem long.

But I'm trying to fill them, using tasks from without and within. I'm currently taking care of a *within* task by brushing the cats. They both love it more than I do, as I usually wind up with enough hair in the brush to open a branch cat.

The *without* task has been taken up by Carol, who's dropped by to say hi. She's wearing her work clothes, (a black suitcoat over a maroon blouse and black slacks) telling me she's playing hooky from the office. She toys with the key I've left on the counter.

"Universal Fitness?" she says, "Isn't that in South Minneapolis? The big club on Lyndale, just off 62?"

"I think so," I say, running the brush across Lenny's stomach while he purrs along, "It would stand to reason anyway. It's not that far from Brady's and Norah's house."

"This is one of those temporary keys, right?" Carol says, hefting it in her hand, "To those temporary lockers? For the people who don't bring a lock of their own?"

"I think so. My club has them, too. Funny part is: people don't hold on to those keys. They use them for their workouts and leave them in the locker after."

"You think Brady accidently walked out with it?"

"In his workout stuff? I can't imagine he'd get farther than the car before he realized his mistake."

Carol holds up the key. "And Norah didn't know anything about it?"

"Not at all."

"Seems kind of strange,"

"It was in Brady's desk," I say, "I'm guessing that means it was off-limits for Norah."

Carol tosses the key on the counter. "Why would Brady take the key with him?"

"That's an excellent question. Mike and I are going to check it out this afternoon."

Carol's nose wrinkles, an expression she frequently uses when Mike's name comes up. But I get the feeling it's more than just Mike. There's been a dark cloud over Carol from the moment she got here.

"Everything okay?" I ask.

She digs through the cupboard, looking for any sweets I may have stashed. "It's a thing with me and Alan. His daughter almost caught us last night."

I finish brushing Lenny and send him on his way. "That sounds ugly."

"It was. The worst part is that we were at his old house."

Carol comes out of my baking drawer with a half-opened bag of chocolate chips. She carries them to the breakfast bar. While I empty the hair brush into the trash.

"What happened?" I ask.

She tosses in a handful of chocolate chips and talks around them. "All right, Alan and I are hanging out and he tells me he's got to stop by his house and pick up something. He asks me to go along. He doesn't want to face the place alone.

We get in there and one thing leads to another and we're both feeling kind of naughty. And…"

"You start doing the nasty in the kitchen."

Carol stops, mid-chew. "How did you know?"

"It's what I'd do."

"And that's exactly what we started doing. Right on the kitchen counter. My head was bouncing off the cupboards, but, y'know, I wasn't complaining. It was exciting. Probably made us louder than we should have been. But Alan stops. I ask him what's going on. He says he hears something. And then *I* hear it. Someone's coming up the stairs."

I pause in tossing the cat hair in the trash. "Who was it?"

"It was his daughter."

"Haley?"

"Yeah." Carol shoots me a look. "How did *you* know that?"

Danger, Will Robinson. "Mike mentioned it. Once. He's…met her."

Carol adopts the stinkface. As long as she doesn't ask me about Haley and Mike, I'm in the clear. Luckily, she's ready to move on with her own story.

"Alan hears this whole commotion downstairs and he says Haley must be home. He says I've got to hide. Haley's still upset about the divorce. He hasn't told her about us and he doesn't want *this* to be the way she finds out."

"It would be hard to come back from a thing like that."

"I know, right? I get off the counter and Alan ushers me out of the kitchen. Just off the kitchen is this little closet. He shoves me in there and closes the door."

"Quite the gallant," I say.

Carol squares me with a look. "It was a desperation thing. You've never done anything like that?"

"As the perpetrator? I don't think so. But I *have* hid in a closet or two in my time."

"Anyway, I'm trapped in there with a bunch of coats that smell like mothballs and boots that really could use some Odor Eaters. And I'm bare-assed because there wasn't time to grab my clothes before Haley came up the stairs. She starts reading Alan the riot act. Wondering what the hell he's doing. Something about the whore he's with. I nearly jumped out of the closet and kicked her ass."

"Probably better that you didn't."

Carol pushes the bag of chocolate chips aside. "Finally, Alan gets a word in edgewise. He says, 'Why the hell are you in your robe?'"

Ah. This is interesting. "Did she have an answer to that?"

"She said something about just getting out of the shower. But even eavesdropping in the closet, I could tell it was bullshit. Alan says, 'Why isn't your hair wet? What's going on? Do you have a guy downstairs?' Completely turns the tables on her. Then there's this huge crash downstairs. Alan says, 'The son of a bitch is down there, isn't he?'"

My heart is in my throat. Because I know the identity of the son of a bitch in question. "What happened then?" I ask.

"Well, now Haley's on the defensive. And I'm glad. Because my clothes are scattered all over the kitchen. I don't know how she didn't see them. Maybe she was too pissed to notice. Whatever. Haley insists there's no one in the basement. She says it might be a burglar. Alan wonders where his baseball bat is. Haley says it's in the hall closet and that she'll get it."

"Oh crap."

"Exactly, right? Alan tries to stop Haley from getting to the closet, but she's not in a mood to listen. On the bright side, I could find the baseball bat easy enough because it was jammed in my left ass cheek. The hard part was keeping Haley from finding *me*."

"What did you do?" I ask.

Carol sits on the arm of the futon. "I stuck the baseball bat against the door. That way, the first thing that happened when Haley opened the closet was the bat falling out. I hid behind a trench coat and hoped like hell she wouldn't notice the coat had feet."

"I take it she didn't notice?"

"She didn't. They both went downstairs and I don't know how that went. I was busy getting dressed and getting the hell out of there. I was still buttoning up my blouse when I was running across the front lawn. Some guy came around the corner. Thank God, he totally changed direction and ran the other way. No idea why he did that. It was weird. But when you're running around in a state of undress, you don't ask questions."

"That's always been my policy," I say.

"I talked with Alan this morning. After last night, I thought he'd be okay telling Haley about us. There's no reason to have these kinds of incidents. But he kept telling me he didn't think the time was right. I asked him what he was waiting for, but he didn't tell me. That left an even nastier taste in my mouth." She runs a hand through her hair. "It goes without saying that you won't mention this to Mike?"

"Lips are sealed and all."

Carol grabs her purse off the futon. "I've got a meeting. Thanks for letting me bend your ear."

"Anytime. Not like I've got a hell of lot going these days."

I glance at her as I put the cat brush back in its drawer. "This guy really mean that much to you?"

"I like him," Carol says, her tone getting a little defensive, "He's grown up and he's fun. I usually have to choose one or the other. I'm not saying we're going to get serious—it's too early for that—but I…can see the potential."

Wow. Carol getting serious about a guy. (Actually, *anybody* in our group getting serious about someone.) My thoughts risk going down the rabbit hole of envisioning the whole gang breaking up. But then I remember Mike is involved, so we haven't left immature idiocy behind.

Same old, same old.

***

One of the secrets to maintaining a friendship with Mike is not to be too judgmental of his actions. I avoid it for two reasons: 1) It's not going to change Mike's course of action, and 2) I frequently don't have a high horse to get on. Instead, I offer a weary tolerance (and more voyeurism than I care for).

"I'm meeting Amy for a drink tonight," he says, stepping out of my car.

"Amy from Pro Sports?" I say, locking the door, "How does Haley feel about that?"

"Weirdly, I didn't ask her permission. Besides, stuff with Haley is getting a little complicated."

We're walking down Lyndale Avenue in South Minneapolis, past a stretch of garish retail stores. Mike is slouching and his hands are in his pockets. His Sulk Walk.

"What's the deal with Haley?" I ask.

"There was, uh, an incident last night."

Over time, I've gotten to dread Mike's use of the word *incident*. It's his way of euphemizing his latest heinous act. I never know what's going to follow that word, but it's always going to be bad.

"What happened?" I ask, trying to keep the air of resignation out of my voice.

"All right, we're over at Alan's place. Down in the basement. And we're doing it on Alan's piano."

"Alan plays piano?"

"Surprised me, too. Anyway, we're going at it and Haley stops. I ask her what's wrong and she's like, 'Ssh, ssh, ssh.' We stop and then I hear it. The unmistakable sound of two people in the act. Y'know, *the act.*"

Holy shit. I've heard this story before. Just from a completely different angle. Like *Pulp Fiction* with less gruesome violence and more clandestine fucking. Still, I have to play dumb.

"In the act, huh?" I ask.

Mike looks around to make sure the coast is clear. "Haley goes nuts. She's convinced it's her dad up there. She pushes me away and runs toward the stairs."

"Oh boy. Where's her mom in the middle of all this?"

"Out of town. Something like that. It wasn't a high priority. Anyway, I go running after her, telling her she can't go upstairs and yell at her father while she's buck naked. She storms into her bedroom, grabs a robe and goes upstairs. Meantime, I'm looking around for my clothes. Which is not easy. Haley and I were all over the basement before we got to the piano. It was like a fucking scavenger hunt just to find my skivvies. Meantime, Haley and Alan are arguing upstairs. I can't make out what they're saying, but it doesn't sound friendly. I'm listening to see if my name comes up. I got so distracted, I tripped over the damn coffee table. Sounded like someone threw a chair through the window or something. Everyone upstairs stops talking. Then Alan starts yelling. 'Is there somebody down there? What the fuck is going on?' And his voice is getting closer to the stairs."

"Uh-oh."

"Exactly what I was thinking. My first instinct is to run out the door. But all I've found is my underwear and a pair of socks. I'm not going anyplace. Say what you will about society, it operates on a *No shirt, No shoes, No service* basis."

"I've found that."

Mike wipes his brow. "I'm looking around for a place to hide. Closest thing is the sofa. It's a little back from the wall. There's just enough room for me. Tight fit, but in I go."

"Too bad you couldn't grease yourself up."

"I know. That night of all nights, right? I wedge myself in there while Alan storms around the basement. Haley's following him, yelling: 'Daddy, I'm a grown woman. I can have guys down here.' Alan reminds her it's his house and as long as she's under his roof, she'll play by his…blah, blah, blah. Then Haley starts in on Alan again. Wants to know who's the whore in the kitchen? Alan claims there's nobody there. He's not doing anything. She says, 'Then why were you naked?'"

Jesus, it's like my friends have become an Edward Albee play. "That family's weird."

"You don't know that half of it." Mike dashes across the street, staying ahead of the traffic. "Haley and Alan are yelling and screaming about each other's sex lives and I'm hiding behind the couch, praying this whole thing will go away. Literally praying. I don't remember the last time God heard from me. He's probably like, 'I thought that son-of-a-bitch lost My number.' But Alan doesn't find me and the argument dies down. There's a light at the end of the tunnel. I might get out of this. Then I spot them."

"Spot who?"

"Not *who*. *What*. My car keys. They're on the coffee table. Right behind Alan. All he's got to do is turn around and look. What's worse, my keychain has the company logo on it. He sees them, he'll know who's been fucking his daughter. And I am *not* prepared to have that conversation. I'm sweating like a whore in church."

"Which you more or less are."

"And I've got to fart like nobody's business. That seems worth mentioning."

"I wish you hadn't."

Mike ignores me. "Anyway, Alan says, 'We'll talk about this later, young lady' and stalks off. Haley follows him, wanting to keep up the argument. They go upstairs. Next thing, I'm running around that basement like Usain Fucking Bolt, trying to find the rest of my clothes. I get 'em all and hop into my pants on my way to the car."

"The Fifty Yard Dash-And-Dress."

"Can't say college never taught me anything. I go around the corner. My shirt's unbuttoned and my fly's wide open. And there's some chick coming right at me. Damn near my fifth heart attack in ten minutes."

That explains the Mysterious Stranger Carol ran into. I'm surprised she didn't recognize him. Mike approaching a woman while in a state of undress is not unheard of. "What did you do?" I ask.

"Ran the other direction. Wound up going all the way around the block. The chick wasn't there when I got back. I hopped in the car and got the hell out of there."

I shake my head. "You talked to Haley about it?"

"She texted me. The whole thing turned her on. I gotta get out of this deal."

Universal Fitness comes into view. It's a blocky two-story structure with an oversized neon sign out front. It fits right in with the plastic retail shops slashing the neighborhood. I take out the temporary key. Mike takes it from me.

"Just follow my lead," he says.

I'm glad to see Mike focused on the task, no matter the situation with his romantic life. I brought him along because we'll need to concoct some bullshit story. And who better to have along than Michael Griffin, the Upper Midwest Poet Laureate of Bullshit?

I lead the way through the glass double doors. The place looks like an airplane hangar swallowed a Gold's Gym. The spacious main floor is filled with weight machines. On the far side, an Olympic-sized swimming pool is visible through a picture window. Up on the second floor, there's cardio equipment and a basketball court. The staff are all clean-cut, athletic and perky. The Stepford Olympic Team. A buff dude with a white polo shirt, a buzzcut and a vacant blue-eyed stare stands in front of the curved front desk, waiting to pounce on girly men like me and Mike. With the scraggly goatee, he looks like someone stuck an air hose up Maynard G. Krebs' ass. He greets us with a sizable amount of teeth and enthusiasm.

"Hi guys," he says, "What can I do for you today?"

I try to match the dude's enthusiasm. "I'm thinking about joining the club. Wondering if I could get a tour?"

"Sure thing, sure thing."

The dude shakes my hand and introduces himself as Jesse. Mike takes on a skeptical look, as if he's seen better health clubs in his time. It's our low-rent good cop/bad cop routine.

"We got a great place here," Jesse says, unconsciously (at least I think unconsciously) flexing his muscles, "Plenty of stuff for every kind of workout you're looking for."

Jesse takes us past the front desk and points out the various weight machines. Mike hangs back a few feet, still putting on the stink face. Jesse's enthusiasm is undeterred.

"What kind of workout do you like?" he asks.

I'm feeling rather guilty. I already have a membership at a gym that's walking distance from my place. And Mike's only workout involves sitting on the couch and eating Doritos.

"I like to work with weight machines," I say, "Do some running."

"We've got everything you need." He glances at Mike. "How about you?"

Mike looks toward one of the studios at the back. "I've done yoga."

"Just yoga?"

"Yoga instructors, specifically."

Jesse looks confused, but promptly gets back to the tour. We get closer and closer to the locker rooms. My glance at Mike is returned by a short nod. The temporary lockers are visible just inside the entrance to the locker room.

"Excuse me," Mike says, "I've got to take a shit."

With that, he disappears into the locker room. I would have preferred a more tasteful excuse, but it does the job. While we wait, Jesse and I chit-chat about working out and other aspects of the club. I'm thinking of the nicest way to decline a membership. The best policy, I realize, is honesty. The next best (and more frequently used) policy is to say I'll get back to him and never set foot in the place again.

Mike comes out of the locker room about five minutes later. He thanks Jesse and gives me a waggle of the eyebrows, telling me he's got something. Jesse rubs his palms together.

"You guys ready to get the paperwork started?" he says.

Time to backpedal. "It's a great place," I say, "But I want to look at a few other clubs before I make up my mind."

"Lot of a good clubs out there," Jesse says, "But you're not going to find one with these kinds of amenities at the price we're offering."

Mike folds his arms. "What about the gay issue?"

Jesse looks startled. "The, uh, the, uh, gay issue?"

"Yes. What kind of gay men do you have working out here?" Mike says, "The place we used to go was an absolute meat market. That's how we met." Mike grabs my hand. "The point is, we have an open relationship and might be interested in meeting other men. What kind of other men could we expect to find?"

Jesse makes a noise that sounds similar to *Utica*. He looks around for someone who can help him out. I get my hand away from Mike, but he puts his arm around me instead.

"Don't worry about it, Jesse," Mike says, "We're going to check out some other clubs—and I do mean *check out*—and then we'll get back you. Sound okay, sweetie?"

Jesse hastily thanks us for coming in—without shaking our hands or looking either of us in the eye—and scurries back to the front desk. Mike keeps his arm around me while we head for the exit. As soon as we're out of the club, I elbow him in the gut.

"That was the best cover you could think of?" I ask, "The guy looked like he was going to swallow his tongue."

"Got to work with the material you're given," Mike says, "I had that guy pegged as a homophobe the second we walked in."

If there's one thing my closest friends have in common, it's a refusal to express remorse for their actions. Mike leads me around the side of the place and down an alley.

"Did you find anything in the locker?" I ask.

"I did. A gym bag. Big sucker."

"What was in it?"

"Didn't have time to look," Mike says, "There were a lot of people around. Figured it was best if I hid it out back. The janitor should be more careful about leaving the backdoor unattended."

"Let's hope it's still there."

We reach the back of the place and nearly run into a big blue dumpster. Mike thrusts his hand behind the dumpster and comes back with a black gym bag. I make sure the coast is clear.

"Let's get it to the car before we open it," I say.

We try to stay casual. It shouldn't be difficult. After all, what's odd about seeing someone walking away from a health club, carrying a gym bag? Although, when you're sweating profusely and looking around like a coke fiend at a narc convention, it's a little hard to say you're playing it cool. But in spite of ourselves, we make it back without any trouble.

Mike slides into the passenger seat, drops the bag between us and unzips it. There's a bunch of towels on top. We pull them out, trying to see if there's something beneath. Sure enough, beneath the towels is a layer of clear plastic. The plastic comes free easily and we find something hiding. It's a bunch of twenty-dollar bills, stacked neatly and bound by a thick rubber band. The bag is *filled* with them.

"That" Mike says, "Is a shitload of money."

"It is," I say, "I wonder who the rightful owner is?"

***

One of the more bothersome trends on social media is the willingness to overshare. Sure, if you've just graduated from high school or just had a kid, let us know and share a copious number of pictures. If you're having a frozen pizza at home alone, you skip the picture and the status update. Your life makes me sad.

And in that spirit, Facebook doesn't need to know about the fortune I've stumbled across.

I'm on my futon, staring at the giant stack of money on the coffee table. The cats have sniffed it a few times, but since it isn't food or another animal, their interest is limited. Which is more than you can say for my friends. Mike is in the comfy chair, sipping a grape soda. Lars circles the money, eyes glued to it. Carol's at the breakfast bar, sipping a martini.

"How much is there?" she asks.

"About ten thousand dollars," Lars says, having counted it earlier.

"And this belonged to Brady?" Carol says.

"It was in a locker he had the key to," I say.

Mike sets aside his grape soda and joins Lars in eye-fucking the huge stack of cash. "What are you going to do with this?" Mike asks.

"Hand it over to Sergeant Pike," I say.

Lars glides over to the arm of the futon. "Maybe you shouldn't turn it in at all. God knows what the police are going to do with it. It'll probably find its way into the pockets of some rat bastard informant. It can be put to better use. Like investing it. In a small business."

"I'm not giving you the money to use on your pot business," I say.

He smacks his hands together. "I'm not saying it has to be the whole thing. You see that little stack over there? Maybe just—"

"No, Lars."

"Dammit!"

I toss the money back into the gym bag, keeping an eye on Lars in the process. Mike and Carol pitch in (I trust Carol to keep an eye on Mike). Lars is too distraught to help out. When we're done, I zip up the bag and carry it to the closet in my bedroom (not exactly a vault, but the closest thing my apartment has to a secure location). "I'll call Pike in the morning."

Carol twists her mouth to one side as she thinks. "If it belonged to Brady, how do you suppose he got ahold of it?"

I lean against the wall. "Maybe from the store?"

"Legally or illegally?" Carol asks.

Mike taps the bag with his foot. "You don't stash big wads of cash in a gym bag and leave it a locker because you're doing things above board."

Carol twists her mouth to one side. "Who keeps an eye on the books?"

"I'm told Stephanie, the store manager, handles the finances," I say.

"She didn't know Brady was embezzling?" Carol asks.

"It's possible she didn't," I say, "But if he was doing it under her nose and she found out about it…"

"She's got a motive," Mike says.

I nod. "And she didn't tell us the hunting knife—the hunting knife Brady might have been murdered with—was missing from the store. Makes an interesting little stew."

"You think Doug, the brother, knew about all this?" Carol asks.

"If he did, he didn't tell me," I say, stepping over to the futon, "If these people won't talk to me, maybe they'll talk to the police. That's the advantage of turning the money over to

Pike. It gives him a line of investigation that has nothing to do with me and Norah.”

Carol leans her head to one side but says nothing. Meantime, Mike gives his phone a conspicuous glance.

“I have to get going,” he says, “Clean the apartment. I may have a, uh, guest tonight.”

I expect Carol to make some remark or at least throw a dirty look Mike’s direction. Instead, she walks into the kitchen. Mike steps to the door and nearly runs into Lars, who’s also heading out.

“I’m going back down to my place,” Lars says, “I need to do some high-level thinking. Consider my options.”

“You’re plotting to steal the money, aren’t you?” I say.

“No!” he says, “No, no. no, no, no, no.” Then he looks down the hall to where I’ve stashed the money. “Yes.”

They slip out the door. Carol returns to the living room. She folds her arms and looks at me, scrutinizing me the same way she was scrutinizing the money. I hold out my hand, inviting her to ask the question that’s obviously on her mind.

“You really trust Norah?” Carol asks.

“Completely. Why wouldn’t I?”

She stifles a laugh. “Why *wouldn’t* you?”

I’m trying not to get pissed. I go over to the desk, putting some space between us. “Fine, yes, she didn’t tell me about her husband,” I say, “But you saw what a fucking lunatic she was married to, right? We hit it off again and she didn't want to screw it up. What was she supposed to tell me? *By the way, hon, I'm married to a guy who'll go completely ripshit if he finds out about us.*"

"If she had told you that up front, would it have been a deal-breaker?"

"I don't know," I say, "I've put up with all this and I'm still with her. It's not like she's got a unibrow or anything."

Carol bites her cheek to stop herself from laughing. She steps toward the front door. She stops and turns back to me. She leans against the door.

"Since you put me on the spot earlier," she says, "It's my turn. What is it you like so much about Norah?"

I sit at my desk chair and stare at the floor as I think. "She works with kids. Not because she can make money at it—nobody makes money doing that—but because she loves it. Because she makes a difference. She's a substantial person. I don't date many people like that. I don't *know* many people like that."

Carol arches an eyebrow. "Present company excepted?"

I hold up a hand. "Present company definitely excepted. At any rate, I figure that's not the kind of person you let get away easily."

We sit there for several moments, not saying anything. Carol pushes off from the door, grabs the knob and pulls the door open in one swift move. She glances back at me.

"Fair enough about Norah," she says, "Just do me a favor: make sure you're seeing what's actually there and not just what you want to see. Okay?"

The urge to get pissed rises, briefly. But I realize Carol's looking out for me. No malice or other agenda intended. I tilt my head toward her, acknowledging I got her message. She nods, satisfied, and heads out the door. I try to remember that Carol doesn't know Norah the way I do.

And hope I'm seeing things clearly.

***

I call Pike first thing in the morning and give him a magnificently vague statement about having some information. I volunteer to come to his office, but he's already out and about. He agrees to stop by my place. His ETA leaves me time enough to go for a run. I need to clear my head before the meeting. The weather's a tad warmer than I prefer (a reminder the Philippines-like humidity we get during the summer is on its way) and it doesn't take long to work up a pretty good sweat.

Running, as it always does, puts me at ease. It's disconcerting that my friends (Carol specifically) have their doubts about Norah. I'm not sure why it bothers me. Maybe it's the feeling that if their Spidey Senses are tingling, mine

145

should be as well. Every time I find myself thinking that way, my pace picks up, as if I can outrun any negative thoughts.

Pike's standing in front of my building as I come down Summit. He's sweaty as well, though I'm guessing the reasons have nothing to do with exercise. His suit is more rumpled than usual and what's left of his hair sticks up as if it's trying to escape his skull.

"All right, what have you got that's so important?" he asks, his hands tucked in his pockets and his slouch giving off a definite attitude.

"Follow me," I say, unlocking the front door to my building.

Pike puts a hand on the door, stopping it. "You can't tell me right here?"

"Sure, I could, but where's the suspense? Where's the showmanship? Where's the recognition you almost certainly hate suspense and showmanship and I love irritating you?"

Pike's lip curls, like someone's holding a small turd under his nose. He pulls his hand away from the door. "This better be good," he says.

He follows me up the stairs to my apartment. As soon as we're inside, I head down the hallway. Pike tries to avoid my cats, who are running a Chinese Fire Drill around and through his legs.

"It's in the bedroom," I say, heading that direction, "I'll be right back."

I grab a towel off the bed and wipe myself down (don't want to get sweat on the loot). I step over to the closet, where I've stashed the money, and open the door.

And the murder weapon falls out.

CHAPTER EIGHT

I'm not what Michael Jackson would refer to as a smooth *criminal. My few forays to the wrong side of law-and-order have proven that. The worst example was when I was in college and tried to "steal" popcorn from a movie theater I was working at.*

Now, I didn't really think of it as theft. At the end of every evening, we were required to throw out the unpurchased popcorn. After several nights of carrying giant garbage bags full of the stuff out to a dumpster, I realized this was a waste. Wouldn't it be more useful to bring it back to my apartment? I knew my roommates wouldn't mind. And by ordering its removal, hadn't the movie theater relinquished ownership of said salty snack? I was well within my rights to toss the bag into the back of my crapbox car.

Unfortunately, I didn't notice a slit had developed in the bag. When it burst open as I was stuffing it into my backseat, I panicked. I hopped in the car and hauled ass back to my apartment. Most of the popcorn went floating out the window, leaving a trail back to the parking lot of my building. The theater gave me a reprimand and told me not to steal anymore popcorn. And at every closing shift after that, my manager stuck to me like glue (or that horrible butter-like substance we used to put on the popcorn).

I've stayed on the straight and narrow, theft-wise, ever since. While I like to think it's due to maturity, a small corner of my mind suspects the truth: I suck at being a criminal.

I didn't realize I sucked this much, though.

At first, I don't know what the hell I'm looking at. The second I open the closet door, something falls off the gym bag and crashes to the hardwood floor, making a *thunk* as it lands. Not as loud a *thunk* as it could make because it's wrapped in layers of plastic so thick I can't see what's inside. I'm so surprised by its appearance, I forget all about the loot.

I unwrap the plastic. It's not fun work. It reminds me of various roasts and hams my mom has sent home over the years. She wraps them in so much plastic I usually get bored and order a pizza before I get to the meat. The closer I get to the middle, the more I can see the blade. By the time I pull away the last of the plastic, I get a view of a serrated hunting knife, covered with blood. Exactly like the one that killed Brady Perkins.

"Everything okay in there?" Pike asks.

I throw the plastic back around the weapon. Yes, I said all that shit about Pike being reasonable, but that was *before* I had incriminating evidence in my bedroom. Pike's steps echo in the hallway. There's no time to do a proper wrap job on the knife, so I toss it, plastic and all, back into the closet.

Pike steps into the bedroom doorway, cop suspicion in fourth gear. "Counselor?" he asks.

"Something fell in the closet. You know what it's like."

"I suppose."

I doubt Pike spends much time at home. He's eyeballing me, like something's off but he's not sure what. I pull the gym bag out of the closet and offer it to him.

"I found this," I say.

Pike takes the bag from me, looking doubtful. He opens it and glances inside. It appears to temporarily wipe away any suspicion about the goings on in my closet.

"What's this?" he asks.

"Some money I found. Might have belonged to Brady Perkins."

I go through the whole story of stumbling across the key and following the trail to the fitness club and finding the money. Pike uses his cop radar, looking for signs I'm bullshitting him.

"You're sure the money belongs to Brady Perkins?" he asks.

"Seems like a decent assumption," I say.

While Pike contemplates the money, Lenny walks into the bedroom and over to the closet. He starts sniffing around the murder weapon. Son of a bitch. Normally, I'd shoo him away, but I don't want to draw attention to the closet. Pike, not a cat person, is too caught up in his own thinking to notice Lenny. I step between Pike and the closet. He stares at the gym bag.

"Maybe it did belong to Brady," he says, "Doesn't mean it's related to the murder."

"Other than establishing motive for someone at the store. The brother, maybe. Or the manager."

"Or your girlfriend. Depending on what Brady was going to do with the money."

My stomach drops. Here I was, thinking this might get the police moving *away* from me and Norah, and now Pike's trying to tie it into Norah. Son of a bitch.

"You're just *not* going to cut Norah any slack, are you?"

"Why should I? A woman carries on an affair and then her husband is murdered? You think that's someone I'm supposed to trust? For all I know, she and Brady had a disagreement over the money and she killed him. Set her boyfriend up to take the fall."

I put my head in my hands and start to laugh. "You thought about writing fiction? You can turn anything into a decent story."

Pike clutches the bag a little tighter. "Seems to me…is there a problem with your cat?"

Lenny has been digging in the plastic. I hook my foot around his midsection and guide him out of the closet, faster and with more force than Lenny probably finds necessary.

"He's just an idiot," I say.

Pike doesn't seem convinced. (Although I'm sure if I told him *I* was an idiot, he'd be all over that.) He sets the gym bag down and adjusts his glasses. "I'll tell you this much: you're not entirely wrong about the brother. There's something strange there."

That's hopeful. I'd feel better about it if Lenny didn't keep trying to get through my legs and back to the closet. "I know he hated Brady," I say.

"So did a lot of people. Gives him motive, sure. The part that's strange is his hand."

"What about it?"

"It's all taped up. You noticed that much, right? When I asked him about it, he just said, 'Car door.' And that was it."

"Same with me."

Pike bobs his head from side to side. "That's the thing, counselor. There's a sweet spot where you can be sure someone's telling the truth. If they tell you too much, they're covering. If they tell you too little, they're covering. There's something about how Doug Perkins' hurt his hand that he's not telling us."

I'm happy about Pike being reasonable, but only half my mind is on this discussion. You see, Lenny is like a teenager. He interprets every attempt at discipline as a license to keep screwing around. In that spirit, he's heading back for the closet. Pike watches him.

"What do you keep in the closet?" he asks.

"All sorts of stuff," I say, "Catnip and the like."

"Uh-huh. And you don't want him to get into the catnip?"

"And the like. No. I do not."

"You sure it's just that?"

I can see how this is going to play out. Pike's going to shove past me and inspect the closet. He's going to find the murder weapon and I'll be spending several months in the Ramsey County Detention Center prior to my trial, conviction and transfer to the state prison in Stillwater. (Yes, I'm spiraling, but this is how I work. My brain is fifty percent worst case scenarios. The other fifty percent is TV trivia.) I've only got one gambit.

"You're welcomed to look in the closet," I say, spinning around to pick up Lenny.

With my back to Pike, I bend over and scoop up Lenny. I also manage to corral the knife and the plastic surrounding it. I keep my back to Pike as I move everything toward my bed. It's not an easy balancing act, what with the delicacy of the plastic and Lenny's big fat ass. Pike checks out the closet. He doesn't follow my movements. It gives me a second to toss Lenny on top of the bed and stash the knife under it. Pike and I both turn to each other at the same time.

"I don't see anything," he says.

"I figured."

"I mean, anything the cat might be interested in. I thought you had catnip or something in there."

"Maybe I'm out. Or maybe there's a mouse in one of my shoes. You're welcomed to look. But I *will* spread rumors about your obvious foot fetish."

Pike weighs the merits of digging though my old shoes. I sit on the bed and pull Lenny on to my lap. (Petting him is the only way to distract him from his obsession with the blood-stained knife.) Pike picks up the gym bag and heads down the hallway.

"I'll keep this as evidence," he says, "But I don't think it's going to lead to anything."

"I appreciate your confidence," I say, following him out of the bedroom and closing the door behind me.

"I'll give you one more piece of advice," Pike says, "I'm probably wasting my time, but here I go. You keep looking into this thing, you're risking your ass. Best bet is to back out of this and let us do our jobs. Clear?"

"Clear," I say. Which implies I understood him but doesn't bind me to listening to him.

Pike seems aware of that. There's a sense of defeat as he walks to the door. "You be safe, counselor."

When the front door closes, I'm tempted to run to the bedroom and toss either the knife or Lenny out the window. Instead, I sit at the breakfast bar, in case Pike comes back with a Columbo-esque, "Oh, one more thing." The seconds pass, but Pike doesn't return. There's a crinkling of plastic coming from the bedroom as Lenny goes back to work.

First thing tomorrow, I'm looking into cat obedience classes.

***

"I've got to tell you, brother," Lars says, staring at the package lying next to me, "That's pretty disgusting."

I'm not going to disagree. The creepiness of my storage area only adds to the effect. It's located in the basement of my apartment building, meaning it's about a hundred years old. The air is dank and cobwebs hang from the corners of the ceiling. Only about half the floor has been paved. The "storage units" are little chicken-wire cages just big enough to hold a handful of boxes. If you told me there are bodies buried down here, I'd believe you. A plastic-wrapped, blood-covered hunting knife fits right in.

I need to get the damn thing hidden and then figure out what to do next. I open a box marked *Wrestling Magazines* and discover there's a little space in it. If I clear out the magazines, I can put the knife in and bury it under the magazines. I start piling them on the floor while Lars mimes baseball pitches.

"You sure it's a good idea to keep that thing down here?" he asks.

"It's not like I can throw it out. And I've got a thing about leaving incriminating evidence where the cops can find it."

Lars squats next to the plastic bundle. "How did it get into your apartment?"

"I was out for a run before Pike got here," I say, "Someone must have broken in and planted it while I was out."

"You think it was the same guy who attacked you?"

"Wouldn't surprise me. The thing I can't figure out is how they go into my apartment."

"Good question. This is, after all, a security building."

Lars has more faith in said security than anyone else. Most tenants realize it isn't exactly Fort Knox. Or even Fort Dix. In the interest of diplomacy, I don't share that opinion with Lars.

"I didn't see any signs of a break-in," I say, "Both doors are fine. I'm on the third floor, so nobody's coming in through the window."

"They must have had a key."

And that's been bothering me. If someone didn't break in then they had access to my spare key. Mike has one and the other is hidden under a potted plant on my deck (in case I lock myself out). The only ones who know the plant key exists are Carol, Mike and Lars.

And Norah.

It's a milestone in my relationships when I let a girlfriend know the existence of this key. The last several women I've dated haven't made the cut. (And I have no regrets about that.) If I trusted Norah enough to let her know about the key, I trust her enough not to use the damn thing to frame me. But there's no evidence someone rooted around my deck, searching for the key. If it was grabbed, someone knew where to look.

Lars is still miming pitches. "I was just thinking about the money."

"The ship's sailed on that, Lars. The cops have it now."

"That's a shame," he says, "Perfectly good wad of cash gone to the government when it could be out there, doing some good."

"If Brady *did* embezzle the stuff, it wasn't circulating in the private sector, either."

"That's dirty pool. No way to prove he embezzled the stuff, though?"

"Not off the top of my head."

Lars stops miming pitches. "You said Brady hired a divorce lawyer?"

"Sheila Grant. Word on the street is she's pretty vicious."

He cringes, like Igor in old horror movie. "Oh, I know her. She *is* bad news. Chuck and I talked to her a few years ago. We had an idea about adding a shuttle service to her firm. Y'know, getting divorcees to and from her office in the event they're too emotionally distraught to drive themselves."

"How did that work out?"

"She threatened to call the police and have us removed from her office. Chuck found it arousing. Anyway, if Sheila Grant was Brady's attorney, maybe she'd know about the money."

Huh. It's an avenue I haven't explored. But I'm not entirely convinced. Certainly, Brady's divorce attorney would know about his financial affairs. I'm not sure if that extends to funds he's embezzled, but I should leave no stone unturned. Assuming Sheila Grant would talk to me.

"Maybe I can give her a call," I say, without a lot of conviction.

"You can play the celebrity card," Lars says, "I've noticed you like to do that."

He either ignores or misses the dirty look I give him. But he's right. The last time I dealt with a divorce lawyer, he was a big fan of celebrities. Maybe Sheila Grant is similar.

"I'll give it a shot," I say, "Problem is, I don't have much of a celebrity card to play. I'm suspended."

Lars strokes his beard. "You having money troubles?"

"I'm hanging in there."

"Chuck and I could use help in the new venture. We currently have openings in muscle work and public relations."

Obviously, I'm more qualified for the latter. But I can't help wondering about the former, despite my better instincts. "What do you need muscle work for?" I ask.

Lars lets out a sigh; the disappointed father. "I'm having some trouble with Billy."

"Your old dealer?"

"The very one. He got word of my new enterprise. Thinks I'm cutting in on his turf. He's not totally off the mark there. It *was* the first thing I wrote in my business plan. He called me up, said if even one of his customers went to me, he'd take out both of us. I told him unless he could produce a non-compete clause, his clientele was fair game."

"What did he say to that?" I ask.

"I won't quote it directly, but it was highly unprofessional and anatomically impossible. There's no reasoning with him."

I'm not surprised. Sending Lars to reason with someone is like asking Justin Bieber for etiquette lessons. I finish hiding the knife and close up the storage locker.

"Just be careful with this Billy guy," I say, "You don't want someone stalking around, looking to kill you. It's no fun. Believe me."

I head back up to my apartment, dropping Lars off on the way. When last seen, he's reciting a list of possible muscle guys. I'm almost back to my deck when my cell phone rings. Norah is giving me a call.

"Justice League of America," I say, in my most suave voice, "This is Gleek, the space monkey, speaking. How may I help you?"

Norah laughs. Her voice has that bubbly quality it gets at the end of the day. Like *she's* like a kid who just got out of school.

"I'm wondering if you're doing anything tomorrow night?" she asks.

"Oh, the usual. Dinner with a few heads of state. Brief confab with the Pope. Bowling with Elon Musk."

"I don't suppose you can fit me in? I have a late start on Wednesday. I'd love to spend some quality time with you."

I've come to love those words. Quality time. "I'll check with my social secretary. But I think I'll be able to talk her into it. Maybe eight o'clock? We can go to The Tav. See where the evening goes from there."

"Sounds good. Elon won't mind?"

"If he does, I'll give him a wedgie."

Norah gives that a purring laugh. "I'll see you tomorrow night."

I ring off and lean against the deck railing. The giant bloodstain covers a good chunk of my deck. (Lars tells me management has finally hired a professional cleaner to get rid of it, but I shouldn't hold my breath, timeline-wise.) As if the bloodstain wasn't pleasant enough, the thought of entering my apartment now fills me with anxiety. I don't know if someone's waiting to attack me or plant evidence to implicate me. This is *not* how I should be viewing home sweet home. I've got to make this go away as soon as possible.

I start looking up information on Sheila Grant.

***

I'll be the first to admit: I'm a weird kind of celebrity. I don't mean *weird* in the Marlon Brando/J.D. Salinger sense. I'm at a weird level of celebrity. For example, everybody knows who George Clooney is. But if you go further down the

Celebrity Food Chain, things get more localized. If you don't read books that often, you probably don't know who Dennis Lehane or Janet Evanovich are. Most politicians aren't known outside of their states or cities. Celebrity-wise, my part of the food chain is very specific. If you live outside the Twin Cities, are over fifty and aren't a total smartass, you probably don't know who I am. When I use my weenie bit of celebrity, there's always half-a-chance I'll get a negative answer to *Do you know who I am?*

Sheila Grant *does* know who I am. And she's willing to meet me for coffee.

Sheila's offices are in Edina, a snooty, old money suburb bordering the southwest part of Minneapolis. The only things I know about it are: 1) Its high school hockey team is easily the most hated in the history of the state; 2) Drivers there will back up traffic halfway to Rangoon while waiting for someone to pull out of a parking space; and 3) It is protected from any form of gangland violence by a veneer of sheer snootiness (and a solid foundation of racial profiling). Sheila suggests we meet at a Caribou Coffee located in Lund's Byerly's, an upscale grocery store whose unwieldy name is the result of a merger between two separate upscale grocery stores, thus creating a vortex of snobbery. I need this meeting, but I'm not looking forward to it. Not only am I going to be interrogating a potentially hostile witness, but there's a finite amount of money in my coffee and gas budgets. A mocha, even a small one, is out of the question. I wonder if the Joad family felt this way.

Sheila's at a high-top table when I walk in. She looks just like the picture on her website. Short black hair, perfectly coiffed. A dark dress suit over a slim frame. Cold blue eyes, set deep in a hard and angular face. Her thin smile exposes a set of perfectly straight, white teeth (though I can't help noticing the canines are a tad sharp). When we eventually create a Lawyer Bot, it will look a lot like Sheila. She greets me with a dry handshake.

"I enjoy your column," she says, "You *do* take a few too many shots at lawyers, though."

"Sorry. My older brother's a lawyer. I think of it as teasing him."

"No offense taken. Just pointing it out." She wraps her hands around her coffee cup. "What can I help you with, Mr. Davis?"

"You can call me Joe."

"Let me guess: Mr. Davis was your father?"

"No, *his* father was Mr. Davis. My dad is Henry. Don't call him Hank. He hates that." I take a bracing sip of my small coffee. "I understand you were going to represent Brady Perkins in his divorce."

"And I understand you were sleeping with his wife?"

Ah. Guess she's done her research. "I, uh, I'm seeing his wife. I have been. For a little while."

There's absolutely no reaction from Sheila, which is more unnerving than if she *had* reacted. "Brady told me all about the affair," she says, "I have to say, I'm a little disappointed."

"There's a lot of that going around. What do you know about Brady being killed?"

"I heard it happened outside your apartment. And you haven't been arrested. Beyond that, I know I don't have Brady as a client anymore."

That's the kind of pragmatism you normally find in a lawyer or your average serial killer. It's made worse by the drone in Sheila's voice, like she's constantly citing precedent. Her eyes flick around occasionally, as if concerned that someone might be listening.

"If you know all that," I say, "Then you know he threatened me over the phone and in person. And there's an excellent chance he came to my apartment to kill me."

"I think most of that is in the public domain. Is there something specific you're wondering about? That isn't covered under attorney-client privilege?"

Somewhere, my brother, Kevin is chuckling and isn't sure why. I drum my fingers on the side of my cup.

"Would it be alright if I asked some very general questions about Brady's finances?" I ask, "If there's anything you can't share with me, you'll let me know."

"You can be sure of that."

It dawns on me: Sheila's bantering with me. She's just doing it such a smug and humorless way that only one of us is enjoying it.

"Brady was going to take Norah to the cleaners in the divorce," I say.

"He was responsible for most of their income. The house was in his name. He had purchased most of what they owned. If you classify protecting your possessions as *taking someone to the cleaners*, then yes. That's what Brady was going to do."

"You knew all about his income?" I ask.

"Yes." Sheila draws that out a tad, as if she doesn't like where I'm going with it.

"It was mainly from the store, right?"

"Mainly. There were some investments."

"Such as?"

Sheila gives that a single shake of the head. "I'm not going into that. I'm sure his wife must have an idea, if you'd like to talk to her."

She puts a little ring around *wife* that I don't care much for. "It's just that I found some money that I think belonged to Brady," I say.

I go into the story about finding the bag. Sheila's eyes dart about the room. She wipes her nose a couple of times, as if trying to remove an unpleasant smell. She tries to give off a general air of boredom, but her hand trembles when she picks up her coffee.

"I don't know anything about a gym bag," she says.

I slide my coffee to the edge of the table. "Can I just put a question to you straight?"

"I'd love to hear you put a question straight, Mr. Davis."

"Brady was up to something and I'm wondering if you know anything about it?"

"I don't."

"You willing to stake your reputation on that?" I ask.

And we've come to the part of our show where Joe bluffs madly in an attempt to get answers. I've read a few biographies of Theodore Roosevelt and TR's way of combating shadowy personalities was to put them in the full glare of the public spotlight. Sheila Grant's reputation is such that I'm guessing she wouldn't want anyone messing with it. In fact, I'm counting on that.

Sheila's face is cold and controlled, but something murderous flickers in her dark eyes. "What are you talking about?"

"Brady was embezzling from the store. His co-workers will back me up on that. And I'll enjoy writing that for *The Bugle*."

This is where the bluff comes in. First, I haven't talked to anybody at Pro Sports since I found the money. And while I'm not on good terms with *The Bugle*, they've done me one favor (although it's probably *The Bugle* doing *themselves* a favor): they haven't publicized my suspension. *Cup o' Joe* is still up on the website. They're publicizing some of my past columns. If a reader (or many readers) complains about a lack of new *Cup o' Joe*s, someone from *The Bugle* will politely and vaguely tell them I'm taking time off to research new projects. And since there hasn't yet been a hue-and-cry regarding my absence, the Circle of Knowledge around my suspension is limited to me, the staff at *The Bugle* and my friends. I hope no part of that Circle has reached Sheila Grant.

Sheila grips the table, her fingernails clawing the sides. "You don't have anything."

"I beg to differ. I'll be more than happy to add how uncooperative you've been. We've been off the record up to now, but since you know about the article, let's change that."

"There's nothing to tell you."

"Can I quote you? It'll be a hell of a lead into the paragraph where I imply you're hiding something."

Sheila talks to me through clenched teeth. "You want to get sued that badly?"

"For what? Is it libelous to point out that Brady committed a crime and you haven't been forthcoming on the subject?"

"Because I'm citing attorney—"

"Client privilege. They always quote that on *Better Call Saul*. God knows *that's* the reputation you want.

"I'm not—"

"Bullshit. What were you and Brady up to?"

"Nothing! I don't care if you believe me or not. It's like I told your girlfriend—"

Sheila stops, realizing the mistake she's made. Her eyes flick around the place again and she vigorously rubs her nose. I lean toward her.

"You told Norah something…when?" I ask.

"I didn't."

"You just said—"

"It's none of your business."

"I didn't realize attorney-client privilege extended to people who aren't your clients. You have a Cone of Secrecy you take every place you go?"

Sheila gets up, leaving her coffee on the table. "Good afternoon, Joe."

"Oh, please. Call me Mr. Davis."

Her high heels click on the floor as she walks away. I swallow the rest of my now-cold coffee and toss the cup in the trash.

I didn't get any more information about the embezzling, though it certainly feels like a third rail subject with Sheila. There's something there, but despite what I said in my bluff, I have no solid information. The mention of the conversation between Norah and Sheila was interesting, though.

I wonder why Norah didn't mention it.

CHAPTER NINE

There was a drunken night in college when Mike and I were both reeling from recent breakups; situations in which the girls who had broken our hearts turned out to be completely different from the girls we thought they were. (Although, looking back, maybe we were expecting a bit much from girls we met on Nickel Beer Night at the Front Street Bar and Grill.) The wisdom of our entire twenty-one years brought us to the conclusion that women simply cannot be trusted. We made a booze-driven vow never to trust another. Given that most of the women Mike dates have Potential Felon written all over them, that was probably a decent idea. And while the majority of my relationships could be tossed into the Cheap and Superficial Bin, I have allowed myself to trust from time to time.

Despite evidence to the contrary, Norah has been one of those I've trusted. But now I'm wondering if maybe Twenty-One-Year-Old Joe was right.

"This is your favorite hangout?" Norah asks, looking around The Tav.

"Long as the doors are open and the liquor license is good, this is where you'll find me."

The Tav is a combination restaurant, sports bar and pub. Picture windows look out over Selby Avenue. Big screen TVs hang from various corners. There's a pool table and a few dart boards. With its cozy atmosphere, friendly staff and collection of quality craft beers, there are times when The Tav feels like an extension of me. Love me, love The Tav.

Norah loves The Tav, at least. And she loves darts.

"I'm glad no one wants to play us for the board," she says, assessing my latest turn, "That last one nearly missed it altogether."

I've never been great at darts. But usually I'm at least competent, with occasional flashes of being good. And I do okay at Cricket, the game Norah and I are currently playing. Tonight, though, I'm distracted by this gnawing in my guts, dreading the conversation I need to have with Norah. It's not doing much for my dart game.

It doesn't help to see Norah enjoying herself. She sips a Long Island Iced Tea as she watches me take another crappy turn. It's one of the few times lately I've seen her happy; abandoning herself to the moment. Norah takes her turn and hits triple 17s, double 15s and a 19. I glance up at the points. No doubt about it. I'm getting my ass handed to me.

Norah sashays back from the board and hands me the darts. "Sorry about this."

"No biggie," I say, "But think how well you'd be doing if you threw with the hand God intended you to throw with."

Norah playfully threatens to go upside my head with that left hand of hers. She goes back to her Long Island, swaying to the music playing on the speakers.

"I should slow down," she says, rattling the ice in her glass, "Even with the late start tomorrow. We've got the final performances of the *Macbeth* scenes."

My next throw hits a 4. Great. "*Macbeth* scenes?"

"The kids are performing scenes from the play for class. I'm one of those rare English teachers who thinks Shakespeare should be performed and not just read. If you do it the way Shakespeare intended, you understand the material so much better."

As a guy with an English degree who's performed in a few plays, I'd like to agree with her. But my only experience performing Shakespeare was a production of *As You Like It* in high school. It only made me understand how the material could bore an auditorium full of high school kids.

"Sounds like fun," I say, imagining hitting a 1 is karmic retribution for my obvious lie.

Norah sets her drink on the table. "Normally, it is. I'm afraid the story of *Macbeth* hits a little close to home."

I imagine. The story of a woman manipulating someone into a series of bloody murders must be getting

Norah a few interesting looks. She looks a little distracted as I hand her the darts. I change the subject slightly.

"Speaking of close to home," I say, "Is Doug going to miss having you around tonight?"

Norah gives that a flip of her hand. "Probably not. We don't see that much of each other. Besides, we both know the arrangement's temporary." She steps up for her turn. "I always liked Doug. I didn't like the way Brady treated him. But Doug, even when he knew I was a sympathetic ear, would not talk the same way about Brady. He's a good guy."

"Did he ever say anything about Brady embezzling from the store?"

It comes out of my mouth without me thinking too terribly hard about it. This is the thing: when I was much younger, I was terrified of calling up girls. I'd make a multi-hour production number out of it. Sometimes I'd get as far as picking the phone up, but then I'd scurry away like an ape from a monolith. If the call ever did get placed (never a guarantee) it would be because I turned my brain off and dialed the number without thinking. Blurting out the suspected embezzlement feels very similar.

Norah sets the darts down on the table. "Embezzling? No, he never said anything like that. Why do you ask?"

I fold my hands on the table. "You remember the key I found in the study? It was for a locker at Universal Fitness. I checked it out and found a bag with ten thousand dollars in it."

Her mouth drops open. "You're fucking kidding me."

"I'm afraid not. I'm not sure where the money came from. I turned it over to the police. And I talked to Sheila Grant, Brady's lawyer. I thought she might know something."

A shadow passes across Norah's face. "And did she?"

"No. She lawyered her way around the bush. But she said the two of you had talked."

I learned a long time ago—and apparently have to keep learning—that you can phrase a question as casually as you please, but people are still going to look right past the tone and seize on the phrasing. Norah's face goes Queen-of-Narnia cold.

"Okay. Sheila and I talked," Norah says.

"When did this happen?"

She stares at me, not blinking. "It was the night Brady was killed."

An electric shock goes through me. It must register on my face because Norah looks away. I wait for her to add more to the story, but she says nothing. I lean on the table.

"The night Brady was killed," I say, "Before or after you left my place?"

"After. We met and I went home. Simple as that."

Norah's not throwing the darts, not sipping her drink and not looking at me. The vibe makes me feel very alone.

"What did you two talk about?" I ask.

She looks at me, her face barely moving. "Nothing."

I can't stop myself from scoffing (although the reaction I get from Norah makes me wish I had). "You had a conversation with your soon-to-be-ex-husband's divorce lawyer and you're going to tell me you didn't talk about anything?"

"That's what I'm going to tell you. Yes."

We stare at each other; one of those *I'm not going to say anything. Are you going to say something?* sort of uncomfortable silences. Norah juts her chin out.

"Is this a problem?" she asks.

"It presents…a problem. According to your alibi, you went home right after you left my place. If you were meeting Sheila Grant, how can I believe your alibi?"

"You think I need an alibi?"

I take a second to consider my answer, then hear myself saying: "I think you do."

Norah grabs her purse, digs out a few bucks and throws them on the table. "I have to go."

She pushes past me. I follow her toward the door, not knowing what to say. I'm stuck with the guy's dilemma of knowing I should apologize and not feeling like I have anything to apologize for. The dilemma keeps me silent. Which is the worst thing I could be.

"I just wanted—" I say.

"Whatever."

Norah stops at the front door, barely avoiding a bunch of frat dudes coming in. Her eyes are wet, but the cold look on her face tells me she's not going to let herself cry. I continue to fumble.

"I don't see why you're so upset," I say.

Her voice is quiet but not angry. Hurt. "I didn't think I needed an alibi with you."

A second later, she's out the door. I know it's no good following her. Wow. Thirty seconds ago, we were throwing darts, all giggly and silly. One question and I might be without a girlfriend.

That went…exactly like I thought it would.

***

I've never been a big one for drowning my sorrows. Alcohol is, at best, a temporary fix. Then again, when faced with personal chaos and a soul-sucking sense of depression, a temporary fix sounds pretty good.

At least, it sounded good last night.

The morning sun feels like someone gently laying a hot poker against my eyeballs. My stomach lurches as I roll on my side. Apparently, I decided to sleep naked (pajamas must have seemed like too much effort when I stumbled into bed). I sit up and reach for the ax someone used to cleave my skull. I'm not feeling good, but I think I can get through this without vomiting. That's something to build on.

I pad down the hallway toward the kitchen. The hangover checklist goes through my head. Stay upright. Get some coffee. Feed the cats. Take a shower. If I can survive the morning, I'll be good for the rest of the day. Don't think about Norah right now. I'm like society in microcosm: cover basic survival needs before moving on to the bigger issues.

Like, for example, why Lars is in my kitchen.

"Morning, boss," he says, peeling off some strips of bacon, "You ready for breakfast?"

I put a hand to my aching head and look down, hoping Lars will be gone when I look up again. Looking down, though, reminds me I'm in the buff. I hop back down the hallway. Lars chuckles.

"We go to the same health club, brother" he says, "You're not showing me anything I haven't already seen."

"Lars, what the fuck are you doing here?"

"Making breakfast. Obviously. Although, it's almost noon. More accurately, I'm making brunch. Don't you remember me walking you home last night?"

That stops me short. I *don't* have any recollection of Lars walking me home. Or *me* walking me home. Or much of anything after using the phrase, "Another kamikaze would be great!" for roughly the fifth time. I stumble back into the kitchen, freshly-clad in boxer shorts and a red t-shirt.

"I don't remember you walking me home," I say, "I don't remember you even being at The Tav."

"You were pretty far gone by the time I got there. I was going to play darts, but you needed looking after."

He lays the bacon on the frying pan and it begins to sizzle. Normally, I love that sound, but right now it makes my stomach do flips.

"I appreciate that," I say, "I suppose I needed looking after. I think I drank most of the available liquor supply in the Twin Cities."

"I don't usually see you like that, brother. Everything okay?"

I get my Batman mug out of the cupboard and discover Lars has made coffee. "No," I say, "Things are not okay."

"You were saying something about being alone for the rest of your life."

"Was I pro or con?"

"It sounded like con at first. But then you started talking about going out into the woods and living like a wolf."

I pour myself a cuppa. "I can't believe I'm not sick this morning."

"You can probably thank that Tav Burger I bought you before we left."

"You bought me a burger?" I ask.

"It seemed like the best plan."

I've got to admit: I'm touched. For all Lars' mooching off me, storming into my apartment with idiot schemes and creating noise by doing God-knows-what-because-*I*-certainly-don't-want-to-know, it's nice he had my back when I needed it. (On the other hand, this means I have to give him a longer leash with the stuff that irritates me. At least until I figure out a way to pay him back. Mental note: start scheming to pay Lars back.)

"Norah and I had a little chat last night," I say, "It didn't go well."

I fill him in on what happened as he shovels breakfast on to two plates and we take seats at my breakfast bar (being used for breakfast, for a change). He gives away little as I describe the meeting with Sheila Grant and Norah's reaction to my questioning her. When I'm done, Lars takes a contemplative bite of his bacon.

"No information from Sheila about Brady," he says, "And no information from Norah about Sheila. And you still need to know what Brady was up to with the money."

"That's about the size of it."

"Have you considered breaking into Brady's place?" he says.

Geez. "Lars, is your solution to everything a break-in?"

"No. But frequently, yes."

I walk over to the fridge to get some salsa for my eggs. "It's not going to work in this case. Norah's mostly moved out. She's boxed up all of Brady's stuff. If there was anything to find, it would have been found."

Lars takes the salsa and dumps a healthy amount on his eggs. "You don't know that unless you look. Doesn't seem like you can take Norah's word on it."

Shit. He's got a point. The time when I could go to Norah and get reliable information out of her has passed (assuming it ever really existed). There's a chance this idiot play would put me in a jail cell. But there's also the sneaking feeling that if I sit around and wait, I'll wind up in a jail cell anyway. Better to be doing something—even something stupid—than nothing.

"All right, if I do this," I say, "Are you going to come along?"

"Yes. I thought was obvious. You should talk to Mike and Carol. We always do better when we get the band back together."

Problem is: this band resembles Spinal Tap. Still, misery loves a certain amount of company. I give Lars the a-okay on his plan. He grabs my empty plate and brings it to the sink with a certain air of triumph. Between the food and the coffee, I'm starting to feel human again.

"How's the new business going?" I ask.

"Not as well as I hoped," he says, "Billy trashed my car. It was a warning from him and his goons. Although, I'm impressed. I didn't think Billy had goons. He never fails to surprise."

"What kind of damage did they do?"

"There are giant rips in the front seat. One of the windows is gone. A headlight is smashed. And there are scratches all up and down the sides."

"Isn't that the condition of your car at all times?"

"Yes, but the ashtray was full of pennies. I won't be getting those back."

Thankfully, the hangover—and the depression back of it—means I don't get annoyed with Lars. Instead, I view the whole thing with a sense of detached bemusement. I drain my coffee and step over to the pot for another.

"What are you going to do about Billy?" I ask.

"I thought I'd take the issue up with Chuck."

That idea makes me want to up with Chuck. While Chuck is a creative genius (I'm taking Lars' word there) he's not exactly a subtle guy. Cut him off traffic and his revenge may take the form of a twenty-seven car pileup. Or at least he'd have the idea for one. Follow through is not Chuck's specialty (that much, *I* know).

Lars heads for the front door. "Let's peg ten o'clock. I'll pick you up. Let Mike and Carol know."

"You're going to drive?"

"No, my car's in no condition. I'm sure Carol will be glad to do it. See you then."

Lars slides out the door. Between saving me last night and bringing me back to life this morning, I definitely owe him. He's a good friend.

I hope I still feel this way when his idiot scheme gets us all arrested.

***

It takes a bit of palaver, but Carol is willing to drive us to the break-in. Lars is not wrong in recommending her. Her Lexus has better acceleration than any of our cars. And if she dings it up, hey, nobody said she *had* to come along.

She drops us off a few blocks from Brady's house. We use the alleys to get behind the place and go in through the back gate. There are a few lights on in the house by way of security. The neighborhood seems dark and unnaturally quiet. It gives me the willies, but that's nothing compared to how the neighbors will feel if they spot us. We make our way up to the backdoor. Mike slips past the screen door and goes to work on the lock.

"Just be careful," I say, "Don't break the—"

"Okay, I'm in."

I may have mentioned this in the past, but when we were in college, Mike had a sideline business as a cat burglar. Nothing huge. He generally stole small ticket items and only when he was short of money and couldn't hit his parents up for a loan. I like to imagine that, beyond some scrapes we've gotten into in recent months, he hasn't done anything like that since. Although, when he *has* used these skills, he doesn't look, um…rusty.

Mike opens the door and gestures me and Lars inside. The backdoor leads into the kitchen. There's some light spill from the living room. I tiptoe through the kitchen while Mike carefully closes the backdoor and Lars rummages through the fridge.

I smack Lars on the back of the head. "Would you knock it off?"

"I can't help it," Lars says, "Break-ins make me hungry."

"Is that why you're always suggesting them?" I ask.

Lars leans on the refrigerator door. "Interesting theory. I'd never considered it."

"And don't consider the fridge," I say, kicking the door closed, "Let's get to work."

Lars groans but falls into line. We stand at the edge of the kitchen. The dining room and living room are well-lit, but almost certainly a waste of time. They've been cleared of any boxes, furniture or decoration.

"Let's try the study," I say, "It's where I found the key."

We sneak through the dining room, sticking close to the walls, as the drapes are wide open. When we reach the study, I fire up the flashlight app on my phone and run it over the room. All the boxes I packed for Norah are still here. I rummage through them while Lars meanders into another room and Mike digs out his own cell phone.

"Call to the girlfriend?" I ask.

"Not a current one," Mike says, punching in a number.

A few seconds later, Carol is on Mike's phone. He's got her on speaker. "How's it looking out there?" Mike asks.

"Dark. If not for the street lights, I'd think there'd been a power outage."

"This doesn't even feel like Minneapolis," Mike says, "This is like the suburbs."

I open one of the boxes and lay some paperwork on the floor. "I guess this is what having money affords you."

"In that case, I'll pass," Mike says.

Lars comes in, eating a sandwich. He and Mike join me in going through the boxes. Norah told me she wasn't keeping this stuff, so we don't have to be careful. Everything gets a glance then gets stuffed back into the box. We go through box and after box but get nothing.

Lars glances around. "You sure this is the only place to look?"

He's got a point. I stand and look around, hands on hips. "Let's search the rest of the house. Lars, you try the basement. Mike, you do the upstairs. I'll look around the main floor."

"Sounds good." Mike starts toward the stairs.

"And stay out of Norah's personal stuff," I say, calling after Mike, "No panty-sniffing."

"I don't do that."

"What about Launa Hughes' dorm room?"

"That was an isolated, alcohol-related incident."

"I don't think campus security would've seen it that way."

Mike stomps up the stairs, mumbling about *Barney Fife* and a *campus gestapo*. Lars goes back through the kitchen to get to the basement. I take another glance around the study, then move into the living room. It's not long before I've gone through the main floor and found nothing. I'm wondering where to look next when Mike's voice calls from upstairs.

"Joe? Joe, come here. I think I found something."

I head for the stairs. I'm at the first landing when I catch a glimpse of Mike's flashlight in the master bedroom.

And I hear someone coming through the front door.

CHAPTER TEN

Nothing forces you to think faster than when someone walks in on you when you least expect it. On those occasions, you must think and act in one smooth, coordinated movement. And if you're like me, you'll fail miserably.

The classic example was the time in high school when I was fooling around with my girlfriend, Lisa. We were upstairs in her room when her parents came home early from the movies, leaving us about thirty seconds to set up the cover story that we'd been studying the whole time. Somehow, we managed to go from buck naked to fully clothed in the time required. The only problem? I was wearing Lisa's underwear instead of my own. After the adrenaline wore off, I realized my fellas were far more constricted than normal. Since her parents began walking past Lisa's open bedroom door at thirty second intervals, I had to spend the rest of the evening passing off the pained look on my face as the struggle to grasp algebra.

To this day, I would never consider cross-dressing. And I can't do algebra to save my ass.

The only advantages I have are that I'm halfway up the steps and said steps are carpeted. This allows me to move without being heard. When I get to the top of the stairs, Mike's in the doorway to the bedroom. The stricken look on his face tells me he's heard the front door.

"Who is that?" he whispers.

"Shockingly, I didn't stop to look."

"I called Carol," he says, "She'll be here in thirty seconds."

"Good. We've just got to wait it out."

Footsteps cross the living room floor, possibly heading for the stairs. Mike and I skulk into the bedroom, hoping like hell neither of us steps on a loose floorboard. The bedroom has the requisite king-sized bed and a walk-in closet. And Mike manages to find a loose floorboard.

Somewhere downstairs, the footsteps come to a halt. Then they start up the stairs. Mike slips inside the walk-in closet and, I'm assuming out of habit, whips the door shut behind him. The sound echoes through the house.

I freeze, going through the mental database of possible escape routes. There aren't any. Any second now, someone's going to come up the stairs and my only options are to jump out a second story window or hide under the bed.

"Hello?"

It's Norah's voice. She's near the top of the stairs.

I flip on the bedroom light and busy myself with looking busy. Norah comes through the door and jumps when she sees me. She puts a hand to her chest. I turn into Mr. Friendly.

"Hey, there you are," I say.

Norah looks nonplussed, to say the least. "What the hell are you doing here?"

I'm in full improv mode. "I saw the light on. I thought you were working on moving. I…I wanted to see you."

She ignores that last part and is still working on why the hell I'm in her house. "You saw the light on?"

"I was hoping you were here."

Norah's eyes soften. She's warming, but wary. "I must have left it on the last time I was here. It was late and I was tired." She leans back. "How did you get in?"

"The backdoor was unlocked."

She leans against the doorway. Her posture becomes a little less rigid. "You wanted to see me?"

"After last night. I…I couldn't let things go like that."

"Let things go? Did we break up?"

There's a light at the end of the tunnel. "I was hoping not. But it felt like it."

Some of Norah's hair tumbles down the side of her face. Somewhere, Mike must be thrilled with my improvisational horseshit. Then I remember *somewhere* is about six feet away.

"I was hurt," Norah says, "But I…I didn't want to give you the idea we were finished."

Relief floods through me. "I'm sorry I brought up the thing with Sheila Grant. I'm just trying to find answers and…I got pushy."

Norah's eyes are big and clear. When she speaks, her voice is hushed. "I want you to trust me."

"I do. I never wanted you to think anything else."

"Because if we don't stick together…"

"I know."

Norah puts her arms around my waist. Her face is close to my chin. "I'm sorry, too."

Sometimes, you can only screw things up by talking. Since I've done plenty of that lately, the best bet is to kiss Norah. She presses into me and runs her fingernails down my back. For both of us, there's a ferocity and a desperation to it. Those who have engaged in any variety of Make Up Sex will know what I'm talking about.

And then my cell phone buzzes in my pocket.

Fortunately, it's on vibrate. I slip the damn thing out of my pocket and, while I'm kissing Norah's neck, sneak a glance at it. One message is from Mike, begging me to knock this off. The other is from Carol, wondering where the hell I am.

"The bedroom," I mutter, absently.

Norah pulls back, her fingernails clawing my ass. "The bedroom? You want to do it right in this bedroom? In the bed I used to share with Brady? That would be so very, very wrong."

"I'm sorry. It—"

"Let's do it."

Before I can say anything, Norah gives me a kiss that nearly takes me out of my shoes. I have a vague realization this is wrong, but my brain is not driving the bus. Within seconds, Norah's t-shirt is in one corner, her jeans in another, her bra is hanging from a lamp and her panties were last seen heading south. I'm fumbling out of my jeans and underwear as I move toward the bed. She dives under the covers and drags me in with her. Just before I slide on top of her, I catch a glimpse of the closet door. Mike's trapped and there's nothing I can do to help.

"Take me, Joe," Norah whispers, "Take me right in this bed."

Not that I'm thinking too much about Mike right now.

***

"That was the most goddamn disgusting thing I've ever been a part of," Mike says, stalking my living room floor, "You have any idea how traumatizing that was? The only thing worse would have been watching my parents…God, I can't even finish that thought."

I look at Carol, who rolls her eyes. This isn't how I like to have morning coffee with my friends. Mike managed to escape Norah's closet after she and I fell asleep. Lars had been hiding out in the basement and was able to escape unnoticed. Carol drove all over the neighborhood before finding them. No one is happy with me right now.

"I am terribly sorry," I say, "For like the eighth time. I don't know what else to tell you."

"I may have had my last woody." Mike uses a flask to Irish up his java. "This is why you and I could never do a three way with a chick."

Carol bows slightly. "On behalf of all the chicks, thank the Lord in Heaven for that."

Mike ignores her. "There are certain levels even a good friendship shouldn't go to. Listening to you and Norah is one of those."

I swing my desk chair toward him. "Is this where I have to remind you of all the times in college where you brought a girl back to your dorm room and *the entire floor* got to listen to the two of you go at it?"

"That's not the issue."

"What is the issue?"

Mike drops into the comfy chair and mumbles, "I had to hear you have sex and it was really gross."

I'm not going to apologize to Mike again. Given there was make up sex involved, I don't even feel all that sorry. Besides, Mike's in the minority. Lars, never one to judge anyway, didn't demand an apology. Carol, perhaps remembering her recent close call, didn't get on my case (at least, not about the sex). And somewhere in his fouled-up cranium, Mike knows he would have done the same thing in my position.

Carol, stepping into the kitchen for a refill, plays peacemaker.. "If you two are over your lover's tiff, I think Mike found something last night."

And that *does* pull Mike out of his snit. He grabs his briefcase and pulls out a file. He sets it on the breakfast bar between me and Carol. I flip through it. There's a bunch of receipts and financial statements. The name listed on the papers, though, is Bruce Hives. And the address appears to be redacted by a heavy black marker.

"Where did you find it?" I ask.

"It was in the closet," Mike says, "Loose floorboard right behind the suits."

"Who is Bruce Hives?" I say.

"I was hoping you'd know," Mike says.

"Doesn't ring a bell." I flip through a few more pages, but they're not any more enlightening. "Think this has something to do with Brady embezzling from the store?"

Carol peers over my shoulder. "It might just be someone's financial records."

Mike laughs. "That you keep under a loose floorboard in the closet?"

I tap the file against my chin. Mike takes a hit from the flask. Carol gives him the stink eye, then looks at the file.

"If Brady was embezzling from the store," Carol says, "He could have been funneling the money to this Bruce Hives."

"Could be someone Brady owed money to," Mike ventures.

"Or someone Brady was working with," I say.

"Or Brady himself," Carol says.

Those are all good theories, but they founder on one important thing: we have no way of proving them. Or even knowing where to begin proving them. Carol takes the file from me.

"You think Brady's divorce lawyer would know anything about this?" she asks.

"Sheila Grant?" I say, "Maybe. But I doubt she'll talk to me."

Carol tosses the file on the futon and sets her coffee cup on the breakfast. Mike pages through the file.

"Maybe you could ask Norah about it," he says.

I wince. "Norah and I just got back on good terms."

"Don't remind me," Mike says.

I spin back toward the computer and punch "Bruce Hives" into a search engine. I don't get anyone local. I adjust it to *Bruce Hives Minnesota* and get absolutely nothing. I spin away from the computer again.

"Forget it," I say, "I'll hand the name over to Pike and see if he comes up with anything."

Carol's eyes widen. "Does this mean you're going to let the police handle this now?"

"No," I say, "It means I'm going to let Pike handle the Bruce Hives thing. I doubt anything will come of it. Meantime, I have to figure out what *I'm* going to do."

Since neither of them have an immediate solution and they both have day jobs, Mike and Carol decide to take off. Mike's out the door right away. Carol grabs her purse off the futon but doesn't follow.

"You broke into her house in the interest of leaving no stone unturned," she says, "Your own words. And now that you found something, you're going to leave *that* stone unturned?"

I wither under Carol's gaze and then say: "I want Norah to know I trust her."

"And that means you can't even ask her questions?"

I hate how mealy-mouthed I sound. "It's just…it didn't go well the first time."

Carol starts out the door. "Seems Norah always get what she wants."

She's gone before I can respond. I'm tempted to storm down the stairs and give her a piece of mind. But the only way to prove her wrong is to talk to Norah and find out what she knows. And there's no reason to be afraid of that conversation.

Keep telling yourself that, Joe.

***

The gymnastics of last night leave me anxious to see Norah again. Sadly, she's got to work early and is smart enough to know a visit to my place will result in a decreased likelihood of her getting up on time for work. I have to content myself with a phone call. Not that I'm giving up easily.

"Last chance," I tell her, "I'm just sitting here in the nude."

Norah giggles. "Are you really?"

"No. But it could be arranged by the time you get here."

"Tempting. *Very* tempting. But I need to get some sleep, sweetie. I'll make it up to you some other time."

"I look forward to it."

I'm trying to find an easy way to slip in a question that hopefully won't ruin the conversation. During a pause, I reach for my most casual tone of voice.

"I was wondering," I say, "The name Bruce Hives ring a bell?"

"No," Norah says, not missing a beat, "Should it?"

I stay relaxed. "Just a name I ran across. Sounds familiar, but I can't remember who mentioned him. It wasn't any of my friends, so I figured I'd ask you."

"No. Nobody I've heard of."

She's quick, but not overly quick, with both answers. If Pike were here, he'd confirm she's telling the truth. Suspicion-wise, there's nothing to see here.

We chit-chat a little longer and then wish each other a good night. I toss my cell phone on the bed and saunter into the kitchen, surprised by the buoyancy in my step. I grab a beer out of the fridge and settle in next to an open arch window. The air is pleasantly warm. For the first time in a while, I start to relax. True, Norah's not here, but neither are any friends to badger me about how I should suspect her and am being manipulated by her.

The "no friends" thing, however, was not meant to last. Lars bursts into the apartment, wearing a cooking apron over a pair of baggy shorts and a bowling shirt. (I long ago gave up questioning his sartorial choices.)

"Hey, brother, don't mean to interrupt," he says, "But I wanted to let you know: somebody's breaking into your car."

It takes a second to sink in, thanks in no small part to Lars' offhanded delivery. Once it does, I run down the hallway.

"Who's breaking into my car?" I say.

"I don't know," Lars says, "Big guy, dressed in black. I saw him out my window."

"And you didn't do anything?" I say.

"What do you mean? I came up here and told you. How is that not doing anything?"

I duck into my bedroom and look out the window facing the parking lot. Sure enough, there's a guy attempting to break into the driver's door of my car. He bears a striking resemblance to the guy I found on my deck. I charge out of the bedroom and head toward the front door. Lars watches.

"Where are you going?" he asks,

"Down to the first floor and out the backdoor of the building. If I go down the backsteps, he's going to hear me coming a mile away."

Lars follows, but bails on when we pass his apartment. "I've got a soufflé in the oven," he says, "I can't leave that now. Best of luck."

I haul ass to the first floor, then cut back down a long hallway toward the backdoor. Beyond the door is a grassy commons area with a few picnic tables. The Saturn is parked next to the grass. The guy looks up in time to see me closing in on him.

Once again, he's wearing all black and the light only gives me a good look at his beard. The guy swears and starts across the parking lot. I slide past the Saturn and go after him. He ducks around the carriage house at the edge of the parking lot and into the alley. The stale smell of sweat trails after him. The guy's surprisingly fast. But I've still got the speed advantage. I make a lunge and hit him at waist level. We tumble to the pavement.

Everything stops. I'm on the ground, pain rolling through my skinned arms and knees. The guy is nearby, groaning. Somewhere, there's a tinny voice saying, "Bart? Bart, what's going on?" Someone calling from a nearby window? Or does the guy have an accomplice?

Then I spot it. There's a cell phone lying between us. The guy rolls to his side and reaches for it. I snatch it before he does.

And he punches me in the face.

It's not a hard blow, but it does the trick. I roll back against the pavement, the lights in the alley moving in a swirl.

The guy stands over me. There's a large hunting knife in his hand.

"You stupid fuck!" he shouts, waving the knife, "You could have fucking killed me!"

Something about the way he's carrying the knife tells me he's not going to use it. But he *is* going to kick my ass. I curl into a ball. He boots me in the side. Twice.

"Joe! Joe, are you all right?"

The guy looks back toward the carriage house. Someone is coming. The guy swears and gives me one last kick. Footsteps ring off the pavement, fading away.

When I look up again, Lars is kneeling over me, cradling my head in his hands. I'm still holding the cell phone. The guy is nowhere to be found.

"You okay, brother?" Lars asks.

"Absolutely. I've always found a little ass-kicking tends to straighten the spine."

Slowly, I get to my feet. The right side of my face feels heavy. Throw in the skinned-up hands and knees and the pain in my side and I'm not in fighting trim. Lars holds me up.

"What have you got there?" he says, nodding toward my hand.

"It's the guy's cell phone. He was on the line with somebody."

I glance at the phone. Whoever was on the line has hung up. But the face hasn't gone dark. I can still see the number of the last call. The guy was nice enough to put the name in his address book.

It's Doug Perkins.

CHAPTER ELEVEN

I've developed a theory that stress in a relationship accelerates the getting-to-know-you process. I have plenty of evidence for this. For example, Mike was once so entranced with a woman named Emily Zuga, he asked her to spend a week in Puerto Rico with him. As luck would have it, Emily was menstruating at the beginning of the vacation and not comfortable with any sexual activity during this…well, period. Mike was completely okay with this. For about a day. Then he started getting pissy, which resulted in Emily getting pissy right back. By the end of the week, they were not having sex for reasons that had nothing to do with a menstrual cycle. When I picked them up at the airport, only Mike was waiting for me. The last he'd seen Emily, she punched him in the stomach and called a cab.

I'm going through a similar thing with Norah (absent menstruation and physical violence). The deeper I get into this investigation, the more we learn about each other. Currently, I'm learning she has a fierce loyalty to those who do her a kindness.

"I don't believe it," Norah says, staring at the cell phone, "This is some mistake."

"I guess it's possible a completely different guy named Doug Perkins hired a thug to break into my car. But it's not bloody likely."

Norah glances up from the phone. The look on her face tells me she doesn't appreciate my snark. She wanders the floor of her basement apartment. I've come here to confront Doug and I'm pissed that my girlfriend is not on my side.

"I can't believe Doug would do something like that," Norah says.

I fall back into the easy chair. "Look, this guy had Doug's phone number. That's at least suspicious, right?"

Norah stops by the stairs, all the way across the room from me. She leans against the wall and some of her hair falls across her eyes.

"There's got to be an explanation," she says.

"Maybe Doug can give it to me," I say, "Is he going to be down soon?"

Norah's shoulders sag. "I'll go get him."

She heads up the stairs. I appreciate Norah's loyalty to Doug. It's a quality that makes me like her as much as I do. It's why she believed I didn't kill Brady without me explaining myself. But in this case, loyalty is blinding her to the (more than likely) truth. Hopefully, this chat with Doug will open her eyes.

A few minutes later, Doug tromps down the stairs behind Norah. His sulky look is firmly in place. He reminds me of a teenager trying to explain a crappy report card to his parents. He slouches and looks to every corner of the room except the one I'm sitting in. Neither of us attempts to shake hands. Doug's right hand is still wrapped anyway, so we'll pretend that's the reason.

"Norah said you wanted to talk," he says.

Since we're not on a small talk basis, I get right to the point. "Someone tried to break into my car. Probably the same guy I found on my deck about a few weeks back. Seems interested in me confessing to your brother's murder." I hand the cell phone to him. "The guy had this on him. You might want to look over the recent calls."

Doug looks at the phone. It doesn't take him long to find his name. (It's not like there are a lot to choose from.) His expression remains sullen. He hands the phone back to me and slips his hands back into his pockets.

"What did the guy look like?" he asks.

"About my height. Kind of hefty. Black beard."

"Kind of piggy eyes?"

I try to bring the guy's face (what I saw of it anyway) to mind. "I think so," I say, "I didn't get a good look at him. Kicks like a mule, I can tell you that much."

Doug stares at the carpeting as he thinks. "Sounds like Bart."

A little thrill runs through me. This was not how I expected this conversation to go. "Who's Bart?"

"A friend of my brother's," he says, and I don't know which word he finds more distasteful, *friend* or *brother*, "They were drinking buddies in college. They stayed in touch. Brady was always giving him money. For what, I don't know. He talked me into hiring Bart at the store. It didn't last long. Let's leave it at that."

"Have you talked to Bart since Brady died?"

"A couple times. He's been calling, to see if there's anything I need. I get the feeling he's sniffing around for money. That's probably how my name wound up in his phone."

I heft the phone in my hand. "Your name and no one else's."

Doug flicks his head to one side, unconcerned. "Bart's a little on the shady side. He might have multiple phones for multiple purposes. I don't know."

Norah looks satisfied with the explanation. Doug's eye cut toward the stairs. I'm not buying his explanation. It's too vague and he's too anxious to get away from this conversation. He's covering something. But I don't have the information needed to call bullshit. I slip the phone into my pocket.

"Thanks," I tell him, "Guess that clears it up."

Doug ambles toward the stairs. Norah gives him a pat on the arm as he passes. He trots upstairs without a look back. I plunk down into a chair. Norah sits on the ottoman, her legs situated between mine. She studies my face.

"Get what you needed?" she asks.

"I guess. Seems awfully convenient, though. This Bart guy happens to call Doug as he's breaking into my car?"

"Sounds like you guys were jostling around. Maybe he butt-dialed Doug."

I'm not convinced and the look on my face probably tells her that. It's not a particularly friendly atmosphere. Norah knows there's every reason to suspect Doug—she must know that—but she doesn't want to admit it. I'm frustrated she believes him so unquestioningly. But if I push it, I can kiss our little détente goodbye. I kiss her on the forehead and start for the door.

"I've got a few errands to run," I say, "Okay if I call you later?"

"Of course."

I head out to the car, parked just off the driveway. I can't help feeling a little betrayed, but I've got to get over that. I'm in a bit of a daze as I reach for the car door.

"Is something on your mind?"

I look up, startled, and see a woman coming across her lawn toward me. She's small and round and at an age where I'm guessing the blonde in her hair came out of a bottle. She's got bright, inquisitive eyes and a happy demeanor. A busybody if I ever saw one.

"I'm fine," I say, "Just on my way out."

"You're a friend of Doug's?"

"More a friend of a friend." And even that feels like a stretch.

The neighbor gestures toward Doug's house. "You mean that pretty girl who moved into the basement apartment?"

Yep, busybody. "Norah. I'm friends with her."

"So sad about her husband." I can't agree, but I'll keep that to myself. "I saw him once," the woman says, "The night he was killed."

This just got a whole lot more interesting. I put my hand out. "Joe Davis."

"Kathy," the neighbor says, shaking my hand, "Yes, the husband. He was Doug's brother, right? He didn't seem very nice. It was a terrible fight they had. I could hear the shouting in my living room."

Probably because she turned the TV off and had the windows open. Again, I keep that on the down-low. "What was the fight about?" I ask.

"I don't know. I couldn't make out what they were saying. But they were definitely yelling. And I heard something crash."

"Crash?"

"Like it got knocked over. Maybe in a fight. I can't say for sure."

But you will wildly speculate, won't you? "A fight? Anything else you heard or saw?"

"No. I saw the brother storm out. Then a little while later, Doug took off. I don't know when he got back. And I stay up pretty late, too. He must have been out most of the night."

Whether she's aware of it or not, Kathy just blew a hole in Doug's alibi. If he was out most of the night, what he was doing? It's a decent question. But I'm not going to get the chance to ask it, at least not right away. The garage door opens and Doug's car pulls out. He gives me and Kathy a dark look as he swings out of the driveway. Kathy and I watch him head down the street.

"Have you talked to Doug about that night?" I ask.

Kathy seems taken aback. "Not at all. It's really none of my business, is it?"

That's the problem with busybodies. They have a strange sense of what is and isn't their business. And usually, they're overcome with bashfulness when they get to the good parts. I thank Kathy and head to my car. She beams at me and waves, but I get the sneaking suspicion I'm going to be the topic of conversation between her and some other neighbor. I debate whether or not to bring this up to Norah. It's starting to feel like we're not on the same page.

Congratulations, Carol. You're getting your wish.

CHAPTER TWELVE

One of the saddest things you'll see is a guy trying to save a relationship that's souring. It's like watching a hamster negotiate a maze of increasing despair.

Part of the problem is that some guys (most guys, really) are clueless as to how they wound up in the relationship in the first place. They have no idea what a nice, attractive young lady would want with them, so they're always feeling they're just along for the ride. Which means they can't dial up a workable solution when things start to go south. And many women have an expectation that a guy should just know *what's wrong and proceed from there. So, we keep trying things that don't work until our little hamster hearts give out and the relationship dies. At which point, we're tossed into the Relationship Trash.*

I'm not quite in that situation with Norah, although things have been crazy enough that I think I can see it from here. Mike, on the other hand, is up to his eyeballs in it.

"I think Haley's getting attached," Mike says, cracking a Grand Brewing Maibock and stepping out of my kitchen.

I swing my desk chair toward him. "What makes you say that?"

"She's been asking all sorts of questions about whereabouts and who I've been with. I think she suspects something."

"Just because you've been sneaking around with Amy? Heavens above."

Mike leans on the breakfast bar. "Haley and I are dating, yes. I didn't think we were dating *exclusively*. Why shouldn't Amy and I have a little fun?"

If not for his obvious deficiencies in work ethic and general intelligence, I've always thought Mike would have made a good fit as a lawyer. The man's forever in search of loopholes.

"Haley would not be cool with you and Amy?" I say.

"No. Cool is the last thing she would be. Especially because she's making noises about taking our relationship to the next level."

"What level would that be?"

Mike tucks his beer under his chin. "For her, it would be telling her father about us. That whole almost-getting-caught thing freaked her out. She doesn't want to keep sneaking around. Says our love should be strong enough to survive anything."

"Your love?"

"It came as news to me, too."

I head into the kitchen to grab a Maibock of my own. "Isn't Haley worried about what Alan is going to say? Or do? Or sue?"

"No. She figures when he sees the two of us, arm in arm, he'll be so entranced, there's no way he'll get mad."

"She actually said this?"

"Word for word. I was waiting for the part where the Easter Bunny was going to get involved." He gulps the beer. "If she tells her father, Alan will fire my ass."

"Can he do that?" I ask, "Doesn't he have to fire you with cause?"

"Joe, you have any idea how many man hours I spend here versus at work? You think Alan can't find cause?"

I sit at the breakfast bar, opposite Mike. Sometimes misery could do without company. I crack the Maibock and realize, distressingly, I have no beer money left to replace these Maibocks when they go.

"What about Amy?" I ask, "How are things going there?"

"Not good. It was fun for a couple of nights. Very enthusiastic, but a little loopy."

"Loopy how?"

"Ah, she's all bright and bubbly and stuff. Then she gets quiet. It was the same way in bed. Like I was getting nothing out of her and then she's on me like an animal. Very strange."

"You ask her about it?"

"No, that would mean getting to know each other." His cell phone buzzes. He glances at it and lets out a cluck of disgust. "*And* she keeps texting me, wanting to get together. I just got another one. This is not the not casual sex I pictured."

A thought occurs. Amy's not been shy about sharing the goings-on at her place of work. Maybe she's got some information on the embezzling. Maybe she'd be willing to tell Mike. I might want to make use of this source before Mike shits the proverbial bed. If that's really the metaphor I want.

"You should get together with her," I say.

"Not a good idea," Mike says, putting the phone back in his pocket, "No point in leading her on."

"As opposed to sleeping with her and ignoring her?"

"Y'know, for a suspected murderer and a confirmed adulterer, you *do* rush to judgment."

All right, Joe, relax. Take the diplomatic approach. "Pick a neutral spot," I tell him, "A place you can meet for a drink. I'll come with you."

"Come with me? I thought I was clear on the idea of you and me in a three way."

"We're not going to have sex with her, you overheated moron! I need to talk to her."

"I assume this is about your investigation?"

"You assume correctly."

Mike debates this, tapping his beer bottle on the breakfast bar (even though he knows that drives me nuts). He takes out his cell phone and works on a return message.

"You realize you owe me one," he says.

"I won't tell Haley about you and Amy. There. Debt paid. And I won't tell Amy about you and Haley. There. You owe *me* one."

Mike looks like he's passing a kidney stone. He sends the message and jams his phone back into his pocket. I hold my beer up in a toast. He doesn't return. Sorry, Mike. You're not the only one who can lawyer your way out of a situation.

***

As could be expected, Amy is not thrilled to see me arrive with Mike. The agreed-upon meeting place is The Tav, since it's reasonably accessible for Amy and an easy escape route for Mike. I hope Amy doesn't create a scene. Freddie, the former neighborhood menace who serves as The Tav's bouncer, has never liked Mike and frequently looks for excuses to throw him out.

Amy's at a high-top table near the picture window. She slides off the stool as we reach the table. She and Mike exchange an awkward half-hug, half-kiss. The top of her head barely reaches his sternum. Her happiness fades as she looks at me.

"Hi Joe," she says, with little enthusiasm, "Are you…joining us?"

"Just for a minute," I say, "I walked Mike over here. I wanted to see you. Thought maybe we could chat."

Amy's big eyes widen. "Oh? About what?"

"Just a few things. It will only take a minute."

We sit at the high-top. I debate ordering a drink. I'm not sure how long I'm going to be here. I certainly get the feeling Amy doesn't want it to be long. My debate adds a few drops of silence into this already-awkward brew. I fumble with the unlit candle on the table.

"I, uh, I wanted to ask you a few questions about the store," I say.

Amy stares at her glass of white wine. "Okay, go ahead."

I try to find a comfortable position on the stool, but my ass is not having it. "Did Doug think Brady was up to something?"

Her face tightens. "What would Brady have been up to?"

I come clean to Amy about Brady's possible embezzling, giving her the rundown on stumbling across the key to the locker and then the money. When I finish, Amy's mouth is open.

"What did you do with the money?" she asks.

"I turned it in to the police," I say, "But they don't see a connection between Brady's murder and the money."

"And you do?" she asks.

"If Doug knew about it, I can't imagine he was too happy."

Amy doesn't seem shocked. "He was pissed. No doubt."

I'm still half-debating the drink. Maybe that's why it takes me a second before I realize Amy's phrasing. I look away from the bar and set the candle aside.

"Doug knew about the embezzling?"

"I heard him talking about it with Stephanie." Amy hastily sips her drink. "It was at the store one night. They were back in the storage area. The floor was dead, so I went back there to grab a magazine I'd left in my bag. I overheard them. I didn't mean to. But you know what it's like when people are talking in a certain tone of voice and you *know* something's wrong?"

It's the same tone my parents used when standing in the kitchen and having whispered conversations about my deadbeat uncle Gordie's latest screw up. But I leave out my family history and let Amy carry on.

"I tried to pick up what I could," she says, "Doug was really pissed. He said he'd been looking at the inventory and stuff wasn't adding up. He said Stephanie ran the books and she ought to know. Stephanie said she didn't know what was going on. She didn't work directly with the inventory. Doug was convinced Brady had something to do with it. He wanted to call the police, call an attorney, anybody. He kept saying what a lying son of a bitch Brady was and how he never should have trusted him in the first place. He was going to make him pay."

The cause of the fight between Brady and Doug is becoming clearer. "What did Stephanie say to that?" I ask.

"She was more careful. She said it looked bad, but they should double-check before they did anything. But Doug was unreasonable. Said he wanted to talk to Brady before Brady went on vacation."

"Brady was going on vacation?" I ask, "Where was he going?"

Amy knocks back the rest of her drink. "I think to Bermuda. For a week. He wound up not going because…you know."

Interesting. The embezzling money could have been funding that little vacation. I'll bet Doug thought so. Stephanie might not have, but she *did* know about the possible embezzling. Yet another instance in which Stephanie didn't mention something she knew.

"I heard Doug and Brady had a big fight the night Brady was killed," I say, "A neighbor said Doug left the house right after the fight and wasn't seen for the rest of the night."

Amy's bright eyes darken. If I had to guess, she suspects something. But all she says is: "I don't know. You'd have to ask Doug."

It keeps coming back to that, doesn't it? I'm anxious to talk to Doug, but the feeling is not mutual. Meantime, I've still got Amy here. (Not that she's anxious to talk to me, either. I sense a trend.)

"You seem pretty tight with Stephanie," I say, "You talked to her about what you heard?"

"No," Amy says, "I wanted to bring it up. I just wasn't sure how. It wasn't something I was supposed to hear."

"You got together with her the night Brady was killed?" I ask.

"We got a drink. Well, I had a drink. Stephanie just had ginger ale."

"How long were you out?"

"Probably until about eleven."

That squares with what Stephanie told me. But it doesn't give her an alibi. "Did you ever talk about the missing knife with her?"

"No. I still haven't."

"And you don't have any idea who took it?" I ask.

"Not for sure."

The inflection in Amy's voice goes up at the end, as if there's more to the story. "It sounds like you have a suspicion," I say.

Amy runs a finger around the rim of her glass. "There was something I didn't tell you before. I…I didn't think you'd want to hear it."

Mike and I exchange a look. I incline my head toward Amy. Mike frowns but does what I (silently) ask. He pats Amy's arm.

"It's okay," he says, "Joe can take it. You need to be honest with him."

Amy grips Mike's forearm, buoyed by his approval. She leans in, drawing us into a huddle.

"Norah used to come in and help out with the inventory sometimes. Mostly, she'd chat with Doug. Anyway, I went into the back room one day to help out. And I saw Norah handling one of the hunting knives. It was still in the box, but she was looking it over. As soon as she saw me, she put it back. She tried to chat, but it seemed like she was trying to cover."

Norah didn't mention the knife thing earlier, but why would she? For all I know, she was looking at a box and got startled. Not precisely the kind of thing you need to mention. But I *am* going to have ask Norah about it. Although, that conversation never goes well. Meantime, Mike looks at me like he's stuck his head in a bag of farts. I've overstayed my welcome.

"I think I've intruded on you kids enough for one night," I say, "I'll head home."

Amy takes Mike's hand. He gives her a weak grin and realizes he's now stuck here for the rest of the evening. I'll pay for this later, I'm sure.

From Mike and from others.

CHAPTER THIRTEEN

When you get right down to it, there aren't a lot of redeeming qualities to sex in the great outdoors. Between the bugs, the dirt, the grass, the weeds and various creepy-crawlies, it's an introductory course to the true number of crevices in the human body. And there's always the possibility of getting caught, which like most things sexual, is more an aphrodisiac than a deterrent.

Norah lays her head on my chest and pulls the picnic blanket across us. "You sure no one's going to find us?"

I prop my head up on the backpack I'm using as a pillow. "We're far enough off the trail. I suppose there's always the possibility a spotter plane could come along."

"And spot this? We'd make somebody's day."

Norah's head bounces lightly as I laugh. Obviously, I called Norah after I left The Tav. As could be predicted, a call led to her coming over to my place which led to her spending the night which led to us going for a late morning bike ride by the Mississippi River which led to stopping for a picnic lunch which led to a tryst in the woods. And here we are, lying in the brush with nothing but a blanket on.

Norah props her chin on my chest. "That was fun."

"Couldn't agree more."

"We're really getting our exercise."

"Some of it more fun than others."

She kisses my cheek. "I'm glad you called. It felt like things were a little tense at Doug's."

"I guess it was," I say, "Sorry about that. It's just everything's that going on. We can try our best, but it's going to intrude sometimes."

Hopefully, these intrusions won't involve one of us getting hauled away for the murder. I keep that thought to myself. It will only kill the mood. Norah looks up at me.

"I actually tried calling you last night," she says, "Before you called me. You didn't answer. Were you doing something?"

"I met Mike and a girl at The Tav," I say.

"A girl?"

"Someone Mike's seeing."

"Then why were you there?"

I could lie to Norah, but I won't. Honesty is the best— and only—policy from here on out. "It was somebody I wanted to question," I say, "You remember Amy? From Pro Sports."

Norah sits up on one elbow. "I remember her. How do *you* know her?"

I keep my tone casual, explaining how Mike and I met Amy while stopping into Pro Sports to question Stephanie, how Mike started flirting with Amy and how they're involved in…there's no easy term for what they're involved in.

"I thought Mike had a girlfriend," Norah says.

"You don't know Mike."

Norah sits up, letting the blanket fall away. She throws a casual look in the direction of the biking path, but the brush disguises us well enough. "Why did you want to talk to Amy?"

"Just to get more information about the store," I say, "About the stuff going on between Doug and Brady. She talked about how they hated each other. Nothing new under the sun."

"And that was it?"

"Not entirely."

Norah's eyes are cold and penetrating. Two words. *Not entirely.* That's all it took to cross the conversational Rubicon. But if I go down the road of avoiding things, it's going to end in mistrust. I have to believe Norah will be okay with what I tell her and accept the consequences if she's not.

"Amy said she saw you handling a knife in the backroom one day," I say, "The same kind that was used in the murder."

Norah unconsciously lays a hand across her breasts. It's a gesture with more vulnerability than defiance. Her foot paws at her jeans, lying at the foot of the blanket.

"Are you asking me something?" she says.

Whenever Norah turns away from me, I feel like she's gone a thousand miles away. And the only thing to do is reach for her and pull her back to me. I sit up.

"I'm not asking anything," I say, "Just telling you what we talked about."

"I might have looked over a knife," she ways, "I honestly don't remember. That's all I can tell you."

"I thought as much. Doesn't sound like any big deal."

She looks at me through the curtain of hair falling across her face. "Then we're okay?"

"Completely."

Norah brushes the hair from her eyes. She takes my face in her hands but doesn't kiss me. Instead, she looks into my eyes. She's thinking something over.

"My meeting with Sheila Grant," Norah says, "She was offering me a settlement."

I gently take her arms. "A settlement?"

"In the divorce. She said Brady was off the deep end. She was worried that handling a client like him might hurt her reputation. She wanted to wash her hands of it."

"Why did she talk to you?" I ask, "Instead of your lawyer."

"Because I didn't have a lawyer. I couldn't afford one. At least, not one that could take on Sheila Grant." Norah shakes her head, ruefully "It wasn't out of the kindness of Sheila's heart, believe me. She knew a clusterfuck when she saw one. Better to cut a deal—one that slightly favored Brady— and let us move on with their lives. I was more than ready to do that."

"Was Brady?" I ask, "He *was* off the deep end. Could Sheila have talked him into any kind of fair deal?"

"Sheila thought she could. You met her. You know what a high opinion she has of herself. Anyway, it was a moot point a few hours later."

It's like an oak tree's been lifted off my shoulders. All that doubt about Norah and there's a perfectly good explanation for it. I stroke her cheek with my thumb.

"Why didn't you tell me this before?" I ask.

"Because of the way you asked me. Like I needed an alibi. I just…I made it about something it wasn't. It was an honest question about meeting with Sheila and I made it a thing about trust. I'm sorry."

"You don't have to be."

Norah lays her face in my hands, as if she could melt into them. I gently pull her toward me. After we kiss, she leans her forehead against mine.

"I need you to stick with me," Norah whispers, "If you aren't with me…I don't even want to think about that."

Norah kisses me again. She slides on top of me while my hands caress her back. Things are about to get exceedingly friendly when voices can be heard on the bike path. They're loud and numerous. Some kind of riding group, probably. The voices linger, leading me to believe they're stopping for a break. Norah and I freeze in position.

A smile creeps across her face. *"Bikus interruptus."*

We start laughing, then hush ourselves, lest someone in the biking group investigates the source of the laughter. Norah slides off me.

"If we get dressed quickly, they probably won't notice us," she says.

"What do we tell them when we come out of the woods?"

"Let them figure it out for themselves."

That brings another round of hushed laughter. We sort out our clothing and dress as smoothly as one can in a lying position. When we stand up, I pick a few leaves out of Norah's hair, which brings more giggling. We're about to walk the bikes out of the brush when Norah stops. She grabs my hand and speaks without looking at me.

"I really like being with you," she says, "It's the kind of thing I…I feel like I could do all the time. For a long time. Do you know what I mean?"

I know exactly what she means. All I say is: "I do."

"I've got this tendency to fall too hard, too fast. It's what got me involved with Brady. I know you're different. Completely different, but still…"

This is not my finest hour, dealing with real feelings and vulnerabilities. I specialize in glib. I like being with Norah, pretty much all the time. But I live my life from paycheck to paycheck, column to column, drinking session to drinking session, girlfriend to girlfriend. That's not the kind of person who thinks in big picture terms.

"Tell you what," I say, "Why don't we ride back to my place, pick up where we left off here and…let that be all we worry about? For now."

Norah squeezes my hand. "Sounds like a plan. For now."

We walk our bikes down to the path, single file. I enjoy the sway of her body and her little conspiratorial looks back. My heart's like a Ferris Wheel; rising at moments like this, sinking when I think about everything working against us. I have to follow my own advice. Just ride home with Norah and, for an afternoon anyway, lose myself in her. That's good enough.

For now.

***

As soon as Norah leaves, I decide to ambush Doug at Pro Sports.

It's only been about twenty-four hours, but I get the feeling the man is avoiding me. I've left him a few messages and followed up with some additional calls. No response. I thought about asking Norah to call him, but I don't want to put her between the two of us again. Best to handle this on my own.

The drive to Bloomington isn't long, but it allows me time to do some thinking. This case, for lack of a better term, is bending my mind like a pretzel. Nobody involved has an alibi, but that doesn't mean anything. I'm down to motive. But what was the motive to kill Brady? If it was the embezzling, then Doug or maybe Stephanie has a motive. If it was the divorce, then…

Norah. Dammit. Why does that keep popping into my head?

I'll try the embezzlement end first. Specifically, the *Possibly hiring some goon to go after me* and *Having a fight with his probably-larcenous brother* portions. Those are things worth talking to Doug about. Whether he likes it or not.

It's a Sunday, so Pro Sports is slow. Amy spots me from the information desk right after I walk in. She waves and I half-raise my hand in response. I haven't talked to Mike, so I have no idea how last night went. I approach the desk with a due sense of trepidation. Amy beams at me as I arrive.

"Hi Joe," she says, "How are you doing?"

"I'm gr—"

"Are you going to see Mike tonight?"

Since I strong-armed Mike into meeting Amy, this must be some kind of karmic retribution. Doesn't mean I have to enjoy it, though.

"I'm not sure," I say, "No plans at the moment."

So much for the beaming. "Oh. I just wanted to know if he was okay. He seemed a little distracted last night."

"Really?" I ask, "Must be something with work."

"That's probably it," Amy says, "Since he's going back to work for the CIA."

I nearly stumble into a display of energy gel packs. "The CIA?"

"He's been called back to active service. He could leave any moment. If I suddenly don't hear from him, that's why."

On one hand, I'm repulsed by Mike lying to a girl who's only mistake was liking him in the first place. On the other hand, it's been years since Mike pulled the *Fake CIA agent* gambit and I can't deny the feeling of nostalgia it gives me.

"He's a man of mystery," I say, "No doubt about it."

"Tell him I said hi," she says, "Ask him to call me, please."

"Uh, sure. Next time I see him. I'll make sure he gets everything he deserves." I clear my throat. "Meantime, is Doug around? I need to talk to him."

Amy gives that a little shake of her head. "Sorry. No. He left early this afternoon. Stephanie's around, if you want to talk to her."

It wasn't who I came for, but there are a few things I need to talk to Stephanie about. I give Amy the go-ahead and she does the paging. Thankfully, Stephanie's doesn't take long to arrive at the information desk, so I'm not left chatting with Amy (and covering for Mike) any longer than necessary. Stephanie holds a clipboard tight to her chest. Her eyes are intense and wary, but she still shakes my hand.

"I'm surprised to see you again," Stephanie says, "Is there something else you need?"

"Yeah. I don't suppose we can talk? In your office?"

She doesn't look thrilled, but she consents to it. I follow her up to the office and again cram myself into the chair across from her. (My kneecaps haven't recovered from my last visit.) Stephanie closes whatever she was working on and turns away from the computer.

"What's on your mind?" she says.

I put my hands around my knees, trying not to look like one of *The Little Rascals*. "Brady was embezzling from the store," I say, "I know you know about it. Amy told me."

Stephanie's face remains placid. "Are you the one who told the police? I've already talked to them about this. They didn't seem too interested."

"I'm not surprised," I say, "And I'm the one who told the police. In a roundabout way. Amy said she overheard you and Doug talking. Doug was convinced Brady was embezzling." I sit back and start to steeple my fingers. It might have looked intimidating, but I crack my knee against the desk. "Why was Doug so sure?"

Stephanie lightly taps her fingers on the desk. Whatever debate she's having, she comes down on the side of helping me.

"Doug had a theory," she says, "It sounded plausible." Stephanie looks toward the ceiling, figuring out the best way to explain to an idiot like me. "If Brady was embezzling, it would have worked like this: you claim you ordered ten of something. Let's say backpacks, just for the sake of explanation. You take out the money to order ten. But you only order five and you pocket the money for the other five. Doctor the receipts to show ten came in."

"You get rich five backpacks at a time?" I ask.

"It would have to be something small," Stephanie says, patiently, "Something no one was likely to notice. You see how much merchandise we have out there. If you nickel-and-dime enough different things—and do it randomly enough—it can add up after a while."

"And you think this is what Brady was doing?"

"This is what *Doug* thinks Brady was doing. He came to me and asked to look at the books. I didn't have an explanation. Doug decided to talk to Brady."

Hence, the confrontation at Doug's house the night Brady was killed. I lean forward, which practically puts me on Stephanie's desk.

"You said it sounded plausible," I ask, "Did Doug convince you?"

Stephanie folds her hands. "Not entirely. Embezzling here wouldn't be easy. If you're the sole owner of a store, sure. There's nothing stopping you. As long as you don't stiff your distributors or your employees. But here? You'd have to cover up on the inventory end or you'd have to cook the books. Either way, you're risking me or Doug catching you."

"He would have needed some help, then."

"Cooking the books would have been hard without my noticing. With some help, he could handle the inventory side, though."

"Any idea who could've helped him?"

"No. We get a lot of turnover here. I'd imagine it would be hard to trust someone enough to help you with that kind of thing."

I look around the room, noticing again how cramped it is. It's probably underscored by the fact I have to ask Stephanie some uncomfortable questions.

"Is that why you didn't mention the embezzling the first time we talked?" I asked.

I need not have worried. Stephanie's face lightens up like she's about to start laughing. Like she's amused by my suspicion. Not the worst reaction, I suppose.

"I don't know for sure that Brady was even embezzling," she says, "So no, it didn't seem worth mentioning."

"Same reason you didn't mention the murder weapon probably came from this store?"

Stephanie inclines her head, the amusement dying away. "I didn't even know about it. Amy hadn't told me yet. And I don't work much with inventory."

Seems a tad convenient. Then again, as Carol's fond of reminding me, I'm not a cop. It's not like I come bearing the power of subpoena. If people share information with me, it's out of their own generosity. (Or a reasonable facsimile.)

"Did you get the idea the police are going to do anything about the embezzling?" I ask.

"No. For them to investigate, Doug would have to present evidence and press charges. Even if he had evidence, who would he press charges against?"

I'll give it this much: between the divorce and other legal proceedings, Brady's death seems to have spared everyone a lot of paperwork. I push the chair back, hoping to clear some room to cross my legs. Instead, the wall comes up faster than I expect and I'm left to sit here like a torture victim.

"Did Doug have any theories about what Brady was doing with the money?" I ask.

"Not that he told me. It's one of the reasons I had a hard time believing him. Why would Brady need to take the money? He lived in a nice house. Owned his own car. He was the breadwinner in the family. We weren't friends, but we worked closely. I think I'd have known if he had a substance abuse problem or a gambling problem or something. The whole thing didn't make any sense."

I sit back, a tad defeated. "There was Bermuda. For whatever that's worth."

Stephanie sits up a little. "Bermuda?"

"Amy told me Brady was taking a trip to Bermuda."

"Amy said something about Bermuda?" It's like I told her Amy had the nuclear launch codes. "Don't know what to tell you there."

"Guess I should talk to Doug," I say, wedging myself out of the chair, "Maybe he has more theories."

"Good luck," Stephanie says, standing as well, "He was barely in the store today. He might be avoiding you."

"Maybe. He certainly wouldn't be the only one."

Stephanie gives me a smile. Her eyes have softened and the smile actually makes me feel welcomed. "I'm here if you need me," she says.

I head out the door. Stephanie watches me go. I get the feeling she sympathizes. Certainly, she was helpful. Strangely, I feel like I've got someone in my corner.

That's one, anyway.

***

When we were in high school, Lisa introduced me to a band called Soul Driver. They were one of those hard-to-define outfits. They were too edgy to be a pop band, too catchy to be a punk band, too eclectic to be mainstream. They were a thing all their own. In short order, I would come to love them as much as Lisa did.

Only two things about Soul Driver ever disappointed me. One, the band was almost broken up at the time Lisa introduced me to them, meaning I missed their all-too-brief heyday. Two, I can't listen to them without thinking of Lisa, meaning I have to be a certain mood to do so.

As a result, I've gravitated to the solo work of Brian Douglas, the band's guitarist and half of their songwriting duo. It's not a popular choice among Soul Driver fans, since Brian's solo work has been decidedly downbeat and a tad shoe-gaze, as if he's sold out his harder rocking roots. I prefer to think of Brian's albums as an acquired taste. When I'm brooding or contemplative, they're a pretty good soundtrack.

I've put on Brian Douglas' fourth solo album, *Last Night of the World,* which is as upbeat as the title would indicate. I'm sitting on what I call the front stoop of my apartment. It's a cement lip extending out from the arch windows. A few years ago, I discovered the recessed area in the center is just large enough to hold a couple of chairs. It affords me a beautiful view of Summit Avenue. My feet are kicked up on the cement ledge and a glass of wine rests in my lap. The window behind me is open and I can barely hear the music (I tend not to crank it for fear of disturbing neighbors who aren't Lars) but it's still there. Brooding and contemplative is my jam at moment. It's what happens when you're thinking about a murder.

There's a lot of stuff to recommend Doug as the murderer. Brady's embezzling, the time-honored hatred toward his brother, their fight the night of the murder. The thug who keeps showing up at my place had Doug's name in his phone and I'm not buying Doug's explanation.

But looked at it in the cool light of reason (or the closest thing I have to it) I can't entirely condemn Doug. Stephanie didn't originally tell me about the missing knife or Doug's suspicions about the embezzling. Norah has treated a few facts on a need-to-know basis. Norah and Stephanie have both explained themselves, but why am I buying their explanations and not Doug's? Do I have some kind of gender-bias going? Or is Carol right and I'm only seeing what I want to see?

A car door slams in the street. I glance down over the cement lip. A dark sedan is parked in front of my building. It's the person walking from the car who gets my attention.

I'm getting a late visit from Sergeant Pike. Oh joy.

I buzz him in without using the intercom then plunk down on the landing outside my apartment, like I'm a kid welcoming dad home from work. Pike stops on the landing outside Lars' place. I raise the wine in a toast.

"Hi, pal," I say, "Something on your mind?"

It's only then I notice how taut Pike's face is. "Yeah, there's something on my mind. You want to step inside or you want your neighbors to hear this?"

I'm disconcerted, but also in a mood to be defiant. I stick my chin out (shades of Norah) and say: "I have nothing to hide."

Pike takes a breath in through his nose. "Fine. You know Amy Page?"

I start to shake my head, but then the name rings a bell. "Amy from Pro Sports? I don't think I ever got her last name."

"You got it now. But you're not going to get anything else from her. She's dead."

CHAPTER FOURTEEN

When I was in college, I had a buddy named Ted, who was quite the ladies man. At least that was Ted's take on it. Yes, he was good-looking and yes, he had a decent line of BS. But any success he had was due to his relentless infliction of his company on any attractive young lady in the vicinity. As Ted himself would tell you, "Nine out of ten times, I get my face slapped. But that tenth time…" As a result of this persistence, I have, over the years, run across a litany of women whose faces purse at the mention of Ted's name.

On one of those occasions, I was at a party, having a casual conversation with a woman named Samantha. I mentioned going to Adams College and she asked, "Did you know Ted Rossini?"

"I remember Ted," I said (I'd had four beers), "Why? Did he hit on you?"

"No," Samantha said, "He's the father of my child."

I haven't talked to Samantha (or Ted, for that matter) since. I bring it up because if you get the impression I'm always quick with a joke (or to light up your smoke) please realize I have an equally-large capacity for sticking my foot in my mouth.

Such as when I try to get cute with Pike and find out Amy's been killed.

We go into my apartment and Pike closes the door behind him. I look toward the bottle of wine on the window ledge. I'm tempted to pour myself another glass. Or start slugging directly from the bottle.

I look to Pike and ask: "What happened?"

"She was found dead in her car, in the parking lot of Pro Sports in Bloomington. Bloomington PD saw we had questioned her about Brady Perkins' murder and called it in."

"How did she, uh…?"

"Stop me if you've heard this one before. Her throat was cut. Similar blade to the one that killed Brady Perkins. Could be the exact same one."

Actually, no. The *exact* one is lying in my storage unit three floors below. But if I wasn't comfortable telling about it Pike before…

"Any idea who did it?" I ask.

Pike takes off his glasses and pinches the bridge of his nose. "Not yet. I know you've been looking into all of this. I'm here to find out if you know something I don't."

Strange. Pike has always seemed like an enemy to me. Last fall, he was convinced Mike was guilty of murder and wouldn't hear otherwise. This time, he's convinced Norah is the one he's after. On the other hand, Pike saved my ass last fall. And this time out, his faith in me is the only reason I'm still a free man. Maybe I need to give him the benefit of the doubt.

I jerk a thumb toward the liquor shelf. "You want something to drink?"

"I'm on duty," he says, "So, yes."

I don't figure Pike for a wine connoisseur so I pour him a shot a whiskey and follow up with a beer out of the fridge. He flops on to my futon. I pour myself another glass of vino and sit on the arm of the comfy chair. I run down the investigation to this point (omitting the discovery of the murder weapon). Pike takes a healthy swallow of the beer then makes his way over to my liquor shelf to refill the whiskey.

"You still haven't found anything on your girlfriend," he says, "Big surprise."

"Because there's nothing to find. I just saw Norah today, so I'm guessing *you* haven't found anything."

Pike glares at me, like he'd love to chuck the beer or the whiskey glass at my head. (And given he's armed and has the power to incarcerate me, glass-chucking might be the most benign option.) Instead, he sets the drink down, removes his wire frames and uses the heels of his hands to rub his eyes.

"I don't have anything," he says, "I can't keep fucking around with this. Two murders, both related. No arrests yet. I don't bring somebody in soon, there's going to be a shit storm raining down on me."

That makes me uneasy, and not just because the imagery is disgusting. Pike's a decent guy, but he's still got a job to do. If he decides he's got enough to haul me or Norah in, he might do it, just to make it seem like the investigation is going somewhere. Best to buddy up to Pike.

"You talked to anyone from the store yet?" I ask.

"Doug Perkins and Stephanie Montella. They were at home when Amy was killed. You said you saw your girlfriend today?"

"Yep. Saw almost all of her."

Pike's not touching that. "When was the last time you talked to her?"

"Later part of the afternoon."

"I'll be talking to her soon enough." He leans his back against the top of the futon. "If the two murders are related—and it would be a fuck of a coincidence if they weren't—I'm thinking Amy Page knew something about the murderer; something that made them nervous. What did she know?"

It doesn't sound like he's asking me, but I'll take the opening anyway. "She knew Doug suspected Brady of embezzling. She knew Stephanie had been told about it. She knew the murder weapon might have been taken from the store. I've been throwing the embezzlement out there as a possible motive and even *I'm* not sure it's related to the murder."

"We agree on that much, anyway." He gets up from the futon and puts his beer bottle and shot glass on the breakfast bar. "The old thing from the detective books. Motive, opportunity and means. It's overrated. You realize O.J. Simpson went to trial on nothing but motive?"

"How did that work out?"

"Would've worked out fine if that trial hadn't been a damn circus." He says it with such a bitterness, I wonder if he worked for the LAPD at the time. He gets it together. "We can establish opportunity for pretty much the entire Twin Cities area. The means is the murder weapon, which could be lying at the bottom of the river for all I know. All I've got to go on is motive. And who has a better motive than your girlfriend?"

"What motive would she have with Amy?" I ask.

"Depends. How well did she know Amy Page?"

"She knew Amy worked at the store," I say, "I think that's about it."

"I guess I'll find out. Meantime, is there anything else you have for me?"

"Not at the moment." Or at least nothing I'll share.

"You still going to nose around this?"

"My attorneys have advised me not to comment."

Pike flicks his tongue over his teeth, like he just tasted something not to his liking. He abandons the beer and starts toward the door. He pauses as he reaches for the knob.

"Something to think about," he says, "If the murderer went after Amy Page because she accidentally knew something, what do you think they'll do to you if you keep poking around intentionally? Leave this thing up to me. And watch yourself, counselor."

With that, Pike heads out the door, leaving both my booze supply and my sense of well-being a little dented. But he's right. If the murderer is getting rid of people who know too much, how long before they come after me?

Just to be on the safe side, I'm sleeping with the tennis racket tonight.

***

When I was suspended from *The Daily Bugle*, a few worries automatically sprang to mind. Loss of income was first and foremost. Loss of identity followed. Losing my weenie bit of celebrity was disheartening, yes, but more than that, I'm one of those guys (and it's generally guys) who let their job become their defining element. I can flip burgers to pay the bills (and it appears I'm headed that direction) but the loss of *Joe Davis: Smartass Columnist* cannot be easily overcome.

One thing I *didn't* expect, though, was boredom. I loved to tell people my work day was around two hours and that was frequently true. But *thinking* about the column was a full-time job. Cruising the internet, watching TV, people watching; all of this was fodder for writing. In a sense, I was *always* at work.

But losing the column means there's nothing to fill my mental space. Chores and other tasks I used to perform while thinking about a column are now just menial tasks that bore the shit out of me. (Seriously, why didn't someone tell me folding laundry was this tedious?) When I'm not working on the investigation or spending time with Norah, the days seem very, very long.

Having an idiot friend and neighbor, though, *does* add a little spice to the day.

I'm having an evening coffee (my booze budget is *extremely* limited now) when Lars barrel rolls into my apartment. He shuts the door and throws himself against it, still in a crouch. I turn on my stool at the breakfast bar.

"Out for some exercise?" I ask.

"Just being cautious. You got a minute?"

"I've got all day. Literally."

Lars presses his ear to the door until he's satisfied there's nothing out there. He crabwalks over to the futon and leans against it.

"I might have a goon after me," he says.

"A goon? Why would you have a goon after you?"

"Billy could have hired him. I get the feeling he's trying to get revenge on me."

"For trying to steal his customers?" I ask.

Lars scratches the back of his head. "Uh, no. I told Chuck about the situation with Billy. He thought we should make a move. And he went a little overboard."

"Really? Have you ever known Chuck to go a little underboard? What did he do?"

Lars sits on the floor, keeping out of sight of the window. "He decided to hit Billy in a place that was near and dear. Kind of like Billy with my car. He found out Billy's favorite bar was the Autumn Pub."

"Was?"

"It burned down the other night."

"And Chuck...?"

"Had something to do with that. By which I mean, he had everything to do with that."

Leave it to Chuck and Lars to get into a blood feud with a previously-mellow pot dealer. "Chuck burned down Billy's favorite bar?" I ask.

"Ah, no. Chuck burned down a bar, yes. But it turns out Billy's favorite bar is the *Auburn* Pub and not the *Autumn* Pub. It's an easy mistake to make, you understand."

"I understand. I'm not sure the Autumn Pub will, though."

"That's a whole other thing. Point is, Chuck made a move against Billy and he missed. And now Billy's going to come after me. Again."

I set my coffee cup aside. "Lars, I don't suppose there's any point in telling you this whole thing would go away if you just dropped the pot business."

He stands, then catches sight of the windows and drops down again. "You want me to give into these jack-booted thugs? This is America, Joe. The land of opportunity. Where would we be if every prospective business owner gave into some thug swinging a metaphorical nightstick?"

"We'd have capitalism as we know it."

"Well, that's not how I do business."

Which would account for Lars' various spectacular failures. But I'm done debating with him. I resume sipping my coffee while Lars crabwalks to the breakfast bar and scampers up on one of the stools. His resemblance to a hipster orangutan is uncanny.

"By the way, I might have a line on the guy who attacked you," he says.

I nearly do a spit-take. Jesus, talk about burying the lead. "You got a line on Bart?"

"His full name's Bart London. At least that's the one he goes by. He hangs out in Frogtown."

"How did you find this out?" I ask.

"I did some asking around. Talked to Guippetto Intentolla."

Guippetto Intantolla is a local hood, known to everyone as The Guppie. Everyone who isn't face-to-face with him, that is. My group of friends have dealt with The Guppie in the past and he seems cool with all of us except Lars. He certainly knows the local underworld element. If The Guppie's talking, I'm willing to listen.

"Is there an exact place I can find this guy?" I ask.

"He hangs out at a place called the Coffee Klatsch."

Huh. I would've pictured a little tougher place. Then again, he's talking about Frogtown in St. Paul. The daycare centers have bouncers. I set the coffee mug in the sink and head for the front door.

"Okay, The Coffee Klatsch in Frogtown," I say, grabbing my keys off the desk, "I'm going to go check it out."

"I'll come with you."

Lars glides to the front door and gives me an eager look, like a dog ready to be taken out for a walk. I drop the keys into my pocket.

"There's no talking you out of coming with me, is there?" I ask.

"I don't think so. No."

"Then just do me a favor: don't try anything stupid."

"Why would you think I'd do that?"

"Because I've met you."

***

Frogtown spreads north behind the State Capitol. It's not exactly upscale or trendy, though it has a few cool places here and there. The Coffee Klatsch is one of them. It's on the end of a strip mall, next to an antique store that seems to be an antique itself. The décor is fairly simple. A handful of cafe tables and chairs. A display of tea pots sitting on top of a bookshelf lined with dusty old volumes. It's after dark, so there aren't many people in the place. Bart London sits at a small table opposite the front door. His face is buried in a large book. We're right at the table before he notices us.

"Hi," I say, "Remember me?"

Bart taps a highlighter pen against the book. "Joe Davis," he says, almost to himself.

I sit across from him. Lars stands behind me, arms folded. I half-turn to Lars and speak out of the corner of my mouth.

"Maybe you want to get us a couple of lattes," I say.

Lars leans over but looks away, acting like he's not talking to me. "Why?"

"Because this will look more like a conversation and less like a mob hit."

He slides a finger off the side of his nose, ala *The Sting*. He glides to the counter, leaving me alone with the thug. Bart drops the highlighter pen into the book and slides it aside.

"What do you want from me?" he asks.

"It's more about what *you* want from *me*. I found you out on my deck. You jumped me outside my building, threatened to kill me if I didn't confess to Brady's murder. You might have planted a murder weapon in my place. You broke into my car and tried to kick my head in."

He separates the hands briefly. "So?"

"To the best of my knowledge, we've never met and I didn't do anything to piss you off. Why are you doing this?"

Bart's lips part, revealing some yellow and crooked teeth. "I don't talk to geeks."

A simple *no* would have sufficed. Did he have to start calling me names? "Someone hired you to do something to me?"

"Go piss up a rope."

"Look, if someone *did* hire you, I assume you've got your money. If you tell me who paid you, I can take it up with them and you don't have to be part of this anymore."

Seems like a reasonable argument. But Bart's dark, beady eyes narrow. "Or we can do this," he says, "You can get up, walk out of here—while you're still able to—and hope like hell you never see me again."

He drives a hard bargain, I'll give him that. The stony look on his face and the malicious glint in his eyes tell me there's no room for negotiation. Bart goes back to his reading. Lars appears at the table, holding a pair of lattes to go.

"Is Mr. London not cooperating?" Lars says.

"He is not," I say.

"That's a shame. Did you mention that Mr. Intentolla says hello? And that he's still expecting payment?"

That doesn't mean anything to me. But Bart's hand jerks and the highlighter pen slashes across the page. He looks up at Lars.

"What payment?" Bart asks.

"Oh, you know what it's about," Lars says, casually sipping his latte, "What's more: I know it. And he wanted me to give you that message."

Lars doesn't even blink. Bart's sweating and the stale smell of B.O clouds the atmosphere. He chuckles at Lars. Then he turns the table over.

It happens so fast, I don't even react. My latte goes flying past me. The table, though, nearly hits me in the head. I get my hands up in time to block it. When the smoke clears, Bart is running out the front door.

Lars and I are after him. Bart rambles across the parking lot and down the street. We gain on him. (We'd be closer if Lars would stop sipping his damn coffee.) Bart swings a big mitt and slaps a trash can as he runs past. The can falls into my path. For a split-second, I'm not sure if I should jump it like Adrian Peterson in the open field or cut back and dodge it, like Adrian Peterson heading toward the line. The moment of indecision costs me. I just fall over the damn thing (like Adrian Peterson after he left the Vikings). Lars crash lands on top of me, not spilling a drop of his latte.

We scramble to our feet. Bart is fumbling with his car door. He gets the door open and leans into the car.

And comes out with a tire iron.

Needless to say, that brings us to an immediate halt. Over my shoulder, I can hear Lars sucking wind. Bart steps away from the car. He holds the tire iron in front of him.

"You shouldn't have stuck your nose in," Bart says.

He moves toward us, flicking the tire iron toward my face. My heart beating in my ears. We need to get the hell out of here.

Then a voice comes from behind Bart. "Put that fucking thing down, Bart. You're embarrassing yourself."

Someone steps out of the shadows. If you judged him strictly by the silhouette, you'd assume it's the Frankenstein monster. Bart's body tenses. He starts to turn, but stops when the guy behind him says, "Eyes forward, dipshit."

Bart does as he's told. The monster from the shadows comes into view. He casually takes the tire iron out of Bart's hand and claps a hand on Bart's back; one of those *Friendly, but not really* kind of gestures.

It's Guippetto Intantolla. Known to his associates (but not to his face) as The Guppie.

"All right, shithead," The Guppie says, "Let's all have a chat."

CHAPTER FIFTEEN

It's always uncomfortable to run into someone you'd rather avoid. Particularly when you don't have the option of getting away from them.

For example, when I was a kid, I was tormented by a budding psychopath named Garry McNamara. Garry wasn't a bully in the physical sense, but he loved to pull pranks. His favorites included jumping out from behind things to scare me, TP-ing my car or chaining my bike to (the top of) a streetlamp. Garry's only saving graces were: he didn't live in Porter's Bay, so I only had to see him for a couple weeks in the summer when he came to visit his grandma; and he was, by nature, a coward. If I was with my brothers (who were physically intimidating) or even my friends Sam and Andy (who were not) Garry wanted no part of me.

One summer when I was home from college, I had just come back from an afternoon working in my dad's hardware store when my mom called to me and said I had a friend visiting. I walked into the kitchen and found Garry McNamara sitting at our kitchen table, drinking our coffee and eating my mom's blueberry muffins. I would have preferred him urinating on the floor to the smirk he gave me and the Eddie Haskell routine he did for my mom. But I had to pretend we were really friends because I didn't want to create a scene in front of my mother. I spent the next hour making polite conversation while Garry shared every embarrassing detail he knew about me.

Later, I told my mother I had no idea how Garry got a muffin stuck down his pants and was kicked down the front steps of our house. Just one of those things, I guess.

The Guppie's about six-and-a-half feet tall, his face is covered with scars and crags and he sports a haircut only Gomez Addams could love. Judging by the look of terror on Bart's face, The Guppie is his personal Garry McNamara.

"What's this for?" The Guppie asks, twirling the tire iron in his huge mitts, "You going to do something here, Bart?"

"No, no!" Bart says, sweating freely, "I just…I wanted them to leave me alone. I got nothing to say to them."

"That's too damn bad. Because if you're not talking to them, you need to talk to me about the money you owe me."

"No, I'm good! They can ask me anything they want! I live to squeal!"

The Guppie holds the tire iron near Bart's skull. He nods toward me, giving me the go ahead to question Bart. I step forward, tentatively.

"This shit you've been doing," I say, "You're trying to frame me for murder, right?"

"Yeah. I was supposed to plant evidence. First, I was going to put a knife on your deck and call the cops. Second time, I was trying to put it in your car."

"A knife?" I ask.

"A hunting knife. Serrated. Big fucker."

I open my mouth, but something Bart said rewires my thoughts. "Wait, my car was the *second* time? Wasn't breaking into my apartment the second time?"

Bart looks confused. "No. I haven't been in your apartment. I only got as far as the deck."

Shit. He looks confused, like someone's trying to explain cubism to a monkey. He's too terrified to be putting on an act. I have no choice but to believe him. And to get to the heart of the matter.

"Who hired you to frame me?" I ask.

Bart hesitates, but gives a half-glance toward The Guppie looming behind him. "Doug. Brady's brother. It was him."

Son of a bitch. I was ninety-nine percent certain of that, but it *still* pisses me off. "Why would Doug hire you?"

"I needed some cash," Bart says, nodding toward The Guppie, "Fast. I talked to Brady about a loan just before he died. Somehow, Doug found out about it. He said he'd give me the money if I did a little favor for him." He gestures toward me. "Framing you was the favor."

"And Doug gave you a hunting knife to do it?"

"I watched him take it out of the box."

Something isn't clicking here. But I'm too keyed up with adrenaline to piece it together. Best to gather the facts and sort them later. But there is a problem with even gathering the facts. I've only known Bart for a short time, but I get the feeling he's someone who covers his ass at all times. Seems worth a fishing expedition…

"I'd like to believe you," I tell him, "But I've only got your word. It's not going to hold up against Doug's."

Bart bounces up and down, like an anxious schoolboy. "What if I can prove it?"

Prove it. I like the sound of that. "What have you got?"

"I taped one of our conversations. Caught him saying everything he wanted me to do. I thought I might need some backup. I don't trust Doug."

Can I read scumbags or can I read scumbags? "You still have this tape?" I ask.

"Yeah. I can get it for you if I want."

Now I'm on less certain ground. I don't know how to negotiate with criminals. If I let Bart out of my sight, it might be the last I see of him. The Guppie, though, is versed in these negotiations. He grabs Bart by the shoulder, nearly lifting him off his feet.

"Here's the deal," he says, "We're going to go to your place and get that tape. Then we're going to talk about how you can work off the money you owe me."

Bart falters. "Work…work off?"

"There's always shit you can do for me," The Guppie says, "I'll take payment in trade. You just have to ask."

"That's…that's mighty decent of you."

"Fuck off."

Bart steps toward the car, then stops and stares at something on the roof. "Can I keep the text book?"

Lars and I look to The Guppie, who says: "Like I give two shits."

Bart grabs the book off the top of the car. "Thanks. It was kind of spendy. It's for my marketing class. I'm going back to school to get a business degree."

"Gonna refer you back to my 'two shits' answer," The Guppie says.

Bart hops in the car and The Guppie positions himself in front of it, lest Bart get any ideas about taking off. He points Lars and me toward the backseat. I hesitate.

"Um, thanks," I say, "I really appreciate the help."

"Thank your friend over there," he says, nodding toward Lars, "It was his idea. And let's get a fucking move on. I got shit to do and I don't need to spend any more time around you assholes than absolutely necessary."

The Guppie wedges himself into the passenger seat. Lars and I each step around one side of the car. I talk to him over the roof.

"You set up this whole thing with The Guppie?" I ask.

"I thought there was half-a-chance this Bart fella wasn't going to cooperate. Seemed like a backup plan was in order."

I fold my arms on the roof. "You couldn't have mentioned that earlier?"

"I didn't think you needed to know."

Huh. Story of my life lately.

***

Her infidelity not withstanding (and I realize that's not an easy withstanding to cast aside), Norah, as I've pointed out, is loyal to a fault. But she's not unreasonable. Show her overwhelming proof of something and she's willing to play ball. That doesn't mean it's easy for her, though.

"*I want the cops to think Joe Davis did it,*" the voice on the tape recorder says, "*I don't care how you do it. You want that loan Brady promised you? This is how you get it.*"

Norah stops the tape and stares at the recorder. She looks like she wants to rewind it and listen to it again. I wouldn't be surprised. She's done that three times already. After a moment's debate, she sets the tape recorder on the coffee table. I'm sitting next to her on the sofa in her apartment. I don't make a move toward her, letting Norah work things out on her own. Her eyebrows come together as she stares at the recorder.

"I don't believe it," she says.

"I know you don't."

Norah gets up from the sofa. She folds her arms and paces the floor. I had been hoping to confront Doug when I came here, but he's conveniently missing once again. Strangely, though, I'm okay with that. I've got enough of a fight on my hands with Norah. But judging by the forlorn look on her face, there's not much fight in her.

"Why would Doug do this?" Norah asks. Her voice is low and she's genuinely asking.

"I've got a few thoughts," I say, "If Doug was convinced Brady was embezzling, it might have pushed him over the edge. He knew you were having an affair with me. He had a chance to kill Brady and set someone up for it. He could have followed Brady over to my place. Surprised him on my deck. Only thing he couldn't anticipate is: the cop in charge knows me and doesn't think I did it. Doug comes up with Plan B. He hires this Bart guy to frame me."

I fold my hands behind my head. It's nice to finally have Norah in my corner. But it's not as easy as I'm making it sound. Yes, there's a compelling case against Doug. But the flaws in it came to me last night as I was struggling to get to sleep.

When I mentioned breaking into my apartment, Bart looked confused enough for me to believe him. But if Bart didn't plant the murder weapon in my place, who did? If it was Doug, why hire Bart in the first place? Why give Bart a new knife when Doug had the actual murder weapon? If you're capable of killing somebody and planting a murder weapon, why risk bringing someone else into the fold? Particularly someone you barely know and can barely trust? It keeps me from being positive Doug did it.

Norah sits next to me and props her feet up on the coffee table. She lays her head on my shoulder. We don't say anything for a few moments.

"I don't want it to be Doug," she says, "He's been good to me. It's like we were—I don't know—kindred spirits or something. We both had to put up with Brady. We were both…lonely. Now I have you and Doug doesn't have anybody. And he's jealous of you."

It doesn't come as a shock. I had the feeling Doug's objections to my sleeping with Norah under his roof had more to do with envy than a sense of propriety.

"Where can I find Doug?" I ask, "I need to talk to him. If he's innocent, that's great. I'll work to prove it. But I'm not going to get that done if he keeps avoiding me."

I admit: I feel a little dirty about that argument. It's less from the heart and more designed to appeal to Norah. I feel even dirtier when it works. She runs a hand through her hair.

"There's a place called The Bier Garten," she says, "It's over by 494, by the retail outlets. Doug hangs out there. That's where he is now." I get off the couch. Norah grabs my hand. "Just be careful," she says.

"Don't worry. I've got Mike with me."

Norah looks around, startled. "Mike? Where?"

"He's out in the car."

"You knew I'd tell you where Doug was at." She taps my leg. "You're pretty confident in yourself, aren't you?"

"If I have to bring Mike as backup, how confident can I be?"

***

When Mike and I were in college, we were at a house party where one of the guests got out of hand. The guy was a smarmy douche who hit on every girl, made smartass remarks about every guy and was generally the sort of clod you'd prefer seeing in a coma.

The douche's major mistake, though, was hitting on our friend Robbie's girlfriend. When Robbie started stewing over this, Mike, who'd had a few whiskeys (never a good look for Mike), said, "Hey, you want to throw that douche out of here, I got your back."

Robbie set down his beer and stalked over to the douche, who seemed amused by someone threatening him. Mike watched from a distance, half-interested in the scene he'd largely created. Robbie grabbed the douche by his polo shirt and hauled him out the front door. Mike stayed put and I stayed with him. (In my case, plausible deniability in case the cops showed up.)

A few minutes later, someone ran in and said, "Some guy's getting the shit kicked out of him." We rushed to the door and discovered the douche had brought friends to the party and they were doing a Four Horsemen-style beatdown on Robbie. I turned around and Mike was nowhere to be found. Our buddy Stoner found a fire extinguisher and unloaded it on the douche and friends. In the confusion, we got Robbie out of there. Mike's whereabouts remained a mystery.

You'll understand then why I didn't jump for joy when Mike offered to back me up on confronting Doug. Although, he's preoccupied with his relationship situation right now.

"This Haley situation has gotta be resolved," he says, "Nice girl. But her father's breathing down my neck. For the first time since I started working there, he's interested in where I go when I leave the office. It's seriously cramping my style. That's why I tried pulling the train into the station."

"You broke up with her?"

"Tried, but it didn't take," he says, "Thought I had the perfect exit strategy. Swing and a miss, I'm afraid."

"What happened?"

He chews a corner of his goatee. "You know how nearly every relationship I've ever had is built on a solid foundation of lying?"

"I am aware."

"It would stand to reason that the best way *out* of a relationship would be telling the truth. So I told Haley everything that went on with Amy. All the details. Frankly, some of them disgusted even me."

I glance at the GPS on my phone, sitting in the drink holder. "How did Haley react?"

Mike crumbles, like a balloon losing its air. "She was cool with it."

"You're shitting me."

"Oh, I wish I was shitting. But sadly, no. Haley forgave me. Said it would only make our love stronger. Gave me some mumbo-jumbo about loving someone and needing to set them free. But now she's going to hold me tight and if I tried to fly away, she'd clip my wings. Among other things."

Wow. Mike finds the winners, doesn't he? "Been nice knowing you."

He murmurs about needing his Johnson more than my sympathy while I pull the Saturn into the parking lot for The

Bier Garten. It's at the end of a strip mall containing a thrift store, a liquor store and a Chinese food joint. The place is a few steps above dive bar and a few steps below classy. There's a lot of dark wood and stained glass. The lighting lends a certain atmosphere. But the carpeting's threadbare and the whole place needs a cleaning. It's not busy right now. Just a couple of people at the bar and a few more at the tables. And Doug, sitting by himself at a corner booth.

"Let's do this," I say, heading toward the table.

Mike bounces behind me, like a boxer going to the ring. I have to remember to keep him away from the whiskey. Doug nearly spits out his beer when he sees us.

"Something you need?" is how he greets me.

Sounds like an invitation to get right to the point. Mike and I sit at the booth, taking seats on opposite sides of Doug. I take the tape recorder out of my pocket, set in on the table and press *Play*.

"*I want the cops to think Joe Davis did it,*" the voice on the tape recorder says. Doug's eyes get wide. He reaches for the tape recorder, but I pull it out of his way and let it play. Doug slouches and looks around, as if worried someone will overhear this. I click off the tape recorder. Mike picks it up. I keep my eyes on Doug.

"Why don't we skip the part about you not knowing Bart London?" I say, "I don't believe it and I don't think the police will believe it."

Doug sags. There's no cavalry coming to save him. Just two assholes with incriminating evidence. "It was, uh, it was nothing personal," he says.

"That's a nice thought," I say, "But I've got to tell you: if I wind up sitting in a prison cell, the life partner of some three-hundred-pound Aryan supremacist named Bubba Ray, I'm going to take it personally."

"What are you going to do?"

"Excellent question. Why don't we talk and I'll figure it out from there? All you have to do is not bullshit me."

Mike brandishes the tape recorder at Doug. "Because if you do, our next stop is to Sergeant Pike at the St. Paul Police Department. And I can tell you from first-hand experience, he's an asswipe of the highest order."

A waitress comes by and we order a couple of beers. Doug curls into his beer, pointedly not looking at the waitress. She's leaning toward middle age (early to middle forties, by my guess) and has bright blonde hair that doesn't quite seem natural. The makeup's a tad heavy and does nothing for her lean face. She looks at Doug for a few seconds, then tells us the beers will be right up. I prop an arm on the table while Doug comes out of his shell.

"Are we going to talk?" I ask.

"Go right ahead," he says.

There seems to be an obvious place to start. "Why did you try to frame me?"

He picks at the label on his beer bottle. "After everything went down with Brady, I was convinced you did it. I wouldn't blame you. Brady was going to kill you. But Norah swore up and down you couldn't have done it. Then I started to worry."

"About Norah?"

"She's the only other person who had a reason to do it. I was worried the cops were going to start thinking that. Besides…I didn't want it to be her."

It's a nice sentiment, but, since the dude tried framing me, I'm not exactly *end of Titanic* moved. The drinks arrive and we take a moment to get some sips in. I lean toward Doug.

"Did you ever break into my place?" I ask.

Doug looks up, then goes back to his beer bottle. "Why would I break into your place?"

It's either a reasonable question or he's playing dumb. Whichever the case, I'm not going to tell him about finding the murder weapon. He is definitely outside the Circle of Trust.

"You weren't home the night of the murder," I say, "Your neighbor said you got into a fight with Brady. You want to give me the details on that?"

Doug runs his bandaged hand through his thinning hair, leaving the strands sticking up. "You know Brady was embezzling from the store, right? I needed to talk to him about it. I thought I'd have the upper hand if it was at my place. Didn't exactly go that way. We were in my kitchen and I laid the whole thing out. He sat there and sipped my scotch and looked like he didn't give a shit. Then he burped and said, 'Can you prove any of that?' Guess it was a little much to expect decency from a guy like him."

Doug's sweating, intensifying the pit rings under the arms of his white shirt. He's reliving the whole conflict.

"What happened then?" I ask.

"I started yelling at him and he started yelling back. Next thing I know, we're in the living room, trading haymakers. It wasn't much of a trade. I missed a roundhouse and punched a door. I might have broken my damn hand." He painfully flexes his right hand. "After that, I ate more than I gave. End came when he punched me through the living room table. Then he spit on me and walked out."

Ouch. If Doug hadn't been so determined to put me in jail, I might feel sorry for him. "What happened after Brady left?" I ask.

"I came here. Needed to do some drinking."

Makes sense. The Bier Garten is exactly the kind of place one gets shit-faced and tries to forget. "How long were you here?" I ask.

"I don't know. A while. I had some shots. A lot of shots, really. Things got a little unclear. I got home. But I don't know how I got there. I don't even remember leaving here."

Huh. Too drunk to account for the time of Brady's death. "You remember anything else from that night?" I ask.

He squirms a little. "Just…some stuff I've been told about."

"Such as?"

Before he can answer, the waitress stops by to check on us. Again, Doug gets exceedingly interested in his beer bottle. This time, though, the waitress isn't going to be ignored. She taps her long fingernails on the table.

"Good to see you again, Doug," she says, "I'm looking forward to Bermuda. We going to talk about that soon?"

He starts to look up but doesn't get far. "Sure, Tammy. Definitely. Just got to, uh, chat with these guys first."

Tammy looks from me to Mike and her lips purse slightly. Mike gives her a little wave. With one last look at Doug, she heads back toward the bar. Mike points toward Tammy.

"Gonna guess that's one of the things you were told about?" Mike asks.

Doug's head drops a bit. "Apparently, I promised Tammy a week in Bermuda. I don't have the money for it. And if I ever go, I'm not going to go with Tammy. She's nice. Don't get me wrong. But if we got involved and it didn't work out—and I'm ninety-nine percent certain it wouldn't—I couldn't come here anymore. You know what I'm saying?"

I do. It's why I try to steer Mike away from any servers or bartenders at The Tav. (Not that I've been all that successful.) I take a slug of my (regrettably cheap) beer.

"Anything else you've been told?" I ask.

"Um, Pat, the bartender, told me I took my shirt off and started singing *Strokin'* by Clarence Carter while I was standing on a table. He almost asked me to leave, but I promised to buy his daughter a car for her graduation. And I had my hand sitting in a pitcher of ice for a while. When Pat went to get me some more ice, that's when I snuck out of the place. He probably wouldn't have let me drive home otherwise."

"What time was this?" I ask.

"Pat said it was about midnight. He was worried until the next time I came in. Said he thought I might wind up getting hurt or killing somebody."

I assume Pat meant this was due to Doug probably driving drunk, but he might have gotten closer to the mark than he realized. Mike, meanwhile, is staring at Tammy, the waitress. From the look on his face (one I've gotten sadly familiar with over the years), he's contemplating what a week in Bermuda with Tammy might be like (although I'm sure he's reduced the timeframe and made the location somewhere more local). Speaking of Mike's uncontrollable libido…

"What about Amy?" I say, "Where were you when she was killed?"

"I was at home," Doug says, "I left the store around six. Went straight home and stayed there." He holds his hands out. "That's all I got."

"Can Norah back you up on that?" I ask.

"No. I don't even know if she was home."

The line of questioning doesn't seem to bother Doug. He could be telling the truth or he could be a sociopath of the highest order. I look over at Mike and point to his beer.

"Pound that thing," I say, "We're getting out of here." I turn to Doug. "Here's the deal: I won't tell the police about you hiring Bart London."

"Thank you!"

"Yet. But if anyone else tries anything—if someone so much as looks at me funny—I'm calling Sergeant Pike at the SPPD and telling him everything I know. Are we clear?"

Doug's head swings up and down, jowls flapping slightly. "We are. Absolutely. I just…" He turns slightly away from Mike, who he's correctly diagnosed as the less-sensitive of the two of us. "I want you to know I did this for Norah. That's it. I…wanted to help her."

I'm still pissed at him, but we've got Norah welfare in common. And, maybe, guilt that we should have done more to protect her from Brady.

"I'm sure she appreciates that," I say, "In fact, I know she does. Between Brady and the job and the shark lawyer, she needed people in her corner."

Doug lets out a grunt of disgust. "Sheila Grant was Brady's lawyer, right? Heard she's a horrible woman. Perfect lawyer for Brady."

"She is. I met her. Even if Norah *had* hired a lawyer, I think they would have been in deep sewage dealing with Sheila."

He looks up, confused. "Norah *did* have a lawyer."

I'm pounding my beer and nearly spit it back into the glass. "She did?"

"Tom Dashwood. I think that was the guy's name. Norah met with him at least once. I heard he wasn't too encouraging." A corner of his mouth goes up. "She didn't tell you that?"

I push my beer aside. "Must have slipped her mind." Mike and I get up from the table. "Remember: do nothing until you hear from me."

"You got it. I'll just…sit back and hope for the best. Whatever that is."

Wish I could tell him. But I don't know, either.

***

Some people have a powerful (need, really) to see the world in certain ways, even if that view has no basis in fact. (Metaphysicians will tell us *no* world view has a basis in fact because reality can't be proven. Feel free to stuff those assholes in a locker.) For example, my mom has a compulsive need to always believe the best about her sons. While my brothers and I always appreciated her support, we always used it to try and get away with murder. One time, during a summer home from college, I came downstairs hungover to beat the band. My mom simply made me bacon and commented on how working at the hardware store must be wearing me out because I looked really tired. She also speculated about which neighbors' dogs must have vomited in the street. My father waited until mom left the kitchen to inform me I was expected to work my regular shift at the hardware store and clean my own heave off the street.

This is on my mind tonight as I ramble around my apartment, beer in hand, and wonder what's going on with Norah. If I am not choosing to ignore certain facts. She told me she didn't have a lawyer. Turns out she did. If Sheila had a legit offer to put on the table—like Norah said she did—why present it to Norah and not Norah's lawyer? Once again, Norah's leaving out crucial bits of information. Why? Unless she doesn't trust me. Or she's covering.

In addition to thinking about Norah, I'm also weighing the merits of the case against Doug. He was convinced Brady was embezzling and when he confronted his brother, he got his ass handed to him. He was drunk and, by his own confession, not in his right mind. His whereabouts for the time of the murder are not accounted for. Hell of a case. Except…

He *was* drunk off his ass at the time of the murder. Brady's murder involved careful calculation. The murderer knew where Brady was and what he was going to do. They set up a situation where Brady could be killed and an obvious suspect grabbed. It was cold-blooded. But a calculating, cold-blooded individual does not sing hilarious Clarence Carter songs while half-naked or ask aging dive bar waitresses to spend a week in paradise. Given how they left things, how would Doug even know where Brady was or what he was doing? It's a great case, but not a perfect one. And I need a perfect one.

I walk into the kitchen, deposit the empty beer in the recycling and grab another. I'm killing off the beer supply with no incoming funds to replace it, but I don't care. (Sure, I could cultivate a taste for cheap beer, but I have no desire to either ruin my palate or become an ironic hipster douchebag.) I've just grabbed cracked the beer when my cell phone buzzes on the breakfast bar. It's a number I don't recognize. Too late to be a telemarketing call. I'm intrigued enough to answer.

The voice on the other end of the line is frantic. "Joe?" she says, "It's Stephanie. Y'know? From Pro Sports?"

"Hi," I say, "Is everything okay?"

"No, it's not," she says, "Someone just tried to kill me."

CHAPTER SIXTEEN

The thing I ask myself from time to time is how I manage to be someone's go-to when they're in trouble. I don't have a history of being a cool head in a crisis. Or any kind of head in a crisis. In fact, I tend to be a completely different part of the anatomy in a crisis.

So, you'll understand my confusion when someone I've met only a couple of times—and have asked pointed questions about a murder—calls me up and asks for my help.

Stephanie doesn't give me any details on how she almost got killed. She blurts out her address and asks me to come over. I scribble it down (for once, I have a pen handy). It's in Richfield, about ten minutes away. I assure her I'll be there in less.

Stephanie lives in a sprawling apartment complex with multiple buildings and very little upkeep from management. (Pay at Pro Sports must not be great.) She buzzes me into her building. I climb the stairs to the third floor, ignoring the sour smell in the hallway. I knock once before the door's whipped open.

"Thank you," Stephanie says, "Please come in."

The place is a lot nicer than the building would indicate. There's a good-sized living room and dining room, a thin kitchen and a couple of bedrooms at the back. The walls and carpets are beige, but Stephanie has decorated the apartment with posters and plants to give it some personality. She's wearing her uniform from work: coach's pants and a white polo. Her hair is out of its usual ponytail and hangs down past her shoulders. Her face is flushed and her eyes dart about.

"You look like you could use a drink," I say.

"I…no, it's all right."

"Maybe I could use a drink."

Stephanie gestures toward the kitchen. I find a bottle of whiskey in the cupboard above the stove. I pour two fingers and make another offer to Stephanie. She declines again. We sit at the dining room table.

"What happened?" I ask.

Stephanie's foot taps against the carpet. "I got home from work, came in the door and I was about to turn on the lights when someone grabbed me and stuck a knife to my throat."

I don't find that as chilling as I should. People being in places they're not supposed to be—particularly someone's home—has become the norm lately.

"Did this person say anything to you?" I ask.

"Yeah. They said, 'Don't talk to Joe Davis.'"

Okay, *now* I'm getting a chill. "How did you get away?"

"I freaked out. I started throwing elbows. I pushed off with my feet and we both hit the wall. I fell to the floor and started screaming. The next thing I know, whoever it was ran out of the apartment. I went to the door and looked, but I didn't see anything." Stephanie runs a hand through her hair. "That's when I called you."

"Did any of the neighbors check on you?"

Stephanie snorts. "You think there's a lot of *Love thy neighbor* around here?"

Just getting the story out seems to have calmed Stephanie a few degrees. I walk over to the sliding door to the deck. It's locked. No sign of forced entry. I step over to the front door. No sign of scraping or splintering. The deadbolt looks intact. I'm not an expert, but I'm not seeing any sign of a break-in here, either.

"You have a set of spare keys?" I ask.

"Doug has them," Stephanie says, "We're key buddies, or whatever you call it."

"My friends call it The Key Master."

It's possible the attacker could have been Doug. It's been a few hours since I left him at The Bier Garten. Time enough to get over and attack Stephanie. After the way I rattled his cage, maybe Doug's trying to silence everyone. But something in Stephanie's story doesn't jibe with that. I have a plan, but it's admittedly a touchy one.

"This might freak you out," I say, "But can you walk me through the attack? Just show me what you did and, as best you can remember, what the attacker did? I'm, uh, going to have to play the part of the attacker. If that's okay."

The frown on Stephanie's face tells me she's not thrilled with the idea. Her face becomes placid and she nods her assent. She scoops her keys off the dining room table and powerwalks to the front door. She steps into the hallway and mimes unlocking the door.

"I let myself in," she says, stepping into the room and flipping the door shut behind her, "I was heading for the dining room table to throw my keys down. I was almost there when someone grabbed me from behind."

Stephanie looks at me, waiting for me to play my part in this. I feel like a creep, but I step behind her. She takes my left hand and puts it into her hair. Then she takes the right hand brings it up to her neck.

I wiggle the fingers on my right hand. "Did you get a look at the knife?"

"I could see the tip of it in my peripheral vision. It had to be long. And it felt weird. Like little prickles on my skin."

"Like a knife with a serrated blade."

"Exactly." Stephanie goes limp. I draw my hands away, but she puts them back, steeling herself. "Then I started throwing elbows." She gently throws her elbows back in an imitation of her attack. They bounce lightly against my rib cage. "Then I pushed back…" We both take a step backwards. "And we hit the wall…" We lightly bump against the wall. "It was hard enough to knock me loose. Then I fell to the floor…" She sits down and stretches her legs out. "Then I started screaming…" She gently crawls toward the table. "I was going to hide under the table. When I looked up, they were gone. The door was closed. I didn't even hear it slam."

Stephanie gets up and steadies herself against the dining room table. I look back toward where the attack happened, trying to envision it.

"When you threw the elbows," I say, "Did you hit anything?"

"No. Just air."

"And when you shoved the attacker backwards, did you get a lot of resistance? Were they hard to move?"

"No. But I had a shitload of adrenaline."

I check out the wall we bounced against, but there's nothing to see. Not that I expected there to be. "When the attacker whispered in your ear, were they right there? Or maybe a little higher up?"

"I don't know. Probably right there."

I join her at the table. "You keep referring to the attacker as *they*," I say, "I assume you're not concerned about preferred pronouns?"

"That's the thing," Stephanie says, "The voice was kind of low and growly, but it didn't sound…I don't know…*natural?* It was like someone was trying to disguise their voice. Like a woman trying to sound like a man."

Makes sense. Sure, the attacker could have been a smaller, slimmer guy. But the attacker mentioned me. And there aren't any smaller, slimmer guys involved in this situation. Stephanie looks at my whiskey glass. I offer her a sip. She waves me off. I drain the rest of the glass, grimacing as I do. Stephanie gives me a wan smile.

"I'm sorry I called you," she says.

"Don't be."

"It's just that whoever-it-was mentioned your name and you gave me your phone number when we talked. I just…I didn't know who else to call."

I take her hand. "Now you need to call the police."

Stephanie slips her hand away. "I don't want to do that."

"Someone broke into your apartment and put a knife to your throat," I say, "That's the kind of thing you call the police about. They encourage it."

Stephanie circles the room, pulling her hair into a ponytail. "You just gave me the reasons not to call them. No sign of a break-in. I can't tell them the first thing about what the attacker looks like. And I can guaran-damn-tee you my neighbors didn't hear or see anything. Even if they did."

"But the police are supposed to—"

"Find who killed Brady? Or Amy? How's that working out?"

Stephanie marches over to the sofa and plunks down. I take a seat on the arm. The sofa faces the sliding door to the deck. The moon is visible beyond it. We stare at the view for several moments.

"I know you and Amy were friends," I ask, "Do you want to talk about what happened?"

Stephanie looks at me, her eyes a tad weary. "Are you genuinely asking or is this part of your investigation?"

I open my mouth to reply, but realize I was about to defend myself. And tell a lie. I hold up my hands in mock surrender. "It's part of the investigation," I say, "I'm sorry. You don't have to talk about her if you don't want to."

Stephanie folds her hands across her belly. Whatever adrenaline remained appears to have been flushed out of her. "It's okay," she says, "I *would* like to talk about Amy."

Without saying it, Stephanie and I reach a compromise. The first half of the conversation is her talking about her friendship with Amy. They had only been working together for a year but had bonded over a shared love of exercise. They took yoga and spinning classes together. Had lunch or dinner when they were on the same shift. Went out for an occasional drink. A couple of times, Stephanie's voice gets tight and she fights back tears. She then gives me the floor to ask about the murder.

"Was anything going on with Amy?" I ask, "Anything she was worried about?"

"Not really. She was trying to figure out your friend, but I figured that was just a drive-by for him. I didn't want to break that to Amy, but I think she was getting the hint. It was okay. Hate to tell you, but your friend wasn't the love of Amy's life."

"That's okay. He's not the love of his own, either." I slide down to the sofa and sit next to Stephanie. "You were at home when you found about Amy?"

"Yeah. Amy and I were supposed to close that night. I was getting tired. It's been stressful lately. With what happened to Brady and all. Amy told me to go home early. She could close up. I wasn't sure. But I was just so tired. Amy knew everything she needed to close up. I figured I'd take her up on it. I went home early."

"What time was this?"

"About nine. The store closes at ten. I came home and fell asleep. The next thing I know, the police were calling and telling me Amy…"

Stephanie's eyes well up again. I'd feel like a shitheel if I pushed any further. I take the empty whiskey glass into the kitchen and put it in the sink. I'm not sure what to do next. When someone's home has been invaded and they've been threatened at knife-point, you don't make it a drop in. Stephanie meets me at the edge of the kitchen and takes one of my hands.

"Thank you for coming over," she says.

"Did you want me to hang out for a while?" I ask, "I'd be glad to do it."

She pats my forearm. "It's okay. I can handle it. I've bothered you enough."

"You're sure? I could crash here tonight. The couch looks plenty comfortable."

"I'll be fine," Stephanie says, "Head on home. I insist. I'm stronger than you think. Besides, I'm terrible in the mornings. You really don't want to be around."

I don't feel right about leaving, but Stephanie's guiding me toward the door. I tell her: "If you need anything, let me know."

"Thank you."

I step out the door. Stephanie's quick to close it behind me. I head down the stairs, wondering if someone's about to jump out of the shadows. It's not entirely paranoia.

Sleep well, Joe.

***

Now I'm running.

No, not running for my life or anything. I'm out for a midmorning jog around the neighborhood. I've not always been a runner. Or more accurately, a jogger. When I was a kid I liked to run, but it was all sprinting. (Funny how you're in a rush to get places when you're young and have the most time on your hands.) When I got to my twenties, I signed up for the Twin Cities Marathon on a lark after a night of drinking. Training for the damn thing taught me how to pace myself, conserve energy, last longer. And it calms me.

I slip past the carriage house and into my parking lot. I slow to a walk, hands on my hips, taking deep breaths. Lars is up on his deck, pottering about. I decide to visit him. Say what you will about the man (and I say plenty) he is relentlessly cheerful. I need that right now.

I assumed I'd find him holding a watering can, coaxing his pot plants toward maturity. Instead, he's got a drawing pad and he's looking at various corners of the deck.

"What's going on?" I ask, as I walk up.

"I'm going to build a greenhouse."

I should be more surprised than I am. "A greenhouse? Where?"

"Here on the deck. I'm going to convert the whole thing into a greenhouse."

Despite the ridiculous nature of the plan, I find myself looking around the deck, pondering the possibilities. "How are you going to build a greenhouse?"

Lars focuses on his clipboard. "Chuck knows a guy."

"A carpenter?"

"No, just a guy."

I had a landlord once who took the same approach. Which was why my apartment didn't have heat or a functioning stove most of the time. Or, eventually, a tenant.

"Have you cleared this with management?" I ask.

He looks at me. "Do you think I need to?"

"A major remodeling project to one of their decks? They might want a heads-up."

Lars considers this. Then goes back to planning. "A lot of things to think about."

I drop into a deck chair and stare at the deck floor. Lars sets aside his clipboard and pulls up a deck chair of his own.

"How you doing, brother?" he asks.

"I've been better."

He strokes his goatee. "Tell your uncle Lars all about it."

I give Lars the story of the attempt on Stephanie, what I found out about Doug and that Norah lied to me again. He listens patiently and pats the arm of the chair when I'm finished.

"It's a rough situation," he says, "People in relationships need to be completely open and honest with each other. If they were, I wouldn't be in this mess with Billy." He props his feet up on the deck railing. "What are you going to do?"

I look out to the parking lot. "I don't know. Thing is, somewhere out there is someone who's killed twice and is in the market to do it a third time. They didn't get Stephanie. Maybe they'll look for another target. Maybe me."

Lars drops a big hand on my shoulder. "You can't let this thing get the better of you. Every problem I've ever had, I've made sure to get out in front of it. That's my credo."

"What about the depression you went into when your ex wouldn't give you back the black t-shirt?"

"Oy. That was an existential crisis if there ever was one." Lars picks up his clipboard and returns to surveying, as if the t-shirt incident is too horrible to talk about. "Seems like you have to find out what went on with Sheila Grant."

"I've tried that. Norah got pissed at me. Which is going to look like a honeymoon if I call bullshit on what she told me. Besides, at this point…" And here comes the thing that hurts my heart. "No matter what she tells me, I don't know if I'd believe her."

Lars glances up, briefly, but goes back to the clipboard. "Maybe you should talk to Sheila Grant."

"I tried that, too. She wouldn't tell me anything. She's not going to play ball now."

"It's a tough one," Lars says, tapping the clipboard with his pencil, "Beyond her obvious coke habit, you've got no opening."

That last statement takes a second to hit me. When it does, I nearly stumble over the railing. "Coke habit? What the hell are you talking about?"

"You've met her. You couldn't see it? The constant sniffing. The nose running. The redness around the nostrils. The way her eyes kept moving around the room."

"I did notice all that. I didn't put it together. How do you know all this?"

"You remember Chuck and I tried to do business with her? When we talked to her, it was like her eyes were playing pinball. I'm familiar with it. My buddy Chan Perry had a decent coke habit going once. He acted exactly like that. Except for the part where he was a man. And a stripper. The dress code works a little differently."

Holy shit. I had the woman right in front of me and I missed some obvious leverage. Well done, Captain Observant. "You're sure about this?" I ask.

"One can rarely be certain of anything in this life. Descartes taught us that. But I'm certain that woman enjoys some of Columbia's finest."

I sit in the deck chair and tap the arms as I think. "We've got an opening."

"Dealing cocaine? I don't know. I've barely got the marijuana business off the ground."

"Not that, you fucking moron. With Sheila Grant. I know how to get to her."

"How?"

I tuck my hands behind my head. "I believe the term is…honeytrap."

***

The Stone Mill is an upscale, yet cozy kind of place in the heart of Uptown. It has a bar area built around a huge stone fireplace and a restaurant with picture windows looking out over Uptown. A good place for a formal dinner or a drink. There's usually a collection of upscale young urban-types scattered about, all of them in pursuit of a deal, be it business or sexual.

Right now, I'm outside The Stone Mill, sitting in Carol's car. She and I are in the front seat. Mike's in the back, fussing with his dress shirt and sport coat. He rubs his face.

"I hate being clean-shaven," Mike says, "Was this really necessary?"

"This woman is a lawyer," I say, "High-powered type. If you don't look like a guy who'd interest her, this whole thing is a waste of time."

"I'm supposed to be hitting on a woman I'm not going to bed with," Mike says, "I think the *waste of time* ship has sailed."

If Mike's attitude says, "I'm doing you a favor even being here" it's because he's doing me a favor even being here. Our scheme depends on finding someone who can trick Sheila Grant into giving me some information. I'm out. I have no confidence in Lars' ability to pretend he's someone else. (Lars may have a shitload of faults, but insincerity is not among them.) Mike is my man.

"You really think she'll go for this?" Carol asks, patting the steering wheel.

"Depends on Mike and his line of B.S.," I say.

Mike pulls on his collar for the fifteenth time. "Unless I've gotten hit in the head since this morning, I'll be fine."

Carol watches Mike's fussing in the rearview mirror. "You look good," she says, and then immediately adds: "Read nothing into that."

Mike gets the stinkface, but at least he's stopped the OCD routine. "Okay, run this by me again. I go in and meet this woman?"

"According to her receptionist, she usually sits at a table in the bar," I say, "You work your magic, blah, blah, blah."

"And then I suggest partying," Mike says.

He reaches into his coat and comes out with a small baggie out of white powder. Carol's head is on a swivel, oh-so-subtly looking for cops.

"Where did you get that stuff?" she asks, through gritted teeth.

"Compliments of Gold Medal Flour," I say, "Minneapolis is the Mill City, after all."

Mike slips the baggie back into his coat. "Then I get Sheila out of the bar and out here to the car. Set up the flour and…"

"Carol and I move in, cell phone cameras at the ready. Then I have leverage for her to talk to me."

Carol props an arm on the steering wheel. "And why am I here?"

I run a hand across the dashboard. "You own the only car nice enough to fit Mike's scenario. If Mike got Sheila out of the bar and she saw the outdated piece of shit he drives, she'd know something was up."

"So glad I know you guys," Carol mutters.

Mike gives himself one last going over and opens the backdoor. "I'm going in."

"Good luck," I say, "Carol and I will be across the street." I hold up my phone. "Maintain radio contact."

Carol and I walk across Hennepin Avenue and duck into the little coffee shop. We grab over-priced lattes and find a table near the window. There's a perfect view of The Stone Mill.

"You think he's going to pull this off?" Carol says, stirring some sugar into her latte.

"Mike's our best shot," I say.

Carol frowns. "He's not *that* good."

"You didn't always think that way."

Her face flushes. "I used to wear a princess dress to school, too. We all outgrow things."

I drop the subject. Somewhere beneath all the bitterness, in a place she doesn't like to talk about at parties, Carol knows I'm right. If I'm going to set a honey trap for Sheila Grant, I've sent my best man. We sit there, drinking our lattes.

"I guess I'm a little bitter," Carol says, "Things have gotten weird with Alan."

"Weirder than his daughter almost catching you guys doing the nasty in the kitchen?"

Carol's tone gets a few degrees below frosty. "Yes, Joe. Although, things kind of started there. Ever since that night, Alan's been obsessed with the idea Haley's seeing somebody he doesn't like."

"She's a grown woman and all. Capable of making her own mistakes."

"You don't have to tell me," Carol says, "But Alan can't let it go. I don't know what to do. It feels like…I don't know…like he's pulling away from me. Before this whole thing went down, Alan was talking about us going away for a weekend. Now, he can't find the time to get together. When we *do* get together, it's like he's not there. If I didn't know any better, I'd think he was with another woman. In a way, I guess he is. It's just that the other woman is his daughter. Creepy, right?"

There's a definite creepiness there, no doubt. Before we can get any further into the subject, my phone rings. It's Mike.

"This isn't gonna work," he says.

"What do you mean?" I ask.

"What do you think I mean? You've struck out with enough women in your life. You must know what I'm talking about. Although, it's not a total loss."

"Would you get to the fucking point?"

"Hey, hey, relax, Captain Spasmodic. Let me explain. I've got good news and bad news." Mike lowers his voice. "Bad news is: Sheila Grant's a no-go for me. She said if I didn't shut up and leave her alone, she'd get the bartender to throw me out of here. Her lips say 'No, no' but her eyes say, 'I'll have you thrown out of here if you don't knock it off.'"

I don't slam my head into the table, but it takes an effort. "And the good news?"

"I figured out *why* I'm not getting anywhere."

"What is it?" I ask, "Bad breath? Intellectual deficiency? Probable impotency?"

"No. And fuck you. The problem is you sent in the wrong person for this job. Sheila's been flirting with the server for the last ten minutes."

"What's the server got that you haven't got?"

"Offhand, I'd say breasts and a vagina."

My mouth hangs open. Great googly-moogly. I hope none of my gay friends find out about this. They'll mock my already-faulty gaydar.

"Sheila's hitting on the server?" I say, "Is she getting anywhere?"

"Not really. Maya—that's the server—is being very polite, but she's not into it."

"What makes you so sure?"

"Because *I'm* getting somewhere with Maya. Let's get this over with so I can get her phone number." There's a pause on the line. "You know what you need to do, right?"

"Absolutely," I say, "Meet us at the backdoor to the Mill in the five minutes."

I slip the phone into my pocket and head toward the door, tossing the rest of the latte in the trash. Carol grabs her purse and follows me out to the street.

"What's going on?" she asks.

"Suit up. You're in this half."

I explain the new plan as we run toward the backdoor of The Stone Mill. As can be predicted, Carol treats me to a round of *Are you fucking kidding me?* and *There is no fucking way I'm doing this!* By the time we get to the backdoor, her resistance has been worn down to *This is an incredibly stupid idea.*

"It's not ideal," I tell her, "But it's all we've got. I need information from this woman. You're the only one in a position to get it."

The backdoor pops open. Mike holds it for us and we slip inside. He hands the baggie of flour to Carol. She stares at it.

"How am I supposed to do this?" Carol says, "Make sweet talk and then I pull this out and we make bread?"

"Make bread," Mike says, "Is that a euphemism for something?"

Carol rears back to punch Mike with the bag of flour. He retreats down the hallway, probably to resume hitting on the server. Carol stuffs the baggie into her pocket and fusses with her hair and blouse.

"You might want to undo the top button," I say. Carol gives me a death glare and I add: "Or not."

"You realize how much you're going to owe me for this?" she asks.

"If it keeps me safe, I'll owe you my life. After last January, we can call it even."

Carol shakes a fist at me, but she knows I've got her. She starts down the hallway, covertly reaching up to undo the top button of her blouse. I slip out the backdoor. This whole thing will fall apart if Sheila sees me anywhere in the vicinity. I stand in the alley and await further news. Twenty minutes later, my phone goes off. It's Mike.

"This is going great," he says.

"What's happening?"

"Maya wants to get together after her shift ends."

"Hey, that's jiffy," I say, "Meantime, let me remind you that *your sex life is not the point of this whole thing!*"

"Fine, fine. Don't be such a Grumpy Gus. Carol and Sheila are heading for the back."

I position myself next to the backdoor. After a minute, Mike opens it. He makes sure the coast is clear. I step inside and glance toward the women's restroom.

"They in there?" I ask.

"Yepper. No idea what's going on. I'm guessing it's hot."

I put a hand on the restroom door. "Let's get the timing right. One…"

"Two…"

We nod for *three* and burst through the door. For a split-second, we're stopped by the sight of a women's restroom (it's like crossing into Xanadu). Carol and Sheila are at the sinks. Carol's carefully emptying the contents of the baggie on to the countertop. Sheila reacts the way any woman would at the sight of two perverts bursting into the women's restroom.

She screams bloody murder.

Apparently, we're not alone in the restroom. Sheila's scream sets off a round of other screams, coming from the stalls. The din startles Carol, who jumps and throws the contents of the baggie into Sheila's face. Sheila stands there, arms apart, mouth open. Mike whips out his cell phone and snaps a photo of the flour-covered lawyer.

"Just like we planned," he says.

Sheila looks from one of us to the other. If this were a cartoon, red would be rising up through her head like a thermometer. That is, if you could see past the flour.

"What the fuck is going on," Sheila says, through gritted teeth.

"Oh, you know," I say, "Just a little meeting in the ladies' room."

We stand there like pissed off statues while a parade of confused women rush out of the stalls and out of the restroom. Once we're alone, Mike glances toward the door.

"I suggest taking this conversation elsewhere," he says.

"We're parked down the street," I say, "Let's go."

Sheila remains frozen by the sinks. "I'm not going anywhere with you idiots."

Mike takes the phone out of his pocket. "That is absolutely your right. And you're well aware of your rights. Meantime, I'm going to take this little photo and share it with several hundred of my closest friends on social media. I'm sure there's no chance you'll be known as the *Cokehead Lawyer* by tomorrow morning. You know how restrained social media can be."

Sheila licks some of the powder off her lips. "This isn't coke. It's fucking flour."

"I don't think that's clear in the photo," Mike says, "But obviously, people will do the research and not just believe everything they're told on Facebook."

Sheila's resistance crumbles. We hustle her into the hallway and out the backdoor. A minute later, we're piling into Carol's car. Sheila and I sit in the backseat. She brushes some of the flour out of her hair, but it winds up on her skirt.

"All right, Mr. Davis," she says, "What do you want to talk about?"

"You met with Norah the night Brady was killed," I say, "Norah told me you put an offer on the table. You could talk Brady off the ledge, make the divorce go away."

"That's true," Sheila says, "It was simple enough."

"She said the reason you two met directly was that Norah didn't have a lawyer. Except she did. Let's start at the beginning. Was there an actual offer to Norah?"

"Yes. I could make the whole divorce go away without destroying her. I thought I could reason with Brady and get him to moderate his terms. Tell him if he insisted on continuing, I'd drop him as a client and do my best to make sure no reputable attorney would take him on."

"Very generous of you," I say, "I'm not still not seeing why that offer couldn't have been run through a lawyer."

"There was another…personal element," Sheila says, "I'm good friends with a board member at Cornette Academy.

I thought I could prevail upon this person to ensure Norah's job security."

"That's beyond generous," I say, "Why would you do that?"

Sheila glances out the window. "If you want to know, you should go talk to Norah."

I'm about to answer, but Mike puts a hand on my shoulder, stopping me. He shakes his cell phone at Sheila.

"Two options here," Mike says, "You can answer my friend's questions or I can hit *Send* and share this picture with several hundred of my closest friends. Your call, Madam Snortsalot."

Sheila's body tenses. She moves as if to grab at the phone. Mike leans back slightly, keeping the phone in view. Sheila throws herself against the seat.

"It wasn't entirely out of a sense of generosity," she says, "I wanted something from her."

"And what was that?" I ask.

"Her."

The answer's so blunt, I don't catch it right away. Carol does. She spins around, her mouth dropping open. Sheila resolutely looks down. I put it all together.

"You propositioned Norah?" I say.

Sheila goes on the defensive. "I made her an offer. If she had accepted, it would have been a win-win situation."

"All for the low, low price of Norah degrading herself with you."

"It wasn't—"

"If you weren't comfortable with Brady as a client, you could have dropped him outright," I say, "You didn't need to parlay it into cheap nookie. Do me favor and shove that idea right up your ass." I take a second to unclench my fists. "What did Norah say to the offer?"

"At first, she said no. When I mentioned her job, she agreed to think about it. But the offer evaporated when Brady did. I had nothing to save her from."

Dammit. No wonder Norah didn't want to tell me about the meeting. That much unsavory stuff, possibly incriminating and not just to Sheila Grant.

"Speaking of business affairs and Brady," I say, "Who is Bruce Hives?"

Sheila snickers. "Bruce Hives is Brady. It's a name he used to divert the money he was…appropriating from the store. He had a number of accounts he had set up in that name. He had an apartment for Bruce Hives."

"Where?" I ask.

"Not far from here. Over by Lake Calhoun."

I don't have an exact picture of how much money Brady embezzled, but if it's enough to support investments and an apartment, it must be substantial. More than the kind of money you'd use to, say, buy a flat-screen TV.

"You have the exact address?" I say.

"I can get it to you," Sheila says.

"Then do it."

"And when I do," she says, waving a hand toward Mike and his incriminating phone, "You'll delete…*that*?"

Mike laughs. "I don't think you understand. There's no deal to be made here. It's like bargaining with someone who has a gun on you. You don't. You give Joe the address and I'll hold on to this in case we need any other information."

I would have expected a fight from Sheila, but she doesn't have it in her. She slumps against the seat.

"Fine," she says, "I'll give you the address." She looks around the car, as if she'd love to shank all of us. "I hope you people can live with yourselves."

Mike tucks the phone in his pocket. "We've made it this far."

***

Most of what I know about the lakes in Minneapolis I know from having run around them. Lake of the Isles has a lot of nooks and crannies. Lake Harriet's bandshell is visible all the way around. Nokomis has a change of scenery every quarter mile. And Bde Maka Ska (formerly Calhoun). Well, it's large.

But Bde Maka Ska is the most popular of the lakes, probably because of the wide-open spaces and the multiple beaches. On a day like today, with the sun out and no humidity to rear its ugly head, the place is crowded with runners, bikers, frisbee players and strollers. The housing around it isn't as splendid as Isles or Harriet, but there are few high-rises, providing what I'm sure is a spectacular view of Uptown.

Brady's apartment is in one of those high-rises. Judging by the apartment number, it's near the top. The problem is how to get into the building and then into the apartment. Since I'm out of my criminal element, I've brought someone who is not.

"The problem isn't getting in," Mike says, gazing over the place, "That'll be easy-peasy. But I'll bet you there are security cameras in the lobby. If that's the case, someone will come after us the second they see us doing something hinky. Not a deal-breaker. Just means we have to be smooth."

Mike and I are sipping lattes. He drums his fingers on the steering wheel of his piece-of-crap Buick and watches the tenants come and go, waiting for an opening. I'm fidgeting in the passenger seat, trying to be cool and utterly failing.

"I still say we should have done the job last night," I say.

Mike bats away the suggestion. "You want to break into a place, you gotta be subtle about it. We don't have the key to the place. If there *is* a security camera in the lobby—and a security door in the lobby—how are we supposed to get in unnoticed? Trust me, our chances are better in the daylight."

I'm not sure how two guys sitting in a car and staring at a building is more subtle, but I'll follow Mike's lead. I swirl my latte, trying to fight off both boredom and anxiety.

"Seems like a lot of work," I say, "Keeping an apartment on the side. It's all I can do to keep track of one."

"If you got the money, you can swing it. Comes in handy from time to time. Alan, my boss, has an apartment on the side. Strictly for Netflix-and-chill purposes."

A little jolt hits me. "You know this for sure?"

"Most definitely. I knew a chick at the office he used to fool around with. They'd meet up at Alan's love shack. Haley knows about it, even though she's never been there."

"But he's moving in there, right? Now that he's getting divorced?"

Mike looks at me like I just grew a second head. "What the hell are you talking about? Alan's not getting a divorce."

I nearly drop my latte. "You sure about that?"

"I work with him and I've been sleeping with his daughter. Believe me, I'm up on all the family news." Mike sets his cup in the drink holder. "Alan started the agency with money he borrowed from his father-in-law. The father-in-law's rich and well-connected. You think Brady was going to do a number on Norah? That would look like a pinch on the ass compared to what Alan's wife would do to him. So, Alan does the only honorable thing he can do. Fucks everything that walks or crawls." Mike swings his head toward me. "What made you think Alan was getting a divorce?"

Brilliant, Joe. You've not only stepped in it, you're sunk in it up to your waist. I try to look casual (not a good look when I'm under stress). "I assumed. He hits on everyone. Haley thinks he's cheating. You mentioned the apartment. Guess I jumped to the wrong conclusion."

Mike doesn't look sold, but when glances toward the building, he does a double-take. "Coast is clear," he says, "Let's move."

He hops out of the car and darts toward the front entrance. I struggle to keep up. Mike swivels his head about as we approach the lobby doors.

"Looking for something?" I ask.

"You live in a security-in-name-only building, just like I do," he says, "How do most people who don't live there get inside?"

"Wait for somebody who's going in or going out to open the door and then slip inside before the door closes."

"That's our plan."

We step into the spacious lobby. There's carpeting and a few pieces of furniture. A set of locked glass doors lead to an elevator bank. Mike doesn't break stride as he heads for the elevator bank. He starts digging through his pockets.

"I think I left my wallet in the car," he says.

I can see the worn outline of his wallet against his jeans. "You've got it with you."

Mike speaks through gritted teeth. "The security camera doesn't know that."

Ah. This is why I follow Mike's lead. He keeps up the act, even throwing in a few gestures toward the front door as if he's going to step out and search for his supposedly-errant wallet. I'm getting uneasy. No one's coming. How long can Mike keep up this ruse before we have to give up? And with the security cameras, this will be our only shot.

Our savior comes through the front door. It's a woman about our age, mousy brown hair, puffy face, a little too much makeup. She digs in her oversized purse and comes out with a card attached to a key ring. She swipes the card through a reader next to the glass doors. There's a loud click as they unlock. Mike pulls his wallet out and holds it up.

"Here it is," he says, a little louder than normal, "Guess I didn't leave it in the car."

The woman goes through the glass door. Mike reaches out a hand out and stops it before it closes. We follow the woman into the elevator lobby. She looks up, startled. She hastily takes her phone out of her purse. Mike points toward the woman.

"Janet?" he says.

The woman pauses with the phone. "It's Diane."

Mike snaps his fingers. "Diane. That's right. How have you been?"

Diane studies Mike. "Do we know each other?"

"Do we…?" Mike looks hurt. "I'm Mike. You, uh, you don't remember me?"

"No, I'm sorry. I don't."

Mike gives her an uncomfortable laugh. "Wow. That's…wow. I thought we had something there. Guess I read that one wrong." His voice grows tight. "Suppose that's what I get for leading with my heart. Sorry I bothered you."

Diane drops the cell phone back into her purse. "I'm sorry if you…"

Mike gives her a melodramatic wave. "No, no. Let's not make this more awkward than it has to be. Have a good day."

Diane tries to say something. Mike turns away and heaves a louder-than-necessary sigh. The elevator doors open. Diane gives me an apologetic look and hops in. Mike stares at the wall as the doors close.

"Is she gone?" he asks.

"All clear," I say, "Nice work."

"It's nothing," Mike says, "Same chat I once had with a girl at The Tav."

"Sorry to hear that."

"Don't be. I was on Diane's end of the conversation."

We hop on an elevator. The apartment is on the eighteenth floor. I have no idea how we're going to get into the damn thing. Mike laughs off my concerns.

"Getting in is the easy part," he says, "You've seen me operate, right?"

The apartment is located around the corner from the elevator. Mike goes to work on the door and a few seconds later, we're inside. Surprisingly, the apartment isn't much to look at it. Its best feature is a deck with a truly amazing view of Mde Bka Ska and Uptown. Beyond that, it's fairly Spartan. A sofa and TV in the living room. A king-sized bed in the lone bedroom. Nothing visible in the large kitchen. And nothing in the way of decoration.

"I wonder if this guy's got any grape soda," Mike says, heading into the kitchen.

"Don't take anything out of here," I say.

"The guy renting it is dead," Mike says, "If he wants to come out of the grave and hassle me about a soda, he's more than welcome." He opens the fridge. "Shit. Empty."

"We shouldn't be touching anything," I say, "Depending on what we find, this whole place could be evidence. Meantime, as long as we've gone to the trouble of breaking in, let's take a look around."

"This shouldn't take long."

He's right on that one. I search the living room, but it only requires digging in the couch cushions and looking behind the TV. I glance through the door and see the deck is clear. Mike comes out of the kitchen.

"Nothing in there," he says, "I mean, *nothing*. No plates, no glasses, no silverware, no nothing. Not a crumb. Why, he even took the last can of Who Hash."

Mike ducks into the bedroom while I take the bathroom. On the back of the toilet, I find a pamphlet for the Green Clinic in Uptown.

"You heard of the Green Clinic?" I ask.

"It's women's health, isn't it?" Mike says, still exploring the bedroom, "OB/GYN stuff. That kind of thing."

I fold it and put it in my back pocket. It might be nothing, but in an apartment this barren, it represents a major find. Mike's voice calls from the bedroom.

"I think I found something," he says.

I poke my head in. Mike's standing next to the bed. He's got something in his hand. He holds it up. It's a little gold bracelet.

"Found it on the floor under the bed," he says, "I think I know who it belongs to."

He hands it to me. It's a simple gold locket in the shape of a heart. Mike turns it over. There's an inscription on the back reads *To Amy, Here's the key to my secret heart.* My hand closes around the locket.

"I'm assuming this is Amy from Pro Sports," I say, "You coming to the same conclusion I'm coming to?"

Mike leans against the wall. "Amy and Brady were…how to put this discretely…knocking boots?"

I heft the locket in my hand, becoming very aware we've broken into someone's place. We've searched it as thoroughly as we're going to. I shove the bracelet in my pocket and Mike and I slip out of the apartment. As we head for the elevators, Mike runs a hand through his hair.

"I wasn't the only man in Amy's life," he says, "I feel so cheap."

"Wasn't she one of about fifty women in your life?"

"So, clearly I know cheap when I see it."

We manage to escape the building and get back to Mike's car. As we pull away from the building, I stare at my phone, sitting in my lap. Mike glances over at me.

"You okay?" he asks.

"I need to talk to Norah. Some of the things she's told me. They're not adding up."

"Which things?"

I slip the phone into my pocket. "Offhand…all of them."

***

I spend a few hours stewing about it then I call Norah and ask if she's available to get together tonight. On the bright side, she is. And that's about the only bright side.

We settle out on the deck with a bottle of wine and I throw a couple burgers on the grill. It's the first time I've broken it out this year. The advantage of having a father who owns a hardware store is that I have a propane grill much larger and more elaborate than someone of my meager income can afford. Management has helped out by power-washing away the giant bloodstain. I focus on the grilling while Norah makes herself comfortable in a deck chair.

"I think I found a new place," she says, "It's over by Lexington. Not far from here."

"That sounds good."

"It's on the second floor of a converted house. Kind of reminds me of yours. Hardwood floors. A lot of character."

I should be thrilled to hear that. Norah practically living in my neighborhood. But I'm feeling uneasy, knowing the conversation we have to have. I haven't been doing a good job of covering, what with the silences and the reluctance to look at Norah. The sort of stuff she's eventually going to pick up on.

311

"Is something on your mind?" she asks, tucking her wine glass under her chin.

My instinct is to tell her I'm fine. But she won't buy that. I close the grill and pull up one of the deck chairs. We sit close, facing each other.

"I've had some stuff on my mind," I say.

Norah puts a hand on my knee. "What is it?"

"I talked to Sheila Grant," I say.

It's like tearing off a Band Aid. Norah's hand disappears from my knee. There's a cold wind blowing in from her direction. I venture a look at her. Her face is as frigid as I expected.

"You talked to her again?" she asks.

"It wasn't exactly her idea, but I, uh, persuaded her. Mike and Carol helped me out. It's a long story. And stupid."

A smile flickers on Norah's face. "I'm sure it was." Then it's gone. "What did she say?"

"She told me about the, uh, *offer* she made to you."

"Offer," she says, spitting the word out, "That's a nice euphemism." Norah takes a healthy drink of her wine. She studies me over the glass. "Did she tell you what I said?"

"She did. I'm sorry you had to go through that."

"Thank you." She sits back in her chair. The distance between us feels very large. "Is that what's on your mind?"

"Seems like the offer disappeared when Brady was killed."

Norah stares at me, her mouth slightly open. There's a change in the air, like a thunderclap. Her eyes are on me, but I give nothing away. She asks: "What are you saying?"

"Amy was sleeping with Brady," I say, "Did you know that?"

Norah's face is frozen. She doesn't even blink. "I didn't know that. How do *you* know?"

I retrace the steps that brought me to Brady's apartment and the necklace found within. I take it out of my pocket and hand it to Norah. She glances at the locket. I turn it over and she studies the back.

"The son of a bitch," she says, quietly, "The hypocritical son of a bitch."

"First you know about it?"

Norah looks up, her eyes wide. "Of course it is." I get up and walk over to the grill. I open it up and the smoke blows past my face. Norah gets out of the chair and walks over to me. I don't turn to face her. She asks: "You believe me, don't you?"

I close the grill again. "See, that's the thing. I'd like to believe you. But there's this trend where you don't tell me the whole truth. You didn't tell me about meeting with Sheila. Amy saw you handling one of the knives at the store and you didn't tell me about that." I let out a long sigh. "You didn't tell me about being married in the first place."

Anger and defiance flash across Norah's face. But there's something deeper. It might be fear. Or hurt. "Are you accusing me of something?"

"Brady was going to destroy you. The whole situation drove Sheila Grant to make a completely repugnant offer. But it went away when Brady died. Amy was sleeping with Brady and saw you handling a knife at the store. Dangerous combination. And now she's dead. Someone attacked Stephanie and tried to cut her throat, just like Brady's and Amy's."

"I didn't know—"

"And from what little she was able to tell me, the person who attacked her fit your physical description."

Norah's mouth clamps shut. To be honest, I wish she'd say something. Even a decent harangue would be preferable to the silence. I'm tempted to back down, say I'm wrong or that we should drop the whole thing. But it's too late for that. Norah sets her wine glass down.

"I thought you trusted me," she says.

"Trust is a two-way street," I say, "And you don't trust me enough to tell me the truth."

There it is. I can't control the finality in my voice. Norah steps past me, tucking her hands into the pockets of her jean jacket.

"I'm sorry you feel that way," Norah says, not looking back.

"I just—"

"I know you do."

"Can I—?"

"Please don't."

I step to the railing and watch Norah walk down the erector set of stairs behind my building. Sadness washes over me. But I don't go after her. I watch her car pull out of my lot. Rain starts falling.

Thanks for nothing, Mother Nature.

CHAPTER SEVENTEEN

When you go through a breakup, there are different phases of the recovery process. At first, you're hit by Disbelief. ("How could she do this to me? "Where did it all go wrong?" "Why didn't I see this coming?") That gives way to Despondency. You feel like you're missing a limb. Then you get a Lift. You realize you're going to be okay. You had a life before you met her. You'll have a life after. You are much bigger than any person who comes into your life. Then you get Optimistic. You'll meet someone else. You'll be happy again. Without her. Then you realize she is going to meet someone else. She'll be happy again. Without you.

And then comes Disbelief.

Once upon a time, my breakup recovery involved a copious amount of drinking and moping. This moping took the form of lying in bed, listening to sad music and performing only basic tasks (bodily functions, feeding the cats, cleaning the litter box). It did not involve getting dressed or showering. When you work from home, you have plenty of time for this behavior.

But I'm trying to avoid it with the Norah breakup. I force myself to get up and take a shower first thing. I specifically avoid putting on any of Brian Douglas' sad records. (In fact, I avoid most modern music and put The Monkees on Spotify.) I ramble around the apartment, trying to keep my mind and body engaged. By nightfall, I've gotten through the day, but not much more than that. I step out to the deck, hoping the fresh air will help. It's a nice night.

I look over the railing, assuming the same position I was in when Norah walked out last night. I've spent so much time on basic tasks, I haven't thought about Brady's murder and everything I've discovered. I'm not sure where I'm at now that Norah and I are no longer a thing. Does this clear me to go after her? Do I even want to do that? Is she really a suspect?

For the first time, I allow myself to build a case against her. Norah needed Brady to go away, for any number of reasons. Among those were his attempts to ruin her financially, cost her the teaching job she loved and force her into a repugnant bargain with Sheila Grant. She knew Brady was going to make a move against me. She could have been lying in wait for him. In the rush of killing him, she took the knife with her. That way, she wasn't intending to frame me as much as protect me. And that's the *best* case scenario.

However, other events intrude with that idea. The knife was planted in my apartment. Amy was killed. Stephanie was attacked. Those are the kinds of cold-blooded moves someone uses to protect themselves. If Norah was capable of all that, then the act of killing Brady on my deck was a premeditated attempt to make me look guilty. It's all very plausible, if hard to prove.

Not that I won't give it a shot.

This happy little reverie is broken when I hear something on the erector set of steps. I glance down and see someone approaching Lars' deck. It's a guy with long dark hair and a build and wardrobe that best resembles Shaggy from *Scooby-Doo.* As he approaches Lars' deck, he hikes up his shirt and reaches for something in the waistband of his jeans. I get a sick feeling. I've only met this guy once before, but he's in my mental database.

It's Billy. Lars' former drug dealer and current business rival. This can't be good.

My first instinct is to shout at the guy. That's overridden by the thought he'd shoot *me* instead of Lars. I run back through the apartment, looking for my cell phone or my cordless phone so I can warn Lars. Naturally, neither of the damn things can be found. Probably hiding under the futon or wedged into the comfy chair. I dash out the front door and down the interior steps to Lars' place. I knock on the door, hoping like hell he'll either answer quickly or be out of the house altogether. A second later, the door's whipped open and

Lars is standing there in a pair of boxer shorts. There's a studded dog collar around his neck and he's wearing a slightly garish amount of eye makeup.

"Yes?" he says, as if this is a business call.

It takes a second to recover myself. "Okay, first," I say, gesturing toward Lars' outfit, "What the fuck?"

He pushes open the door a little more, revealing a woman with a black bustier, purple hair and a riding crop. "As you can see," Lars says, "I'm entertaining."

"That's a good word for you," I say, "Meantime, you're about to die."

"No, no, it's fine." Lars lowers his voice, "There's a *safe word* we use just in case—"

"I'm not talking about that, you fucking idiot! Billy's on your deck and he's got a gun."

Lars runs over to his houseguest and grabs the riding crop. "Gonna need to borrow this."

I take a few steps inside. "Lars, you're going to use a riding crop against a gun?"

He tosses it back to his guest. "Be right back," he says. He runs into the front bedroom and emerges a minute later, wearing a crash helmet and holding a baseball bat. "Let's do this," he says.

There's a rattling at the backdoor. We all freeze. The rattling becomes a scratching. Someone trying to pick the lock.

I wave Lars and his guest toward the front door. Maybe they can take refuge in my apartment while we call the cops. Another sound comes from the back deck.

"Ow! Hey! What the fuck, dude?"

Then another voice, gravelly and hard-edged, comes through the door. "Lars, get your ass out here!"

Lars whistles. "Smoking that much bud is playing hell with Billy's vocal cords."

I push past Lars and lead everyone down the hallway. I open the door and see Old Man Albertson with a grip on the lobe of Billy's right ear. Billy's eyes water and his knees buckle. Old Man Albertson's other hand is gripping Billy's gun like it's a piece of poo.

"This idiot belong to you?" Old Man Albertson says.

"No," I say, "But I know the idiot this idiot belongs to."

As if on cue, Lars slides past me. Old Man Albertson gets one look at Lars' ensemble and mutters, "Jesus wept."

He lets go of Billy's ear and Billy crumbles to the floor of the deck. A few seconds later, Mr. Albertson has disassembled the weapon and deposited the pieces on the table next to Lars' grill. Billy rubs his ear and looks up at Lars, who folds his arms across his bare chest.

"Billy, what were you going to do?" Lars says.

"Look, man, I—nice outfit, dude—I can't have you out there cutting into my business. There's a sense of propriety here."

Lars scoffs. "You're one to talk about propriety, my friend. I go over to your place to pick up some primo shit and you can't be bothered to make a little connection with me? There's nothing sadder than watching a drug dealer let his business go."

Billy pops to his feet. "Son of a bitch. *That's* why you're doing this? 'Cause I didn't bullshit with you? That's completely insane."

"But that's how it is," Lars says, maintaining an air of haughty indifference, "Not unlike Bill Gates and Apple. You've made a powerful enemy, my friend."

Billy comes at Lars with his fists clenched. "And you're a fucking dead man if you don't knock it off!"

Old Man Albertson slams his hand down on the table, causing everyone, including Lars' date, to jump. He situates himself between Lars and Billy. "Here's how this is going to go down." He sticks a finger in Lars' face. "You are going to get out of this pot dealing business. I see one more drugged-out Nancy boy skulking around here and it's your ass."

Billy stares at the deck floor with a hangdog expression. "That's hate speech, man."

"Yes," Mr. Albertson says, "Because I hate you. And speaking of you—" He moves the finger to Billy's face. "You are going to spend some quality time with this moron. He's one of your customers."

Lars points toward Billy. "The customer is always right."

"No," Mr. Albertson says, "Sometimes the customer's a fucking moron." He puts a hand on Billy's shoulder. "But that's business. These are the headaches you deal with. And if I see your ass around here again—" He gestures toward the disassembled gun. "You're going to look like that gun over there. But spread out over a larger area. You understand me, boy?"

Billy nods, hair and dandruff flying about. He sticks out a hand toward Lars, who takes it without hesitation.

"Glad we could put this behind us," Lars says.

"Me, too, man," Billy says, "You wanna smoke a bowl?"

Lars inclines his head toward the woman in the bustier. "Kind of in the middle of something here."

"Kind of thing that keeps you from smoking a bowl?"

Lars turns toward his date. She shrugs. "Doesn't have to," she says.

Lars, Billy and the woman in the bustier disappear into Lars' apartment. Old Man Albertson retrieves the pieces of the gun. I try not to think about Lars' den of iniquity.

"You're out of your apartment," I say.

"I'm not going to make a habit of it."

"Good thing you spotted Billy."

"Spotting him was nothing. Getting up behind him without him hearing me. That was the hard part. You know what this place is like. One of your cats could wander out here and the whole building would hear them. If that hop head wasn't missing most of his brain cells, there's no way he could have missed me coming up behind him. And then your friend might have been…" Mr. Albertson drags his thumb across his throat.

The gesture might lack sensitivity—I get the feeling it's not Old Man Albertson's strong suit—but it jars something in my brain. The noise on the steps. The throat slashing gesture. Thoughts come to me in a rush, like when I used to write a column. Like I will when I start writing columns again. Because I now believe that day is coming.

"Son of a bitch," I mutter.

"Excuse me?" Old Man Albertson says.

"No, that wasn't directed at you. If anything, it was directed at me. The answer's been right in front of me the whole time and I didn't fucking see it."

I slip around Old Man Albertson and run to the steps leading to my place. I pull my cell phone out. There's a few calls to make. And if I'm lucky—and a little smarter than I have been—a situation to wrap up.

***

It's a couple hours later. I'm on the deck of Brady's apartment, looking over Lake Bde Maka Ska. Far below, moonlight twinkles on the lake. There's a slight chill in the air. The apartment is lit on only by a single lamp and the full moon. All is calm. For now. If I could only get control of that sense of anticipation twisting my guts.

The phone calls went well. The plan that formed in my mind as I ran up to my apartment has played out perfectly so far, but it's just the prologue. For all I know, it could end with me being thrown off this deck.

I step into the apartment and watch the front door. I take out my cell phone and glance at the clock for eight-hundredth time in the last ten minutes. If this were the old days, I'd tap my wristwatch to make sure it's running on time. There's no arguing with Greenwich Mean Time.

My guest will be here any second. They'll come right in, since they have the key. I have absolutely no doubt my guest is the person who murdered Brady Perkins. And Amy. The more I think about it, the more I put the sequence of events together in my head, the more it makes sense. The problem,

324

though, is proving it. Everything has to fall into place. And even then… My phone rings. It's Mike. I scramble to answer.

"T minus ten," he says, "Your murderer is on the way in."

"That really how you want to put it? *My murderer?*"

"You got someone who's killed twice coming up the elevator and you want to argue fucking semantics?"

"Believe it or not, it relaxes me."

"Enjoy it while you can, I guess."

I shake out the tension. "Thanks for keeping an eye out. I can take it from here."

"You sure? I think I should come up."

"No. I need to get a confession. It's got to be just me and the murderer. Don't worry. I got this."

There's a moment where I imagine Mike putting together a smartass response. He says, quietly. "Good luck, man."

I ring off. There's a click at the front door. Someone's coming in. No time to ponder my own fate. There's a rush of blood in my ears. I try to calm myself. Have to stay focused. Make sure everything works like I planned. The door opens and the murderer is silhouetted in the light from the hallway. The silhouette hovers a moment. Then the murderer steps into the light.

"Hi, Norah," I say.

CHAPTER EIGHTEEN

It's never fun to run into ex, particularly when you're not expecting it. There are many degrees of lousy in this area. There's the Casual Bump-Into or The Seeing Them with a New Significant Other. I've even had the Set Up By Tindr When I Didn't Realize It Was My Ex. No matter the situation, it's an invitation to kvetching, hand-wringing and soul-searching. These feelings, though, can often be remedied by vodka. (Then again, if you're in a bar during the Casual Bump-Into, vodka might be the cause of these feelings.)

Given all that's gone down with Norah and me, I can't even tell you which level of weird this breakup has reached.

Norah stops the second she sees me. Even in the thin light, I can see the color drain from her face. We stand there, staring at each other.

"Joe," she says, vacantly, "What are you doing here?"

I've got no better comeback than: "I was going to ask you the same thing."

"I'm going to meet somebody here. It wasn't supposed to be you, though." She steps further into the room, leaving the door open behind her. "What about you?"

"Same reason. But I didn't call you."

Norah cocks her head to one side. "Who did you call?"

A voice comes from the doorway. "That would be me."

Norah spins around and backs toward me. I put my hands on her shoulders. We look toward the doorway. Stephanie steps in, a serrated hunting knife in one gloved hand. Norah and I stare at the knife.

"Hi, Stephanie," I say, "Welcome to the party."

Stephanie kicks the door shut behind her. "Good to be here. I was glad to get your call. I saw right through the reason for it, but it was a relief, really. It's time to bring this whole thing to an end." She brandishes the knife toward us. "The famous final scene."

Nuts. No offense, but I'm not thrilled about spending my last moments on Earth with a Bob Seger tune running through my head. (Though, if I had a choice, it would be *Shame on the Moon*.) Stephanie positions herself between us and the door. I step in front of Norah.

"How did you know?" I ask.

"You wanted to meet because you found new evidence," Stephanie says, "You could trap Norah into confessing to the murders. But you needed my help. I knew you didn't have any new evidence. There's nothing to be found here. And what could you have that's worse than the murder weapon? The one you've had for a few weeks."

"Because you planted it in my apartment," I say.

Stephanie bows slightly. "I found your spare key. Brady knew where it was. You mentioned it to Norah in the email he found; the one that clued him into your little affair."

See, now if I had subpoena power—or bothered to read my outgoing emails—I might have figured this out sooner. I back us away from Stephanie, angling toward the bedroom, even though it can't act as an escape route.

"Sounds like we weren't the only ones having an affair," I say.

A little vein pops out on Stephanie's forehead. "Don't make it sound cheap. I was in love with Brady. This…" She takes a look around. "This was going to be our home." Stephanie purses her lips as she looks at us. "I hate seeing the two of you in it."

"It's a nice place," I say, "Funded by the money you and Brady embezzled."

Stephanie sneers. "The store was more Brady's than Doug's anyway. Doug's a nice guy, but Brady was right. When it comes to business, he's an idiot. The money was going to fund a new life for us. Pardon me if I don't feel guilty."

Norah's eyes seem numb. "Brady was going to leave me?"

"Or so Stephanie thought," I say, "Didn't exactly turn out that way, though, did it?"

Stephanie gestures toward me with the knife. "I should have figured it out. When he went apeshit over Norah sleeping with you. I know this means less than nothing to you, Norah, but in his own completely fucked up way, Brady loved you. He wasn't going to leave you. At least, not for me."

"And I'm sure this means less than nothing to *you*," I say, "But he wouldn't have left Norah for Amy, either." I'll admit: I get a little kick out of the way Stephanie's lip curls in hate when I say that. "Did you know Brady was sleeping with Amy before you killed him?"

"Not exactly," Stephanie says, "I knew he was sleeping with somebody. I found some personal items here at the apartment. Stuff that didn't belong to me. And God knows Brady would never buy that kind of stuff."

Norah mutters: "You got that right."

I'm going to pretend I don't know what they're talking about. "How did you figure out it was Amy?" I ask.

"She knew about the trip to Bermuda," Stephanie says, "Only Brady and I were supposed to know that. But that was way after the fact. At the time, I just knew he cancelled the trip with me. And I started to think he was going to go with someone else. I tried talking to Brady about it, but he was too obsessed with Norah. With you two."

I take another step toward the bedroom. Norah comes with me. Stephanie follows.

"You came with Brady to my apartment," I say, "You were going to help him kill me."

"No, I wasn't," Stephanie says, "I was there to finish things with Brady."

"And to frame me for killing him."

"It was an added benefit. But I panicked and took the knife with me. If I had left it there, you'd be in jail right now." She grips the knife. "How did you figure out it was me?"

"A few things I should have figured out earlier," I say, "First part is my building. You can't take three steps on the decks and stairs outside without someone hearing you. That meant whoever killed Brady was working with him, not sneaking up on him. That definitely ruled out Doug and probably ruled out Norah."

Norah's head swivels toward me. "Probably?"

"Had to leave a little margin for error." I turn back to Stephanie. "And there was the matter of Brady and Amy being killed by someone who was right-handed."

Stephanie looks confused. "I don't get it."

"When we were recreating your so-called attack, I held the knife in my right hand. The murderer was right-handed. The police confirmed as much."

"So what?" Stephanie says.

"So, Doug's right hand was fucked up after the fight with Brady. He couldn't grip a coffee cup, let alone a knife he was using to murder his brother. And Norah, as I'm fond of reminding her, refuses to use the hand God intended her to use." Responding to the look on Stephanie's face, I add: "She's left-handed. She's out. That leaves only one person who could be the murderer."

Stephanie scoffs. "Because I'm right-handed?"

"And you're pregnant."

She damn near drops the knife. Norah's jaw falls, as if she's trying to figure out what *Twilight Zone* episode she's slipped into. Stephanie tightens her grip on the knife.

"How do you know?" she asked.

"You dropped the climbing class. You changed your hours to afternoons, to cover your morning sickness. You claimed you were completely freaked out the night you were supposedly attacked but you wouldn't let me spend the night. Again, because of the morning sickness. You had liquor in the apartment, but you wouldn't drink it. When I was here before, I found a pamphlet from the Green Clinic in Uptown, an OB/GYN clinic. It adds up."

Stephanie's glare takes on a certain *Curse you meddling kids* quality. "Very good."

"Brady was the father, right?" I ask.

"No. The baby never *had* a father," Stephanie says, "Not as far as I'm concerned."

Stephanie's voice has a low, dangerous tone. Her eyes are glazed. She's off the beam. Probably been the case since the night she killed Brady. Maybe earlier. I look toward the bedroom, but we've backed up as far as we can.

She runs a hand over her stomach. "You really do seem like a decent guy, Joe. But I've got someone to protect."

A voice comes from the bedroom. "So do I."

The bedroom door opens behind me. Norah and I clear a path. Sergeant Pike leans against the doorframe and glances at me.

"I'll give you credit, counselor," he says, "I didn't think this dumbass plan would work. Full confession in front of a homicide detective."

Stephanie's face melts into a look that's half-confused and half-infuriated. "You motherfucker."

Her next move comes too quickly for me to react. Stephanie's free arm lashes out and grabs Norah's arm. She yanks Norah toward her and swings the knife up to Norah's throat. Pike reaches for his revolver, but freezes in position, realizing he'd probably only jeopardize Norah's safety. I'm standing there, frozen, staring at Stephanie and Norah. Stephanie backs she and Norah toward the door.

"You're going to stay right there," Stephanie says, "And you're going to do nothing. Do you under—"

Before anything else can happen, the front door swings open and Mike charges in. He crashes into Stephanie. Her arm comes forward, giving Norah an opening. Norah ducks away from Stephanie and sprints over to me. Stephanie backs off, finding a middle ground between all of us, her back to the deck. Mike looks from her to us.

"Motherfucker, what the fuck?" he says.

"I was going to ask you the same thing," I say.

"You were taking forever. I thought something had gone wrong."

"It kind of just did."

Stephanie brandishes the knife Mike's direction. "You stupid motherfucker!

She dives at Mike, making a lunge with the knife. He manages to sidestep her. Mike retreats further into the apartment. Stephanie spins around, ready to make another charge. Pike pulls out his weapon. There's no need.

A beautiful, dark-haired girl comes through the door. She crashes into Stephanie, knocking her toward Mike. He ducks around Stephanie and steps over to the girl. This must be Haley. She's every bit the knockout Mike described. I'd appreciate her more, but this really isn't the time. Not that Haley seems aware of this.

"Mike, what the hell is going on?" she asks.

Mike looks back to Stephanie, over to me and back to Haley in the space of a gnat's fart. "What are you doing here?" he asks.

"I wanted to know what's going on with you," Haley says, "I like to think I can trust you. I had to follow you and find out."

Great. Glad we cleared that up. Stephanie brandishes the knife. It gets Mike's attention, if nothing else. Stephanie prepares another charge.

"Get out!" she screams, "Just…fucking get out of here!"

Stephanie rushes at Mike. He steps behind Haley. Another voice comes from the doorway.

"What the fuck?"

It's Alan, Mike's boss. Several things happen in short order.

Hearing Alan's voice, Mike spins around. He bumps into Haley, knocking her out of Stephanie's path. Stephanie completes the charge, though. She buries the tip of the knife into Mike's right ass cheek. He howls in pain. Alan, though, is oblivious.

"You son of a bitch!" Alan says, his face red, sweat popping out on his forehead, "*You're* the one Haley's been seeing? You lazy, horned-out pile of shit! You couldn't keep your hands off my fucking daughter!"

Haley jumps back over to Mike's side. "Daddy, what are you doing here?"

"I was following you," Alan says, "I knew you were seeing somebody. I just didn't know it was this lousy pile of crap!"

"This is none of your business, Daddy!" Haley says, "You don't know Mike like I do. He's a wonderful man and a magnificent lover!"

Mike drops his head into his hands and mutters, "Oh dear God." Alan steps around Haley and throws a right cross at Mike. Mike leans back, avoiding the punch. Haley screams. Stephanie screams as well. She hoists the knife over her head and takes a swing at Alan. Pike raises the weapon. He doesn't need to use it. Someone *else* appears in the doorway.

"Alan, what the hell is going on?" Carol says.

She grabs Alan and spins him around, unintentionally pulling him out of Stephanie's way. Alan gives Carol a feeble grin.

"Carol," he says, "What…what are you doing here?"

"I followed you," she says, "You've been acting so weird lately. I wanted to know what the hell was going on. I should have known you'd be obsessed with your daughter. Alan, this is not healthy. Don't you see that?"

Pike lowers his weapon again. He mutters: "Didn't I see a Marx Brothers movie that looked a lot like this?"

"Probably," I say, "I didn't have this many people at my last *party*."

Stephanie, meanwhile, is standing in the middle of the floor, rapidly becoming unglued. The parade of idiots is blocking her path out of the apartment. She's trapped in no man's land between them, the group of me, Norah and Pike and the deck.

Carol grabs Alan's shoulders. "Alan, you have to let Haley grow up. You can't act like a jealous fool *and* be in a relationship with me."

Haley's hands fly up like a pair of claws. "Again? You cheated on Mom *again*?"

Carol throws a look at Alan. "Again? What is she talking about Alan? You said you were getting a divorce."

Alan tugs at his collar. "Uh…it's complicated."

Haley slaps Alan on the back of the head. "No, it's not! You cheated on Mom with another one of these whores you picked up at a bar!"

Carol's mouth drops open. "He did not…okay, I'm not a whore." She turns to Alan. "You're still fucking married?"

Mike grumbles. "Still married and fucking anyway."

Alan turns to Mike. "Shut up, asshole! You're fired!"

Carol grabs Alan's arm and spins him around. "Leave him alone, you lying sack of shit!"

Haley screams, "You fucked my fucking father! Fuck you!"

Stephanie, having heard enough, decides to try grabbing Norah again. This time, though, I'm able to slap her hand away. Stephanie brings the knife up, but Pike brings his weapon up at the same time.

"Put down the knife," he says, cold as can be.

Behind Stephanie, Alan pulls Mike's oversized cranium into a headlock. Carol grabs Alan around the neck in a rear naked choke. Haley grabs two handfuls of Carol's hair and begins shaking the shit out of her.

Stephanie takes her eyes off us to watch this live-action telenovela. Norah brings her foot up, booting the knife out of Stephanie's hand. It tumbles through the air and lands near the idiot pile. (I have to hope none of them get the idea of using it.) Stephanie backs away. Pike tracks her with the gun.

"I want you to kneel down," he says, his voice flat and reasonable, "And put your hands behind your head."

Stephanie glares at all of us. Suddenly, she turns and runs for the deck. Pike lowers the weapon a tad. Obviously, he's not going to shoot someone who's not going to get away or present a threat to others. Besides, he doesn't have a clear shot. Norah's taken off after Stephanie. I take off after Norah. She gets to the deck a few steps ahead of me.

Stephanie's standing at the railing, looking out. It's probably dawned on her she's got no chance of navigating the eighteen floors needed to get out of here. Then again, she might not even be interested. Norah approaches her, holding out a cautioning hand.

"Stephanie," she says, her voice firm.

Stephanie flicks a look over her shoulder. "Go away, Norah."

"What are you going to do?"

There's a long moment and Stephanie says, "I don't see a way out of this."

A pang runs through me, witnessing Stephanie's predicament. I'm looking at a woman who's murdered twice and done yeoman's work in framing me. And yet I'm afraid she'll be over that railing before anyone can stop her.

Norah takes another step toward her. "Take a look around, Stephanie. There's no getting out of here. If you can't save yourself, you can't save the baby. You understand that?"

Stephanie's voice is gentle. "Yes."

"No matter what happens if you get arrested," Norah says, "It can't be worse than that." Norah holds out her hand. "Come with me and we'll talk to Sergeant Pike."

Stephanie grips the rail. She pulls away from Norah. My body tenses. Stephanie could make a move and none of us could stop her. She looks toward Norah's hand. Norah's voice remains steady.

"Just come with me," Norah says.

The next several moments feel like they could be measured with a calendar. Nobody moves. Nobody says anything. Pike stands behind me, muttering about how he should have known better, how he should have had backup, how he never should have listened to me. But he has to follow Norah's lead. Stephanie doesn't move a muscle. But neither does Norah. Stephanie takes another look over the railing.

Then she takes Norah's hand.

Norah delicately escorts Stephanie into the apartment. Pike eases Norah out of the way and takes hold of Stephanie's arm. He makes no move to cuff her. Stephanie looks shell-shocked, the last of her manic energy gone. She looks at Norah, glassy-eyed.

"Brady didn't deserve you," Stephanie says.

"He didn't deserve anyone," Norah says.

Pike seats Stephanie in the one chair in the room. Norah stumbles toward me, the adrenaline washing away, leaving her weak. I'm not in much better shape. We fall together, holding each other up.

"Good work," I say.

"You, too," Norah says.

Pike seats Stephanie in the one chair in the room. The headlock daisy chain has paused to watch the action. Pike holsters his weapon and pushes up his wire-frame glasses.

"Not sure how I'm going to massage the paperwork on this one," he says, "But it worked. Good thing I trust you, counselor."

"I appreciate it," I say.

Pike looks over at the headlock clusterfuck and waving toward the door. "The rest of you get the fuck out of here before I shoot you."

They promptly disentangle and head for the exits. Alan doesn't look at anyone. Haley stares hateful daggers at Mike and Carol. Mike slinks out, withering under Carols' glare. Carol pauses in the doorway and looks back at us.

"I've got to be honest with you," she says, "Love sucks."

EPILOGUE

Much as I love my mom, she's not the first person I turn to for advice. Or the fiftieth. Not that my mom isn't smart. But even smart people can fall down in certain areas. (Like I do with gift-giving.)

A classic example is something she said just before my breakup with Lisa, my high school girlfriend. I was moping around the house, not much interested in anything. She made a few feeble attempts at cheering me up before deciding to reason with me. It took this form: "Look at it this way, Joe. Once Lisa goes away to college, you'll probably never see her again." I stared at her for several seconds, then asked her to please stop talking to me. I think she wonders sometimes why I never ask her for relationship advice.

Not that I don't need it from time to time.

It's been a few days since Stephanie's arrest. Norah and I have been taking the time to come down and sort out what the hell happened. We've traded text messages, each making sure the other is okay. She agreed to meet me at Glacier's so we could talk.

I'm at one of the wrought-iron tables on the sidewalk when Norah walks up. Her face lights up as soon as she sees me. For some reason, my heart sinks when I see she's got a to-go cup. She's wearing faded jeans and a jean jacket. Her hair cascades past her shoulders and glistens in the sunlight. There's a buzz of energy about her, a lightness. She gives me a quick peck on the cheek as she sits down.

"How have you been?" Norah asks.

"Hanging in there. Trying not to look over my shoulder. Get a good night's sleep."

"I know the feeling."

There's a pause. That subject is a little too unpleasant to get into this early in the conversation. We avoid eye contact while looking for another topic. I'm quietly hating this. Those moments when what was once free and easy becomes strained and uncomfortable. Norah manages to hit on something.

"How are your friends?" she asks.

"Recovering," I say, relieved to be talking, "I don't think they're freaked out as much as they're pissed off."

Norah winces. "Looked like a rough night all around."

"That's one way to put it," I say, "Mike and Carol aren't speaking to each other. They'll get over it, but…"

"I take it they're both single now?"

"Sadly, yes. If 'sadly' is the word I want. Carol kicked Alan to the curb when she found out he was still married.

Haley was pissed when Mike stood up for Carol. That was the end of both relationships. And Mike's out a job."

"Ouch," Norah says, "You're sure he and Carol are going to be okay?"

"They will," I say, "They both like hanging out at my place. Sooner or later, I'll insist they stay in the same room with each other."

Norah swirls the coffee in her mug. "How about Lars? How's he doing?"

"He's out of the drug business," I say, "Back on good terms with his dealer. Lars is going to consult with him about public relations. Begs the question about who's going to consult Lars, but there we go."

Norah laughs and, for a second, it feels like old times. But it fades faster than I'd like. There's been too much going on to flip a switch and pretend everything's normal. We let the breeze play over us. A shadow crosses Norah's face.

"What do you know about Stephanie?" she asks.

I cringe at the mention of the name, not sure what to think of Stephanie. Yes, Brady did not do right by her and I can sympathize with the string of events that drove her around the bend. It doesn't change the fact, though, that she killed two people and was perfectly willing to add Norah and me to that number to cover up what she did.

"I talked to Pike," I say, "Stephanie's expressed remorse. It's like the whole thing finally hit her."

"She'll go to jail, won't she?" Norah asks.

"Hard to imagine she won't. Too many calculated moves to claim temporary insanity. Maybe the pregnancy will cause a judge to give her some leeway. Remains to be seen, I guess."

Norah looks out into the street. "At least we're still here." She props her elbow on the table and plunks her chin into one of her hands. "How are things at *The Bugle*?"

I tap the table with a little triumph. "Suspension lifted and all is forgiven. When you bring them a story like this—with the reporter right in the middle—it erases a lot of bad publicity. I'm Lance's fair-haired boy again. Which means I'm stuck with him." I sip my coffee. "How about you? Things okay at the job?"

"As far as I know," Norah says, "The school wasn't pleased about the publicity, but I literally talked a woman off a ledge. The publicity would be worse if they fired me now. I'm expected back in the fall." She looks over the street. "And I'm moving out of Doug's place. I signed a lease on the apartment on Lexington."

"How's Doug taking it?" I ask.

"He's got enough to worry about with the store. He's out a partner and a manager."

"You think he'll close down?"

"I don't think so," Norah says, "Brady always acted like the business couldn't survive without him. If Doug closed down, that would prove Brady right."

"Driven by spite."

"Whatever it takes, I guess," Norah says. Then she lays a hand on my arm, a mischievous look on her face. "Oh, and I might be called to testify against Sheila Grant. At her disbarment hearing. I get the impression I'm not the first person she's propositioned."

"Wow. How did they even know?"

Norah scratches her ear. "Some revenge-minded individual must have ratted her out."

I laugh, a lightness filling me. I always suspected crossing Norah was a bad idea. Can't say I feel sorry for the counselor. Although, the mention of Sheila Grant brings us around to the topic we've been sidestepping. It hangs heavy in the air. I'm not sure how to start but feel like it's my job to get the ball rolling.

"The cats have really missed you," I say.

Norah grins, but she doesn't look at me. "Have they said something?"

"Not in so many words. But there's a definite tone in Lenny's meowing. Although, to be fair, that might be him begging for food." I'm not sure where to go next, so I say what's on my mind. "And I've missed you."

There's a long moment where Norah stares at the table. Her face flickers between flattered and mournful. Whatever she's thinking, her thoughts feel far away. She looks at me.

"I feel the same way," she says, "It's amazing when you think about it. We survived all of this."

"We did." Another pause. "Makes me wonder where we're at now."

Norah sets the coffee aside. I look away, not wanting her to feel watched or grilled. "I like you," she says, "A lot."

"This sounds like the kind of thing you say before adding, 'But it's not going to work.'"

Norah takes my hands and runs her thumbs along my fingers. "You were right. I didn't tell you the truth. I'm sorry about that."

"You don't have to apologize. It's done now."

"But that doesn't change what happened, does it?"

I have to be honest, both with Norah and myself. "No, it doesn't."

"I've been thinking about why I did…everything. I trusted Brady. And you saw how that turned out. I was ready to move on from him. I guess I just wasn't ready to trust yet."

I sigh, hating the finality in my voice. "Maybe this wasn't the right time for us."

Norah gently disentangles her hands from mine. "Maybe not."

I lay a hand on her forearm. "But hey, we did better than last time."

She laughs and it again lights up her face. "We did. Give us a couple more years and we could really be something."

"I'd like that." That sounds inadequate, given how much hope it fills me with. I say it one more time. "I'd like that."

Norah takes out her phone and glances at the time (I'm guessing this is a convenient way to end the conversation). "I've got to get going. I've got some stuff to move into get the apartment. I'm done with living out of boxes."

"Understood. It's one of the reasons I'm probably never going to move."

Norah gets up and throws her purse strap over her shoulder. I rise to meet her. She looks at me with that trace of sadness still in place. She gives me a hug.

"You take care of yourself," Norah whispers

"You, too. Say hi to Doug for me."

Norah laughs as we part and punches me on the arm. She looks at me another second, then flutters her fingers and heads down the sidewalk. Away from me.

I sit back down at the table. I've got my laptop and an editor interested in hearing my musings about being at the center of a murder case. But even after a few weeks of desperately missing it, I don't feel like writing. Not just yet. I'll have a lousy night's sleep and then get back to work in the morning.

The phone buzzes on the table. I glance at it, not entirely interested. It's Carol. Probably the only person I feel like talking to right now.

"What's up?" I ask.

"Nothing," she says, "Absolutely nothing." Trepidation sneaks into Carol's voice. "Are you done having coffee with Norah?"

"Just ended," I say, "In more ways than one."

"I'm sorry."

"It's not a surprise. Seems like everybody's on a losing streak."

"Tell me about it," Carol says, "You doing anything tonight?"

"I am completely free."

"Want to grab a drink? Cry in our beers?"

I chuckle. "Strangely enough, that sounds great."

"The Tav? Eight o'clock?"

"I'll be there."

We ring off and I stare at the phone. Yes, I feel bad about Norah. But I still have my friends. I still have my life. The last few weeks have taught me those things are not always guaranteed. And I'm surprised at how much I'm looking forward to talking to Carol. Misery and company, I guess.

I get up from the table, ready for the walk home. The sun is out. It's warm. The lilacs and apple blossoms are in full bloom. It's hard to be gloomy on a day like today. But I'm sure I'll give it a shot.

I know myself too well.

THE END

www.ingramcontent.com/pod-product-compliance
Lightning Source LLC
Chambersburg PA
CBHW060933120726
47910CB00002B/306